Under the Influence

AN ENEMIES TO LOVERS ROMANTIC COMEDY

AVERY KANE
AMANDA M. LEE

KISSINGSHARK PUBLICATIONS

Copyright © 2022 by Avery Kane

All rights reserved.

No part of this book may be reproduced in any form or by any electronic or mechanical means, including information storage and retrieval systems, without written permission from the author, except for the use of brief quotations in a book review.

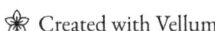 Created with Vellum

One

"What's up, Buttercup?"

Grady Dalton, his lithe frame on display in his normal jeans and T-shirt, leaned against my desk and looked me up and down.

"I have a name," I reminded him. He bothered me on a level that shouldn't have been possible, especially because I'm easygoing. No, really. That's not something I say about myself. Other people say it.

"Yes, but there's nothing that rhymes with Shay or Archer that I find cute. 'What's up, Shay Archer' doesn't have the same ring to it."

He was trying to be charming. Every woman in the office had fallen prey to that dimpled smile of his. Well, every woman but me. I was above such things.

"I'm not even blond," I pointed out, instinctively tucking my shoulder-length brown hair behind an ear. "Buttercup doesn't work for me. That's what you say to blondes."

"I see." His dimple grew deeper. "Do you prefer I call you Poo Boo because of your brown hair?"

From the desk next to mine, Grant Landry laughed. He always laughed at Grady's jokes, even if they weren't funny.

"You could call me by my name. Is there something you find abhorrent about it?"

"Actually, I think Shay is a pretty name."

"Great."

"I was just trying to make conversation." He folded his arms across his chest and regarded me with his unreadable bright blue eyes, which served as a shock against his black hair. Mine were a mundane green, more hazel than anything. He looked intense when staring. I looked bored. That was probably why he was so good at garnering interviews.

We both worked for *The Bourbon Street Bugle*, a newspaper that operated in New Orleans' illustrious French Quarter. I handled entertainment pieces—there were a lot of options in the city—and he considered himself a newshound. Most of the time that meant we didn't butt heads on stories. That didn't mean there wasn't some foot stomping and head ramming in the newsroom. Grady sucked up all the oxygen in the building, and I needed space to breathe. The combination made for a toxic atmosphere.

"Next time just state your business and avoid the cutesy nicknames," I suggested. "I'm guessing that if I were a man you wouldn't bother with such trivialities." I knew I sounded prim—to the point he would ultimately question what had crawled up my ass and died—but I couldn't contain my dislike. He rubbed me the wrong way. He *always* rubbed me the wrong way.

"See, that's not true." Grady vehemently shook his head. "I have nicknames for everybody. Take Grant, for example." He gestured to our co-worker, another tool, but kept his eyes on me. "I call him the newshound who was born to be a boozehound. You don't hear him complaining, do you?"

I narrowed my eyes. "Do you have a reason for being

here?" I'd filed my column for the day—I always beat my deadline by at least thirty minutes—and was trying to figure out a way to entertain myself until the employee meeting that had been called early this morning. After that, I was free to leave, and I was already dreaming about crawfish étouffée for dinner. I didn't have time for Grady and his version of charm.

"Yeah." Grady glanced over his shoulder, his smile slipping. He was serious when he turned back. "I want to know what you've heard about this meeting."

The newsroom had been buzzing with rumors ever since our editor, Edith Felders, announced attendance was mandatory in the conference room at four o'clock. We had many meetings—there was little Edith loved more than being the center of attention—but it was rare for attendance to be mandatory.

"What have you heard?" I demanded. He was up on the office gossip much more than I was.

"Well, Sheila Graham in advertising said that they're cutting the physical publication to two days a week. She said she heard it from the executive secretary."

I frowned. It was no secret that newspapers were in trouble. When I'd decided to get a degree in journalism, my parents warned me it was a bad idea. My father insisted hotel management was a better option—there were always new hotels being built—and my mother suggested that I find a nice man with huge money-making potential to settle down with. I'd politely declined both their ideas...and then watched as they separated to sleep in different bedrooms at opposite ends of the house for the night. That was the norm in my house.

"Do you really think they'll go that route?" I asked. Cutting to two days of print and seven days of online content meant layoffs. I covered entertainment—live music and bar reviews were my favorite—which would make me less necessary than someone like Grady.

He shrugged. "I don't know. Print's days are on borrowed time. If they were cutting publication back, I think we would have heard from the printing plant in Marigny. They would've let us know, if only to put the owners on blast."

He had a point. "Maybe they don't know yet."

Grady glanced over his shoulder again and then back to me. "Rod in the back shop says they're going to kill half the staff and merge us with the *Garden City Gazette*. The coverage would be the same, just split, and with half the staff."

My stomach did an uneasy somersault. "I guess that would make sense," I said after a few seconds. "What do you think?"

"We're in trouble over the long haul regardless. I wish I had a different skill set. My father always said I should be a plumber. I already have the crack and everything. He had an in because my uncle was head of the plumber's union. That's starting to look like a wasted opportunity."

"Yes," I agreed dryly. "You do make me think of toilets whenever I look at you."

His lips curved. "There's the girl I know and love. You're much cleverer than you give yourself credit for. The Buttercup insults of earlier were terrible. You should up your game."

"I'll take it under advisement," I said, my eyes drifting to the clock on the wall. "Two minutes."

"We might as well go in," he said. "It'll be standing room only."

My stomach clenched as I pushed myself to a standing position. I hadn't been all that worried about the meeting until Grady had shared the rumors. Now I was terrified. Much like him, I didn't have a skill set that would allow for easy employment if I lost my job.

Before we could go to the conference room, Edith's office door opened and she stepped out. She didn't even make an attempt at a smile as she glanced around the room.

"Is everybody here?" she asked, her mouth moving as she

counted heads. "There's no need to go into the conference room if everybody is here. The rest of the announcements are being made to the other departments now."

My heart sank. This was going to be worse than any of us thought.

"So, as everybody knows, *The Bugle* has been struggling," she began. "All daily newspapers are facing the same issues. People don't want to pay for news content and advertisers don't want to shell out big bucks for placement. We have to pivot."

I held my breath, and for some reason darted a look toward Grady. His face was immovable, chiseled of granite. Whatever was about to be announced, he would accept it with the sort of grace I could only pray for.

"There will be no more print product," Edith said.

Grant was the first to stir. "None at all? Does that mean *The Bugle* is dead?"

"Not dead." Edith managed a watery laugh. "It's pretty far from dead. However, we won't be the same Bugle you're used to."

Here it comes, I told myself. *She's going to give the entire entertainment division the heave-ho. You're going to be jobless in thirty seconds, and homeless in three months.* Why didn't I make sure to have six months of savings like my father always told me? Oh, right, because he drove me crazy when he said things like that and I'm a stubborn mule.

"Online content is going to be robust," Edith explained. "And when I say robust, I mean it. We're going to update the website nonstop—at least to start. But not with news."

I exhaled heavily as Grady reacted. He was still next to my desk, his shoulders squared. That egotistic smile was gone.

"What do you mean there won't be any news?" Grady demanded. "We're a newspaper."

"We're going to be an entertainment beacon," Edith

replied. She held up her hands when ten people started talking at once. "I don't make the decisions, guys. I simply have to deliver the news...and then adjust. Quite frankly, there's going to be a lot of adjusting."

"What does that mean for us?" Grant demanded. He looked as if he was about to go nuclear.

"Nobody is out of a job right now," Edith supplied. "That's the good news. The bad news is that you're going to have to perform to keep your jobs."

"What does that mean?" I blurted.

"It means that those of you who get the most hits on the website—not just for one day, but repeatedly—will be retained. Those of you who can't get hits will be let go." Edith's smile was grim. "There will be severance packages for those who don't make it. I don't know if I would call them generous, but they'll get you through a few months."

"A few months in a city that hasn't hired a new reporter in five years?" Grant demanded. "How is that supposed to make us feel better?"

"I... can't answer that." Edith held out her hands. "This is a fluid situation. Tomorrow is our last day for the print publication. We announce the change to readers in tomorrow's edition. There will be no wind down. And there will be no office."

Oh, well, the hits just kept on coming. "No office? How is that going to work?" I asked.

"You'll all be issued new laptops. This building is being sold. In fact, in a month, you won't have access to the building. I don't expect you to pack up everything today, but you need to do so within a week. Your keycards will not work after that. The building will be off limits unless you're specifically called here for a meeting."

I felt sick to my stomach. It reminded me of the infamous Tequila Incident morning after.

"If we're not writing news, what are we writing?" Grady demanded.

"Entertainment columns," Edith replied. "They want us to pivot into the influencer stuff. Apparently, that's where the advertising dollars are."

"I don't understand how that works," I admitted. "How are they going to sell advertising for entertainment content?"

"It's New Orleans, Shay," Edith pointed out. "Entertainment is what we do here. The columns need to be entertaining. They're more like blogs than columns, I guess. The goal is to revamp and search for new investors, but we have to get the website numbers up."

To my surprise, Grady's hand landed on my shoulder. It was a comforting move—something he never did. His eyes remained on Edith.

"They're cutting overhead," he said. "The building goes and that makes us more streamlined. The printing plant will be sold—if it hasn't been already—and that will make overhead almost non-existent. Then the staff will fall by the wayside because of the way you've set up the competition for jobs."

Edith's nod was stiff. "I didn't make the decision on this. In fact, I argued against it. I can't change how this is going to play out, though."

"I still don't understand what sort of content you want," I said. "If it's not reviews and stuff, but it has to be entertainment oriented, what do you want us to write?"

"I want you to find your niche," Edith replied. "I can't tell you what to do. Essentially they want lightning in a bottle—those were the words the front office used—and I have no idea who can deliver on this."

"Basically, you're saying that we should all start looking for jobs," Grant surmised. "None of us will survive this. We're dead men walking from here on out."

"And women," I muttered. Grant's eyes flashed.

"I have a family, Shay," he snapped, taking a step in my direction. "I have a wife and two children. You live alone. Heck, you can get a job in a coffee shop and be fine. It's different for those of us with families."

Grady's hand shot out and planted in the center of Grant's chest when he took another step in my direction. "Don't go over there," he warned. His eyes, normally so full of mischief and irritating energy, were serious now. "She's not the one you're angry with."

"Grady is right, Grant," Edith said severely. "I know you're upset, but you really do have a chance to save your job. Everybody has a clean slate as of now. Tomorrow, the competition begins... and believe me, it's going to be fierce."

"What about the others?" I said, my mind drifting to the other departments. "What happens to them?"

"The back shop is being laid off right now. The printing plant employees face the same fate. The advertising department is being given the same offer as you guys. If they sell ads, they keep their jobs. If they don't, they will be out in a month. As for the rest, I can't say. I'm sure most of the smaller departments, like Human Resources and Accounting, will keep one person, but the rest will go."

"And we're just supposed to drum up exciting coverage without any direction?" Grady demanded. "How are we even supposed to know if we're on the right track?"

"I can't answer that, Grady." Edith looked as if she'd aged ten years. This was really taking it out of her. "I only know that if you don't get the numbers you need to sustain your position, you're out."

She turned back to her office and paused, hand on the door. "I really am sorry, and I wish you all the best."

With that, she disappeared inside and shut the door. Several people started in her direction—no doubt to voice their complaints—but I didn't bother. Edith wasn't in a power position. She'd given us everything she could.

"What are you going to do?" Grady asked me. He was one of the few people who hadn't erupted once Edith's door had closed.

I held out my hands. "I don't know, but I need to figure it out fast."

"You and me both."

Two

I didn't get depressed. Like...ever. Sure, I was sad when someone died. When I saw a terrible story on the news —or heard about one in the newsroom—I felt disheartened. But I didn't get depressed about it.

All that changed when I learned I would likely lose my job.

"I'm going to have to throw myself into the Mississippi," I announced to my best friend Cally Hart as I stared at my Voodoo Juice in Moxie's Cantina. The bar had opened only a month ago and had quickly become a favorite hangout. "It's the only thing that'll drown my sorrows."

Cally rolled her eyes. She was one of those women people always described as "adorable" and it was true. She was only five feet tall, could fit into juniors clothing a decade after graduating high school, and boasted a cute shoulder-length bob that showed off her ski-slope nose and blue eyes. And she always wore T-shirts with insulting phrases that nobody else could get away with.

"I'm serious," I insisted. "I'm going to become a drain on society. Do you know how long it takes a person to go from paying bills month to month to becoming homeless? I'll tell you how long. Eight months."

"Eight months, huh?" Cally didn't look convinced. "How did you come up with that figure?"

"That's how long it takes to evict someone once they miss their first month of rent."

Cally leaned back in her chair and drummed her fingernails on the bar. She worked in a nail salon—the artist in residence at Nola Nail—and yet her fingers boasted chewed off husks. She didn't even bother painting her nails a solid color. Still, women lined up for her services because she was just that good. "Have you forgotten that you live in my father's building? He won't evict you. I won't let him."

I hadn't forgotten, but I couldn't take advantage of Cally's father. "I have to be able to pay my rent. Your father can't carry me."

"Of course he can," Cally insisted. "My father owns like seventy million buildings in the French Quarter alone. He can overlook one missed rent check."

I shook my head. "I can't. I'll feel guilty forever...and your father owns like thirty-six buildings in the French Quarter. I read a real estate article about him three months ago."

"You're such a stickler for numbers." Cally sipped her drink. She was a New Orleans native, Bohemian and fun for no other reason than she was born that way. I, on the other hand, came from a suburb of Orlando. My idea of fun was hiding all day from tourists dressed in mouse ears. How I'd ended up in New Orleans remained a mystery.

Okay, it wasn't that much of a mystery. When I graduated college with my fancy new journalism degree—with a minor in radio to fall back on—I applied to one-hundred-and-fifty-seven newspapers. No joke. That was the exact number. Three messaged back for interviews. One was in New York City, and as much as I would've loved to live there it wasn't practical.

The cost of living was too high. The second was in Texas, which wasn't out of the realm of possibility. *The Bourbon Street Bugle* interview had been on my way to Texas, and the second I drove into the city I fell in love.

I'd never considered myself a natural in interviews, and yet it felt kismet when I interviewed that day. I had an answer for everything, came across as smart and driven, and didn't even look like an idiot when I flirted with another guy coming in for an interview right after mine. And I had flirted. Hard. The other person interviewing? Grady Dalton. We both got the two open positions. We both started the same day. The flirtation that had sparked in the elevator on interview day died when we got our desk assignments. We were right next to each other, and the sparks that started flying after that were of a different variety.

"Hey!" Cally snapped her fingers directly in front of my face to get me to focus. "Did you hear me?"

I nodded, even though it wasn't true. "Of course. I always listen to you."

She narrowed her eyes, suspicious slits glittering back at me. "What did I say?"

I focused on her shirt as I debated how to answer. It read "Fun Fact, I Don't Care" and always made people laugh. All her shirts made people laugh. "You were telling me it's not the end of the world," I said. If I was wrong, she would bust me, but odds were that I was correct. "You were saying that I don't know that I'm going to lose my job because I still have a month to prove myself. You were saying that I'm a good worker and I'm masterful at what I do, so I'll be fine." I smiled at her.

Her response was not what I expected.

"I was saying you need to stop feeling sorry for yourself and start brainstorming," she shot back on a very unladylike snort. "I don't say nonsense, I'm practical." She rapped her fist into my forehead, causing me to rear back. "Not everybody is going to lose their job, Shay. You need to get it together so you can be ahead of all those other idiots."

I sipped my drink. It was purple, and the bartender, who was also the owner, was known for slipping dry ice cubes in her theme drinks so they smoked. It didn't make the drinks taste any different, but it was a neat effect. "I don't know what to do. I don't even know what an influencer is."

"It's those idiots on that show about the mom who had a bunch of kids and pimped them out to make them famous."

"You're going to have to be more specific," I said.

"You know." Cally had no patience and always exceeded exasperation -- quickly. "That mom. She had two sets of kids. The older ones were with an O.J. Simpson lawyer, and they became famous because they all had huge...um, assets...and one of them made a sex tape."

I kept my face neutral. "Not ringing a bell."

"Of course it is. The mom then married an Olympian who was trans. They had two other daughters and absolutely nobody held down a real job and yet they were all filthy rich."

"Still have no idea."

Cally jabbed a warning finger toward me. "You know exactly who I'm talking about. You're just trying to get me to say their name."

"Why would I do that?" I was the picture of innocence now.

"Because you know I hate them, and I flog myself every night whenever I say their name."

I did know that. "Just out of curiosity, why are you advising me to act like the first family of being famous for nothing if you hate them?"

"I don't want you to be like them. I want you to realize that anybody can be internet famous." Cally was solemn. "Seriously, have you ever spent an hour on TikTok? There are people who are famous for making faces while watching other people's videos. That's a real freaking thing. They sit there and video themselves watching videos."

I blinked and sipped. "Why would that be a thing?" I asked after several seconds.

"I don't know. TikTok is the place where common sense and decency go to die. Yesterday, for example, I spent the entire day watching this woman melt the fuck down because she'd just found her biological family and they weren't paying enough attention to her, as if she was somehow owed something."

I narrowed my eyes. "I watched you melt down two days ago because your mother bought you an eyelash curler."

Cally slapped her hand on the bar hard enough for it to echo. "Who buys someone an eyelash curler? I'll tell you who. A sociopath, that's who." Cally was under the misguided notion that her mother was not only a borderline sociopath, but also a diagnosable one who could someday turn into a serial killer. The problem was, Cally swore up and down true sociopaths couldn't be diagnosed because they were so good at hiding their real identities. She was convinced her mother was a serial killer in human disguise. She just hadn't yet uncovered any bodies.

"Keep it down, ladies," a happy voice said from the left. Moxie Stone, the bar owner, appeared at our side with a tray balanced on her hip. She was a perky blonde, a bright smile always on her face, the sort of person I strove to be because she never settled for anything less than the best. "You girls are going to force me to cut you off if you're not careful." The sparkle in Moxie's eyes told me she didn't mean it. Ever since we'd started coming in she'd been obsessed with finding out what weird thing Cally would say next.

"We're on our first drink," Cally said reasonably. "We're

nowhere near drunk. Besides, this is Bourbon Street. You can't kick someone out after one drink. It's illegal."

Moxie wasn't a native NOLA girl either. But she wasn't so new she'd fall for that. "If you say so." She set down the tray and rested her elbows on the bar. The place was packed. Three other servers handled the floor, and Moxie's fiancé Gus was behind the bar pouring drinks and holding court. It was a perfect time for her to catch a breath. "What are you guys talking about?"

"My life is over," I replied, taking another sip. Seriously, the Voodoo Juice was strong. I had no idea what was in it—I wasn't what could be considered a cocktail connoisseur—but it had quickly become my favorite drink.

"What's his name?" Moxie asked without batting an eyelash.

Cally snorted. "Chris Hemsworth. He haunts my dreams."

Moxie laughed. "I can see why." She kept her gaze on me. "Does Chris Hemsworth do it for you too?"

I shook my head. "I prefer my guys tall, dark, and lanky. This isn't about a guy. It's about my job."

"She thinks she's going to lose it and be homeless in eight months," Cally volunteered.

Moxie's blue eyes went wide. "Seriously?"

I shrugged, trying hard to keep my shoulders from drooping. My mother was a big fan of perfect posture. My posture was far from perfect, but I knew better than slouching. It would cause back issues later on, and because I was about to lose my job and ultimately my health insurance, I didn't need to be picking up any ailments. "So it seems."

"She's not really losing her job," Cally countered. "They're trying to sell *The Bourbon Street Bugle*. They're streamlining operations and giving all the reporters a month to build up influencer blogs to keep their positions. Shay doesn't think she can pull it off."

"Influencer?" Moxie's eyebrows drew together. She looked to be concentrating really hard, even when Gus came over to see what she was doing.

"You two are stealing my woman," he teased, nudging Moxie with his hip to get her attention. "It's been too long, baby. I need five minutes with you in the storage room."

That knocked Moxie out of her confusion. "Did you just admit in front of the entire bar that we do it in the storage room?"

Gus managed to keep a straight face...although just barely. "I was insinuating we went in there to kiss, but okay." He swooped in for a quick kiss. They were adorable. As far as I could tell, they always had a good time together, even when they were bickering. Watching them interact sometimes made my heart ache.

Moxie rolled her eyes again. She didn't look bothered that people might regard her as a sex fiend. "I don't care what people think. In fact, if customers believe that, we'll be even more popular. We'll tell everyone it's the Voodoo Juice that makes us act like that. We'll sell it by the vat."

"There's my little business genius." Gus tapped the end of her nose and then sobered. "I need you to watch the bar for fifteen minutes. We're out of plastic cups."

Moxie's shoulders dropped. "The plastic cups I was supposed to order last week and forgot?"

"I wasn't going to bring that up," Gus replied. "I was going to let you skate. You're far too honest for your own good."

"I'm really sorry." Moxie reached for her apron. "You shouldn't have to go."

"I'm going to my brother's bar," Gus replied. "He'll loan me cups without embarrassing me too much."

Moxie looked sad when she patted his arm. "That's totally all you. I'll make it up to you later."

"Bet your sweet ass you will." He playfully swatted her. "Hold down the fort. I'll be back in fifteen."

My eyes were on Moxie as she watched him go. She looked completely in love. It was very sweet...and irritating. I had big problems and watching someone else bask in a perfect life was almost more than I could take. "So, back to me," I prodded, waiting for both sets of eyes to swing back around. "I don't know how to be an influencer. I can't be one of those people who can't be named because Cally will melt down if they're mentioned. I'm not built that way."

"You wrote music reviews and bar pieces," Cally pointed out. "Heck, you wrote a piece on this bar."

"You did," Moxie agreed. "We have it framed on the wall. Can't you write pieces like that?"

I shook my head. "No. They want the sort of pieces that people chat about, that gets people talking, imaginations firing."

"You're in New Orleans," Moxie pointed out. "That material is around every corner."

"Is it?" I honestly wasn't certain. "I'm out of my comfort zone and I have no idea what I'm supposed to do. If I don't figure it out, I'll be jobless in a month."

"And then homeless eight months after that," Cally supplied. "You're not going to be homeless, so stop freaking out about that. You can do this. I have faith."

"That's great," I said, "but how do I do it?"

Moxie responded. "You're looking at it wrong." She had her pragmatic face on. I saw it whenever Gus had a new business idea, one too expensive to entertain seriously. "You're looking at this from a news standpoint. You think you need to present stories. You don't."

"I don't?"

She shook her head. "You said it yourself. You just need to get people talking. I'm guessing there will be a narrative when you stumble across something, but you need to find the fun before you find the narrative. The narrative will come naturally."

I was still at a loss. "How do I find the fun?"

"Oh, honey, this is New Orleans," Moxie said. "There's fun on every corner."

"She's right," Cally said. "You're a great writer. You can make nothing into something. You just need to find the fun."

I sipped my drink again. Find the fun? Why did that sound so much harder than it should? "I can find the fun," I said after a few seconds. I was trying to convince myself as much as them. "I can totally find the fun."

"You can," Cally agreed. "But start tomorrow. Tonight is for the Voodoo Juice."

I took another sip. "Tomorrow it is. I'm going to go on an adventure to find the fun. It will be like *The Goonies*."

"Sure." Cally bobbed her head. "You'll get chased by murderous thugs and have to babysit without getting paid. What's not fun about that?"

Three

I woke the next day with a hangover...and a bad attitude. I rolled to my back long enough to stare at the ceiling fan, curse my lot in life, and then trudged to the bathroom. There were no cups—my mind wasn't working well enough to remember things like that—so I proved myself a lady of impeccable manners and drank right from the faucet. Then I grabbed some Tylenol from the medicine cabinet and repeated the process. When I still felt like dying, I staggered to the kitchen for some Gatorade.

I filled up my arms with drinks and snacks, went back to my bedroom, and promptly fell back asleep for two hours. By the time I woke again, I felt better...at least where the hangover was concerned. My career prospects were still in the toilet.

With lackluster enthusiasm, I grabbed my tablet and started scouring some of the NOLA message boards. I was looking for something—anything really—that would be influencer worthy. Other than what I'd seen on television, I still had no idea what an influencer even did. The story I followed closest was that actress from an old sitcom who scammed her influencer daughter's way into college. I tried looking at that kid's videos, but there were only so many makeup tutorials I could endure.

Ugh. I pinched the bridge of my nose and squeezed my eyes shut. *I can't do this,* I repeated over and over in my head. I was incapable of doing this. I simply didn't have the chops. I was a big, fat failure.

I was also feeling sorry for myself, I realized. That's what the previous evening of drinking had been about. That's what this morning was about. I was a self-pitying fool and I hated myself for it.

"You can do this," I said to nobody in particular—I was alone after all—and grabbed my tablet again. "It doesn't have to be makeup. It just has to be something that pushes people to talk...and click. Just think of it as a column that can garner advertising."

I scanned the message boards. Most of it was nonsense. Locals were desperate to keep away from tourists when it came to parties, which meant they eschewed Bourbon Street unless somebody held a gun to their head. Locals were the ones reading our stuff, except...*hmm.* A tiny inkling of an idea nudged at my brain.

Locals read the newspaper more. What if I could somehow change that? The tourists spent money on Bourbon Street. They kept the city afloat. Sure, they often did it through drunken revelry and ridiculous tours, but the key would be finding the balance between the locals and tourists. How was I supposed to do that?

I sat on my bed a minute longer and then forced myself to get up. The answers weren't going to be found in bed. I had to go looking for them. I needed a shower...and some coffee...and some beignets couldn't possibly hurt. After that, I would begin the hunt.

Or at least I would give it a solid try. That had to be enough, at least for today.

NEW ORLEANS WEATHER was steamy even in the dead of winter. In the summer it was practically intolerable. Cally had grown up in the city and didn't notice the heat. I was a more recent transplant, and even though I was familiar with heat and humidity from my time in Florida, it felt somehow more oppressive here.

I filled up on iced coffee and beignets for breakfast. Well, it was closer to lunch by the time I finally made it out of my rental house. Then I started walking, looking for ideas. Something was out there. I just had to find it.

It was still early for Bourbon Street. New Orleans slept like a teenager...at least in the French Quarter. That gave me a clear shot to study the businesses before the revelers took over. The only other people out were the homeless. Cally insisted I had to ignore them because otherwise I would be swamped. That was easier said than done.

I dropped what I had in loose change in the cup of an outstretched hand as I turned the corner to St. Philip Street and pulled up short. There it was. My idea for the day: Bloodline, the vampire store.

Now, I know what you're thinking: a vampire store? Yes, it's beyond corny. Only the tourists bother with such things. The store has a little cafe next door that serves Merlot in a blood bag. No joke. I wasn't interested in writing about the store. Heck, I wasn't interested in writing about the cafe. No, I was interested in the after-hours club they supposedly ran.

I had never been. I wasn't even sure where it was located. I'd heard rumors that customers were given cards so they could attend the after-hours club. It was by invitation only and there seemed to be no pattern as to who was invited. The club would make a good story, so I needed to wrangle an invitation.

I took a moment to collect myself on the corner, sucked in a breath, squared my shoulders, and then crossed the street. I had to dodge traffic to get to the store, and then peered through the window. The mood lighting was so dim it was impossible to make out the shoppers. I had no choice but to go in, no matter how ridiculous I found the prospect of the store.

I forced myself to suck it up and pulled open the door. Just on the other side was a woman with violent pink hair. She wore a bustier top that I always thought looked uber cool but knew I could never carry off. Her crushed velvet skirt cascaded to her ankles, not a hint of skin showing thanks to the black boots below. It was a stark contrast to the white skin visible above the waistline.

"Welcome to Bloodline," she said in a dull voice, as if this was the most boring thing she'd ever had to do. "Only those interested in living in the dark and forsaking the light may enter."

It took everything I had to keep a straight face. "Um...that's me." I smiled brightly. "I love the darkness."

Still bored, the woman made a "get on with it" wave. "If you have any questions, ask the woman behind the counter when you check out."

"I'll do that." I was sure at this point that my smile was deranged, but I kept it in place as I studied the shelves. Even though the decor was all vampires, there was nothing to distinguish the shop from the other voodoo stores throughout the Quarter. Real magic shops—and I was assured there were real ones—couldn't be found by the tourists. They were over on Frenchman Street. Everything here was created for the masses.

"Ooh, tarot cards." Even though I was disappointed with the store's offerings, I couldn't stop myself from reaching for the foil-wrapped deck. I collected tarot cards. I found them beautiful, even if I didn't necessarily believe in the magic associated with them.

As I reached for them, another hand came in from my right. Whoever it was reached for the same deck, and our fingers collided.

"I am so sorry," I offered, instantly contrite. "I didn't mean to...." I trailed off when I got my first glimpse at the person who shared my great taste in tarot cards. "Grady." My tone was dark as I regarded him. "What the hell are you doing here?"

Unlike me, who couldn't hide what I was feeling because my face betrayed every emotion, Grady's expression never changed. "Is that any way to greet your favorite co-worker?"

I glared at him. "You're not even on my top-five list."

"Oh, the horror." He mock clutched at his chest and grinned. "I have to know, who could you possibly like more than me in that office?"

"Um...pretty much everybody."

"Johnny Chan?"

I scowled. "No. Not Johnny Chan. He calls everybody by their full names and smacks them with a wet towel if they walk by him in the kitchenette."

"He is the worst," Grady agreed. "Although...Bob Seward is worse when I think about it. He has that weird religious thing."

"Praying when someone swears?"

"It's not just praying," Grady countered. "It's whispered praying while vigorously moving his head. I swear, if he could get his hands on holy water he would throw it on all of us whenever the chance arose."

To my utter surprise, the woman in the bustier walked straight up to Grady and slapped a small bottle in his hand before she kept walking. "What's that?" I asked.

Grady flipped over the bottle and read the label, grinning as he held it up for me to see.

"Holy water," I muttered, shaking my head. "I guess I should've seen that coming in a vampire store."

"We both should have," Grady agreed. He stared at me a moment and then handed over the tarot cards. "If you want them, you should have them."

I eyed the cards suspiciously, as if he'd offered me anthrax. "That's okay. I was just...browsing."

"I was just browsing."

"Yeah?" I snagged the cards from him. "I guess that brings me back to my original question. What the hell are you doing here?"

His grin was lightning quick. "Has anybody ever told you that you're a delight?"

"No."

"Well, I don't think they'll start today." He grabbed the cards back. "I'm willing to bet that I'm doing the exact same thing you are."

Suddenly, I was the picture of innocence. "I'm not doing anything."

"Right."

"I'm not."

"So you've said."

My eyes narrowed. "Why don't you tell me what you think I was doing, and I'll tell you if you're right."

"Fine." He leaned in close, so close that my natural instinct was to take a step back. That was a mistake, because now I had a shelf at my back and him at my front. He rested one forearm on the wall. His face was so close to mine I could feel his breath on my face. In fact, if I stood on the tips of my toes, our lips would be firmly planted against one another.

Not that I wanted to do that, mind you.

"You're looking for something to write about," Grady

said. He kept his forearm lodged against the wall and brought his other hand up close to my face, causing me to flinch. "Wait...are you afraid of me?" He looked taken aback, and immediately stepped back.

Once I could breathe again, I collected myself quickly. "Of course not. Why would you think that?" I couldn't meet his gaze.

"Because you flinched."

"I did not." I tried to sound haughty, as if I were reacting to the most ridiculous thing in the world. I wasn't certain I pulled it off. "Don't be stupid."

He didn't look convinced. He also didn't invade my personal space again. "I'm sorry. It wasn't right to get up in your face like that. I just...um...was screwing around." He almost looked tortured, which made me think my surprised reaction had thrown him.

"It's fine." I meant it. I might not have liked the guy, but I wasn't afraid of him. "You just...moved really fast. It reminded me of a superhero."

His smile was back in an instant. "Or a vampire." He let loose a loony laugh that reminded me of a *Scooby-Doo* cartoon villain. "Is this really how you plan to keep your job?"

"I...don't...know." Now that he said it like that, I felt like a bit of an idiot. Then something occurred to me. "Hold up. You said you were here for the same reason. Why am I the one who gets made fun of when we both had the same idea?"

"Because I'm simply too handsome to be laughed at," he replied.

I snorted, and he frowned. "Of course," I said when I'd managed to convince myself that I could speak without choking on a laugh. "That's exactly what I was thinking."

"I'm totally hot." Grady feigned hurt. "I can't believe you would deny me that truth."

I didn't want to encourage him. He was already full of

himself. Denying he was hot seemed a ridiculous hill to die on, though. "Fine. You're hot."

He beamed at me.

"You're a total tool." I would never walk back that statement. "But you're a hot tool."

He leaned in again, not as close. His eyes zeroed in on my face. "I'll guess I'll have to live with that." He lingered longer than necessary and then leaned back, his thumbs in his belt loops. "Seriously, you're better at this stuff than I am. What are you doing here? I would think you'd be out killing this assignment elsewhere. I came here because I was desperate."

I held out my hands. "Maybe I'm not as good as you think I am."

"Yeah, that's not it." He was serious. "You're Edith's favorite. On top of that, your entire gig is restaurant and band reviews. You've got this in the bag. How can you be worried?"

"Because what I do isn't what they want. They want something that drives advertising. Bands don't drive advertising."

"Restaurants do."

"Yes, but you can only review every restaurant once and if it's a bad review there's no advertising to gain. That means all good reviews...and nobody wants that. They want the truth. I need to come up with a lot more than that, and believe me, I don't understand this influencer thing any more than you do."

He studied my face for a really long time and then smiled. "You'll be okay. Me, on the other hand, I have no idea what I'm doing. News was my life. This is entirely out of my wheelhouse."

"No, it's not." I shook my head, firm. "You'll do fine."

"I hope that's true." He smiled at the worker in the bustier as she came by again. "Love your store," he drawled to her, his most charming smile on display when she slowed her pace. "Honestly, I think this place might be the coolest store in New Orleans. I can't believe I've never been in here before."

"It is cool," the woman replied. Her voice was still flat and disinterested, although there was a keen look in her eyes as she regarded Grady. "Here." She pressed a card into his hand. "That's my last one of the day. If you want to have a good time later, check that place out." Her eyes darted to me. "The invite is only good for one person."

"Well, I do like a good time." Grady's smile was smug as he slid his eyes to me. "As for no plus-one, I'm fine with that."

"I figured you would be." The woman slid around me and began walking to the front of the store. "I'll look for you later."

Grady fanned the card in front of his face, seemingly reveling in the glare I leveled on him. "I guess this story—whether good or bad—will be mine after all."

Annoyance bubbled up. "Well, good luck with that. I'm going to get something way better."

"I'm sure you will."

"Oh, it's totally going to happen."

"I believe you." His fingers moved toward my face again, this time slower, and I almost fell over when he tracked his thumb across my bottom lip.

"What are you doing?" I asked dumbly.

"I have no idea." He shook his head, as if emerging from a dream, and dropped his hand. "I'll tell you how my party goes tonight. I could call you after...if you want to give me your number."

I rolled my eyes. "I think I'll just read about it with the rest of the world."

"Your loss. I'm a witty conversationalist."

"Yeah, I'll believe that when I hear it."

Four

"I'm on the clock, Cally."

My leg was shaking from the voluminous amount of caffeine I'd imbibed—okay, the endless piles of sugar I'd downed hadn't helped either—and I was starting to panic.

It was eight o'clock. I had to publish something to my page before bed so it could go live in the morning. I had no ideas. Cally, ever an amazing friend, had decided to come over and help.

"Tell me what you have so far," she prodded as she danced in front of the stove. Her idea of helping was making gumbo. Given her background—she grew up with cooks and never had to fend for herself—she should've been a menace in the kitchen, like me. Instead, she was a pro...and I was slightly bitter about it.

"I have nothing," I growled. "I've already told you that."

"You must have something." She used her most rational tone.

"I thought I had a vampire club."

She gave a dismissive wave with a wooden spoon. "The vampire club was always a losing proposition."

"Then why was Grady there with the same idea? He's smart. He clearly thought it was a grand idea."

"I thought you told me he admitted to panicking and went with the first thing he thought of."

"What do you think I'm doing?"

"I think you have a brilliant mind and an even more brilliant friend." Cally refused to panic. It wasn't because she was perpetually calm. Far from it. But we had a rule. Only one of us could lose her mind at a time. Today was clearly my turn. "Just tell me what you think you can make work."

"I could write an article about the time I killed my best friend because she tried to feed me gumbo in the middle of a meltdown," I said.

"Oh, right." Cally rolled her eyes. "Like you could kill me."

"I could right now."

"Without me to help hide the body, how would that work?"

She had a point...and I hated her for it. "Cally...."

"Tell me another idea," she insisted. "We'll figure it out."

"I could rank the bars." I was getting desperate. "But...like for something fun."

"Like what?"

"Like hottest bartenders. It would require me running out and hitting every bar in the Quarter, but I have nothing else."

Cally cocked her head, considering. "That is an interesting idea. I would totally like a list for something like that. You don't have time tonight but keep that in your back pocket. What else do you have?"

"Nothing. Have you not been listening?" She might've been right about me not being able to kill her under normal circumstances. I was so frazzled right now that I was convinced I could carry it off...and then likely get off on a second-degree murder charge because of a mental defect. I was definitely feeling defective this evening.

"Let's think about it." She swished her hips as she returned to stirring the gumbo. My mouth was watering, even if I was too panicked to eat. "Influencers focus on things like makeup and clothes." She looked at my outfit. "You wear T-shirts with bands and insulting messages...although I'm a big fan of your 'Did I roll my eyes out loud' shirt, because I often feel that way." She frowned when her eyes landed on the shoes I'd kicked off in the middle of my living room. "And don't get me started on your shoes."

I grabbed my Converse out of instinct and cradled them to my chest. "Don't you dare insult my shoes. They're all I have right now. When I become homeless, it'll be me and my Chucks. You'll stop being my friend because of the smell."

Lines appeared on Cally's forehead. "Do you plan to begin stinking for some reason?"

"I won't be able to shower regularly."

She waved the spoon again. "Don't be ridiculous. Even if you're homeless, I'll still make sure you shower. I would never be that cruel."

I was back to wanting to throttle her. "Cally!"

"I'm thinking," she snapped. "Don't pressure me. You know I don't do well under pressure."

"Join the club."

She managed a small smile. "It's okay, Shay," she said in her softest voice. "You won't lose your job tomorrow if this doesn't come together."

"Maybe not, but if you think they're not watching everybody's views coming out of the gate, you're a crackhead."

"I would never do crack. It's whack. Pot is another story. It makes you mellow." Her gaze was pointed when it landed on me. "We should totally find some pot. That's what you need to open the flood gates of your mind."

"Oh, here we go." I threw my hands in the air. "You did not momentarily join Mensa when we went to the jazz festival thanks to the wonders of a joint, Cally. You were stoned and imagined it."

"No, it totally happened. You're not open to the possibility, though, so it will never work."

"It definitely won't work," I agreed. I pressed the heel of my hand into my forehead and stared at my blank tablet screen. I hadn't typed a single word. "What am I going to do?"

"You're going to take a breath," Cally insisted. She'd begun doling out gumbo into bowls. "You're going to have some dinner with me, and we're going to talk about things calmly and rationally. I might have a few ideas."

I was so desperate I would entertain any thought at this point.

Cally used her elbow to nudge the tablet out of the way and then sat across from me on the floor. I had a kitchen table, but it was buried under books. "Let's talk," she said when she'd gotten comfortable. "I guarantee your bosses don't want you to focus on makeup and fashion."

"They pretty much said as much," I agreed.

"So, they want you to influence things other than makeup and fashion."

"No, they want buzz," I countered. "That's the word they used. It's our job to get people talking. It doesn't matter about what. If people are talking, directing people to the website, more eyes will be on the advertising. That's the only way to save *The Bugle*."

"Right." Cally tapped her bottom lip, seemingly lost in thought. "How did Grady look when you saw him today?" she asked, throwing me for a loop.

"What?" Perhaps I had a stroke and missed the transition.

"Grady," she repeated. "He's the co-worker you have a crush on, right?"

"No," I sputtered, gripping my spoon so tightly my knuckles turned white. "I don't have a crush on him. Why would you even suggest that?"

"You're always talking about him."

"Because I hate him."

"Okay." She choked on a laugh. "Oh, you're serious," she said when I continued to glare. "You really think you hate him."

"I *know* I hate him," I shot back. "He's horrible."

"I thought he was hot."

"That doesn't preclude him from being horrible."

"Right." She bobbed her head. "But how is he horrible?"

"He constantly talks down to me."

"Because you're a woman and he's a man?"

"Sometimes. Mostly just because he thinks he's smarter than anybody in the room."

"And yet he had the bad idea for the vampire party just like you," Cally mused. "I've yet to meet him. I've only heard stories. Maybe you should arrange for us to meet over drinks one night."

Was she kidding? "I'm not introducing you. Don't be absurd."

"Because you like him and you're afraid he'll take one look at me and fall head over heels."

"Because he's a tool and I'm afraid that I'll kill him if I spend too much time in close proximity to him."

"That's a very smart answer." Cally beamed. There was something knowing about her expression I didn't like. "Maybe you should call him and ask what he's writing about? You might get some ideas."

"He's writing about the underground vampire club."

Cally tapped her spoon against my bowl. "Eat. We'll brainstorm."

"I'm going to write an ode to my Chucks if you're not careful," I warned as I spooned the gumbo into my mouth. It was as good as it always was. "I'm going to talk about how fashion is overrated and comfort is the way to go."

Cally made an O face.

"Whatever you're thinking, don't," I snapped. "I just know it's a terrible idea."

"What if it's not?" she challenged. "What if the thing that gets people talking is you being you?"

I was at a loss. "Me being me?"

"You're funny, Shay," she insisted. "You're self-deprecating and always make people laugh."

"Half the time I'm not trying to make people laugh. They just do."

"That's why everybody likes you. I mean...I make fun of your clothes, but they fit you. Maybe they'll fit New Orleans too."

"I just told you my boss doesn't want me writing about fashion and makeup," I reminded her.

"You won't. You'll be doing the anti-fashion blog...and telling people why Chucks are better than hooker heels and T-shirts are better than spaghetti strap dresses."

"Isn't that a given?"

"To you...and I bet it will be to others."

She looked so hopeful all I could do was nod. "Sure. I'll write a column about why Chucks are the shoes of the Quarter, and it will make me the belle of *The Bugle*."

"Stranger things have happened."

CALLY ENDED UP SPENDING THE NIGHT. Once we finished the gumbo we turned to the gin. It wasn't like me to imbibe two nights in a row, but I was feeling sorry for myself. After two cocktails, I started writing an ode to my Chucks as a joke. I knew I would be in trouble because I would have nothing to turn in the following day, but by my fourth drink I didn't care.

Two sips into that drink, I started to feel sick.

"That shrimp was fresh, right?" I asked as Cally swirled her cocktail and danced in front of the window.

"Of course," she scoffed. "Why?" When she turned to look at me, her eyebrows flew so high they disappeared into her hairline. "You look a little green, Shay."

I felt a little green. Before I even realized what was happening, I rushed into the bathroom and dropped to my knees. I hit so hard I knew I would be feeling it the next day, but it didn't matter. I just managed to dip my head into the toilet before I started puking.

Cally was a sympathetic puker, but it didn't matter. We'd both eaten the gumbo. It took her only three minutes longer than me for the sickness to hit. "Oh, man."

We spent the entire night taking turns throwing up. Then we moved to my bed to pass out. When I opened my eyes again, it was a chore. They were crusted shut—from sweat or tears, I couldn't say—and every muscle in my body hurt.

"I don't know if I'm never drinking again or never eating your cooking again," I growled to my best friend, who was stirring beside me.

"It was the gin," she insisted in a raspy voice. "It had to be."

"I don't usually puke after three cocktails. I might not be a native New Orleans resident, but I have a stronger constitution than that."

"You had four drinks. I counted."

"I had two sips of the fourth drink. That's barely anything."

"Well...." Cally looked as rough as I felt. She'd fallen asleep without removing her makeup, something she never neglected to do. She'd sweated through most of that makeup when doing her regurgitation floor routine, but her eye pencil was the stubborn kind and ran sometime in the middle of the night. "Don't blame my cooking."

"It's clearly food poisoning," I growled as I shifted my legs off the bed. I felt weak and tired. "How am I supposed to go into the office feeling like this?"

"Call in sick. What are they going to do?"

"Um...fire me."

"They already plan to do that if you don't come up with something better than an ode to your Converse. I can't believe you sent that in, by the way. I thought you were joking."

I made a face. "I was joking."

She shifted to stare directly into my face. "You sent it in."

"No, I didn't." To prove it, I forced myself to my feet. I groaned the entire way into the living room, making a quick pit stop at the refrigerator for a bottle of water. I guzzled the entire thing, tossed the empty bottle into the recycling bin, and then grabbed another. When I glanced at the hallway, I found Cally bracing herself in the opening by pressing a hand against each wall.

"I'm going to be in big trouble for not sending anything in, but I might be able to use the food poisoning as an excuse if I'm pathetic enough."

"You're plenty pathetic," she reassured me. "I swear you sent that article in. I remember very distinctly. You said if you were going to go down, you might as well go down in flames...and then you got those Converse that have flames on them out of your closet."

"Don't be ridiculous." My eyes moved to the coffee table in the living room. To my surprise—and horror—my flame

Converse were indeed out. "I did not send that article," I insisted.

I stomped to my tablet and unlocked it. I expected to find the Pages app filling the screen, maybe even still open to the ode to my Chucks, but instead I found the load portal for *The Bugle* website. I could feel what little color I had drain from my face.

"No, no, no." I dropped to my knees and tapped at the screen. I had long since been logged out because the window had sat idle for so long. When I finally managed to get into the system, I found my article had not only been posted, it had been approved by Edith and was live.

"No!"

Cally leaned over my back. "Uh-oh. Do you think this is the part where you have to stop showering?"

I definitely wanted to kill her now. "What am I going to do?"

She held out her hands and shrugged. "Own it, I guess. It's too late to pull it back, right? If anybody asks, just tell them you were trying something new."

That sounded like a terrible idea, and yet I had no other choice. "I blame you for this."

She patted my shoulder. "That's what I'm here for. Do you want me to cook you breakfast before you head out?"

"I feel like death. I don't want to eat."

"Huh. I feel like I'm rebounding."

Of course she did. "I'm getting in the shower. If I get fired today, I don't want to smell like puke."

She flashed me an enthusiastic thumbs-up. "That's the spirit."

Ugh. This day had barely begun and it was already the worst.

Five

Most offices would frown on showing up to work hungover. But this was New Orleans, and nobody bothered giving me grief about my red eyes, lack of makeup, or the fact that all I'd done to fix myself up was throw my wet hair back in a messy bun.

"How was your night?" Grady sidled over to my desk when I sat down and stared at the things that needed to be packed.

"Fine," I replied, refusing to go into detail. "Yours?"

"It left a little to be desired." His smile was rueful when he sat on the corner of my desk. The aftershave I so often admired—from afar—made me want to gag. "The vampire club was a bit of a letdown. I couldn't put that in my piece, of course, because there's no way anyone will pay for advertising if all I do is complain. I turned it into a commentary on horror as entertainment."

Despite my hangover, I was intrigued. "How so?"

"How we try to turn the dangers of the night into fluffy bunnies so we'll be less frightened. That's what that club basically is. It's why vampires are turned into romantic heroes in movies and books. I decided to be above it all."

I admired him for telling the truth. "You're saying you opted to be a douche."

"Pretty much," he agreed on a grin. "It's nothing compared to your ode to your shoes, of course, but I'm not entirely unhappy with how things turned out."

I tried not to cringe...and failed. "Um...have you heard anything about that?" I tugged on my ear, a nervous habit I'd been working overtime to quit since I was fourteen. I'd thought I'd shaken it...right up until this moment.

Dammit!

"You're wondering if anybody has mentioned the fact that you wrote about your Converse." His smile was conspiratorial when he leaned forward. "I think you flew under the radar with that one."

Hope flashed bright. "Really?"

"No." He barked out a laugh. "There's a running bet over who is going to be eliminated on the first day when the month is up -- and you're the odds-on favorite. There's even a rumor they won't really wait until the end of the month."

The nausea I'd thought tamped down returned with a vengeance. "Great." I rubbed my forehead. "That's just...great."

"I have to ask, what were you thinking? Turning in nothing would've been better than that."

I couldn't have agreed more but had no intention of admitting it. Instead, I doubled down on my stupidity. "I think it was a brilliant move," I lied, internally cursing Cally and her need to help. "I mean...people are talking about it, right? That's the point."

Grady stilled. "That's a genius move."

"Right?" I suddenly started feeling better. If I could convince Grady that I'd published the piece about my shoes on purpose—and that I was thinking outside the shoebox, so to speak—then maybe I would be okay.

"Not even remotely." Grady's smile was back as he shook his head. "You can pretend you were trying to be edgy, but I bet you were drunk."

I balked. "I wasn't drunk."

"You're hung-over. He leaned in and sniffed. "Bourbon?"

I was horrified and immediately lifted my arm to scent myself. "How can you possibly know that?"

"Oh, babe, I'm an expert on almost everything. You should already know that."

I glared at him. "Whatever." I was determined to get through this day quickly, and without any bloodshed, which meant he needed to go. "Don't you have something else to do?"

"Not really."

"Well, find something." I made a shooing motion with my hand. "Even if you don't, I do."

He made no move to leave. "What are you doing?"

"I have to pack up my desk. In case you've forgotten, we're getting kicked out of here. I figure it's better to get it done today."

"So...you're basically saying that you're going to throw some pencils and a coffee mug in a box and call it a day."

I glared at him. "Dude, seriously, I'm going to throw up if you don't take that cologne someplace else."

Finally, I got a reaction out of him. "What?" He mimicked my earlier motion and sniffed himself. "Can you really smell my cologne? The woman I bought it from said it was subtle."

"The subtle influences of cedar wood and coriander?"

"How did you know that?"

"Call it a guess." I shooed him away again. "Seriously, I'll puke all over you if you don't leave."

"You say the sweetest things," he drawled as he got to his

feet. His smile stretched wide for a moment and then dissipated. "Just ignore Edith when she comes down on you. I get that you were blowing off steam last night and got frustrated. There's still plenty of time to come up with something to save yourself."

He almost sounded sincere. Almost.

"I'm not falling for your act again," I said. "You're my competition. You want me to fail so you'll be safe."

"Believe it or not, I don't want you to fail."

"I don't believe it."

"I want others to fail." He offered up a cheeky grin. "If Annabelle Chalmers were to fail, I wouldn't shed a tear."

That got my attention. The rumor was that Annabelle and Grady had dated...and more than once. Supposedly they'd had a torrid affair. It burned bright for a month and then the flame was somehow doused. I'd been trying to track down information on the cause of their breakup—something that happened more than six months ago—but I'd come up empty.

"Was your breakup that bad?" I teased.

He made a face. "Don't believe everything you hear." He took one of my pencils and tapped the end of my nose. "Seriously, ignore what everybody says about your shoe piece. I thought it was well-written and funny...even if there was absolutely no point to it."

I had a momentary flash of pride, and then he threw in that last part. "You can go now, Grady."

"Thanks for gracing me with so much of your time," he called back as he started across the room toward his desk. "I know it was torturous for you."

Oh, he had no idea.

AN HOUR LATER AND MY DESK WAS completely bare. I'd dropped little extras like my tape dispenser and computer wipes in the box on the big table in the center of the room, but everything else was packed. The only thing remaining was my work computer...and it looked sad and bereft as I stood several feet away and stared at what had once been my career home base.

"Are you worried?" a female voice asked from behind me.

I didn't have to turn to know who was infringing on my personal space. I blanked my features—my initial reaction had been a sneer—and slowly turned to face Annabelle. Her desk was on the other side of the newsroom, and we'd rarely interacted. I preferred it that way.

"I think everybody is worried," I replied. "It's stressful, even if you think you can work something out. Some people will keep their jobs. Others won't be that lucky. Those who do manage to stay will likely feel guilty because friends will get cut. It's a stressful situation all around."

Annabelle, her black hair loose around her shoulders, blinked several times. "I meant about your stupid shoe post," she said. She had a voice like nails on a chalkboard. Actually, it was worse. What's worse than nails on a chalkboard? I'll tell you, it's Annabelle's voice. "I can't believe you actually loaded that thing."

I pressed the tip of my tongue against the back of my teeth. I wanted to yell at her—you have no idea how much— and it wasn't just the hangover. But an outburst on top of the ridiculous shoe column would have me headed through the door on the arm of security before anybody else.

"I just thought I would try something different," I said. "It's not a big deal."

"Not a big deal?" Annabelle scoffed. "Seriously? You wrote about shoes."

My temper ratcheted up a notch. "What did you write about?"

"They're planning a fashion show at Louis Armstrong Park. A big one, with real models. I broke the news."

My heart sank. That *was* a good tip, and it would cause a lot of buzz in the Quarter.

"But I'm sure your shoe column will get just as many clicks." She gave me a condescending look. "Here comes Edith."

If I hadn't already felt sick, Annabelle's haughty tone would've completely done it for me. I was in big trouble, but it was worse than I feared.

"Hello, everybody." Edith pulled out the sort of smile adults reserve for children about to get some very bad news. "I want to thank everybody for filing their first pieces under what I know had to be daunting circumstances."

I tried to make myself small, dodging behind Grant and his broad shoulders. I did not want Edith catching sight of me.

"Some of the pieces were quite ingenious," she continued. "We even had some breaking news thanks to Annabelle, and that gained several-thousand hits."

Annabelle preened under the compliment, shooting me an "I told you so" grin.

"One piece blew away all the others," Edith continued. She sounded tired, as if she hadn't slept in days. "When I saw the numbers, I thought it must've been some sort of fluke. I couldn't figure it out. Then I tracked the article to where it was getting the most shares, and guess what? It was TikTok."

I was beyond confused. What did a video app have to do with an influencer column?

"Were they talking about my news?" Annabelle asked. She sounded convinced that was the case. "I bet the locals are hoping to get a chance to walk the runway. Apparently, they are going to tap a few girls for the show."

"It wasn't your story," Edith replied, matter-of-fact. "Your story got twenty-five-hundred hits. That's very good for a first try and I'm impressed."

Annabelle kept her smile in place, but she looked frozen, as if she suspected something bad was about to happen.

"The piece I'm talking about got twenty-five-thousand hits."

The revelation stole the oxygen from my lungs.

"And, I have to tell you, when I originally saw the piece, I thought it was the stupidest thing I'd ever read," Edith continued. "Who knew an ode to tennis shoes would make for such fascinating reading?"

I froze. Wait…was she talking about my piece? I snapped up my chin and found Edith looking directly at me.

She nodded encouragingly. "Your piece went viral, Shay. The girls at one of the Tulane dorms were bored last night, it seems. The storm that rolled through had them locked inside…and they found your piece. They loved it, filmed a bunch of videos in their Converse while reading your piece, and it led to twenty-five-thousand hits in less than twelve hours."

That couldn't be right. "But—" I broke off and licked my lips. What was happening?

"The girls liked your take on shoes not defining the woman," Edith explained. "They thought it was a down-to-earth opinion on the many hats a woman must wear in everyday life. I think it was a risk, but in this instance, it paid off. Well done." She lightly applauded. "As for everybody else, I don't want a bunch of columns about shoes. That's not what this is, so don't bother trying to suck up that way. Shay wrote a poignant piece that touched people," she continued. "I'm guessing she had no idea how many people she'd reach."

Well, that was an understatement.

"In this case, it worked out well," Edith continued. "People are talking about us, which is good. Shay's hits put her way ahead in the competition. You all have someone to be worried about." She grinned at me. "Well done. I'm very proud of you." With that, she turned on her heel and headed back to her office.

The newsroom was silent for a full ten seconds before everybody started talking at once. Questions were fired in rapid fashion, at me, and I suddenly found myself the center of attention. That's not where I wanted to be.

"Well, congratulations," Annabelle said stiffly. The look she shot me was hardly friendly. "I guess your willingness to take a chance worked out."

I nodded. Annabelle wasn't the sort to congratulate another woman when there was a competition afoot.

"I guess I need to step up my game," she added. It almost sounded like a threat.

"You're already doing well," I enthused. "I mean...twenty-five-hundred hits. That's amazing."

"Don't patronize me."

"I'm not." I meant it. I couldn't patronize her even if I wanted to. I had no idea what was going on.

"Whatever." Annabelle flounced off, leaving me standing in the middle of a melee. Everybody wanted to know how I'd come up with the idea...and if I'd paid someone at Tulane to do the videos. After answering questions, I slowly made my way back to my desk.

Unsurprisingly, Grady was sitting on it. "Well, that was interesting." Unlike Annabelle, his smile looked legitimate. "How did you pull that off?"

I held out my hands. "I wish I knew. I thought she was going to hold me up as an example of what not to do."

"I think she probably would've if it hadn't been for those hits. It's an interesting strategy."

There was no strategy, but I could hardly admit that. "Well, it worked out." I went for humble. "I feel really lucky."

"Yeah. Now you just have to keep it up. The problem with being the frontrunner is that you always have something to lose going forward."

The relief I'd felt only moments earlier fled. "I...um...."

He flashed a smile and then patted my arm. "Don't let the fear get the better of you. You've got this."

He said it, but I didn't feel it. I'd managed to skate by on a fluke. I needed to get it together...and fast.

Six

I left with little fanfare. I said goodbye to a few co-workers, but I knew I would likely run into them again. It was the French Quarter, and despite the size of New Orleans, we frequented the same places.

I made it to the downstairs lobby with my box before I realized there was only one personal item in it, a framed photograph of Cally and me. I removed it from the pile, dumped the box in the big garbage receptacle in the lobby, and continued out the door.

There was no sense holding onto things that couldn't help me.

"Hey." Grady sidled up as I stepped outside the building. The heat was oppressive this time of day, and that's what I blamed for the hot flash that washed over me.

"Were you waiting for me or something?" I demanded. "Stalking is bad, no matter what the nightly news has told you."

Grady blinked twice. "I was talking with Glenn and Don." He pointed to two men standing on the sidewalk. "We're going to get drinks at the corner bar. We thought you might want to come. Well, you and anybody else who is leaving."

"Oh." I pressed my lips together. "Sorry."

Amusement curved his ridiculously pretty mouth. "It's okay...I guess. But my feelings are definitely hurt."

I didn't bother to hide my eye roll. "I'm not buying you drinks, so forget it. I have to pinch my pennies if I'm going to be homeless in a few months."

"Don't be so dramatic." He laughed at my expense. "Nobody's going to be homeless."

I wasn't so sure. "I guess I could have one drink." I wasn't exactly feeling up to cocktails—the ones I'd imbibed the previous evening still had me unsettled—but I wasn't ready to let go of the camaraderie of the office. Everything had been yanked away from us so fast. "Don't think you can take advantage of me."

"Well, how else would a stalker think?"

I didn't want to laugh. It would only encourage him. But I couldn't help myself. "One drink."

"Sure." He plucked the framed photo from my hands. "Is this your sister?"

"My best friend."

Grady's gaze was serious as he studied the photo. "I know this might come off as an invasive question—and I'm sorry if it offends you—but it never occurred to me to ask you before."

I was confused. "I'm dying to hear this question," I said on a laugh. "Go for it. It's not like there's a Human Resources Department to report you to if I don't like the question."

"I have that working for me," he agreed. "Um...you're not a lesbian, are you?"

It wasn't the question I expected. "Why would you ask that?" I snagged the frame back from him, and then it occurred to me. "Because of this?" I held up the photo.

"I told you I wasn't trying to be offensive," he reiterated. "I'm just curious. I've never seen you with a man."

"So because I haven't had a date pick me up at the office, that makes me a lesbian?"

Grady's cheeks colored under my scrutiny. "I was just curious. Sorry."

"Uh-huh." I had no idea why he was so interested. Well, I had one idea. It didn't make me like him any better, though. "You're not interested in watching us kiss or anything?"

Grady snapped up his chin. "Wait...*are* you a lesbian?" It almost looked as if he was disappointed, which didn't follow the narrative I was building in my head.

"I'm not, but there are times I wish I was. If I could roll that way, I think my life would be so much better. Alas, I'm a slave to the male form...and it's depressing." I took on a far-off expression as we arrived at the bar.

"Wow. What a drama llama." Grady barked out a laugh. His ready smile was back. "I'm sorry you're a slave to the penis, but I am curious why you wish you were a lesbian."

"I didn't say I was a slave to the penis." My scandalized statement escaped just as Don held open the door and I slipped inside the bar. Normally that wouldn't be a problem, because in most New Orleans establishments you had to shout over the loud music. But apparently the band was between sets. My voice echoed throughout the bar and plenty of eyes—including those belonging to Annabelle—snapped in my direction.

"Well, great," I muttered.

Grady let loose a low chuckle and leaned close enough that his breath was warm on my ear. "I liked it." A shudder went down my spine.

"I'm not a slave to the penis," I insisted in a whisper. "That's not what I said."

"You said you were a slave to the male form," Grady

insisted. "If you're not talking about the penis, what are you talking about?"

"Don't worry about it." I was mortified. I couldn't believe he was taking it this far. Well, I *could* believe it, because that's who he was, but I was embarrassed to within an inch of my life.

"It's okay." He gave me a friendly pat on the shoulder. "Your secret is safe with me."

"If you say so." I trudged behind him as he led me to the area of the bar that had been taken over by our co-workers. Several tables had been pushed together so everybody could sit together and commiserate.

"What do you want?" Grady asked when he pulled a chair out for me. "I'm going up to get something for myself. I can get you something too."

"Oh." I felt put on the spot. "I'll just have an iced tea."

Grady cocked a dubious eyebrow.

"I'm still recovering from last night."

"You know what they say: The best cure for a hangover is another drink."

"Yes, I believe that's the New Orleans motto," I said dryly.

He folded his arms across his chest, telling me that he had no intention of getting me an iced tea.

"A gin and tonic will be fine," I said. "Violet gin if they have it."

"That's a very boring drink," he noted. "Clearly I'm going to have to introduce you to better liquor. But today you may have your drink of choice. Just this once."

It was an odd thing to say, and I shook my head as I sank into the chair.

"So, how did you manage to get those kids at Tulane to do videos on you?" Clarissa Davenport asked from her spot next to Annabelle. There was an accusatory glint in her eyes.

I felt like a bug under a microscope when I looked up and

realized all eyes were on me. "I didn't ask anybody to do that." I felt awkward and unsure, not uncommon for me. "It just happened."

"Yeah, but you wrote about shoes," Clarissa insisted. "You didn't even write about good shoes. You wrote about Converse, for crying out loud. Why would college kids care about something like that?"

I'd been asking myself the same question since Edith announced my triumph. "Um...I honestly don't know."

The look Clarissa leveled on me said she didn't believe me. "Right."

"What are we talking about?" Grady asked when he returned with our drinks.

I'd never been so happy to see anyone in my life. He was great at filling awkward silences. "Nothing," I replied, accepting my gin and tonic.

"We were just asking Shay how she managed to upstage us all," Clarissa replied. "She was being cagey."

"Yes, she claims she didn't coordinate what happened," Annabelle added. "It's very...unbelievable."

"Well, why is it so hard to believe?" Grady demanded. "We've done hundreds of stories about viral videos throughout the years. There's never a rhyme or reason to them. That's what happened here."

"Unless it wasn't." Annabelle insisted. "It's possible Shay bribed the students to make the videos. I'm not saying it wasn't a smart move. Obviously, it was brilliant. We just want to know how she did it."

"I didn't do anything," I insisted to Grady. Why I felt the need to plead my case to him was beyond me.

"I know." He patted my back. "Why can't you guys let it go?" Grady demanded. "It was a fluke. It's one of those things that's one in a million. We should be happy that our co-worker managed to do something so fabulous."

Annabelle muttered something I couldn't make out.

"What did she say?" I asked Grady.

"I believe she said she's bitter that she thought she was going to be the big star today and her grand designs to be publicly lauded were snatched from her grasp," Grady replied. "She thought she had the accolades in the bag with that fashion show scoop, even though I happen to know she's been sitting on that tip for a week and only knows about it because her mother does PR for that makeup place on Decatur."

Annabelle's eyes went wide. "That was a real story."

"It was a good story," Grady agreed. "That's the sort of thing people will be buzzing about for weeks. The local teenagers will want to try out for one of those coveted runway spots. That's exactly the sort of thing Edith is looking for."

"Except now it's not," Annabelle fired back. "Now the brass will expect twenty-five-thousand views per story. Shay has screwed us all."

I sank lower in my chair. I felt multiple sets of eyes on me, and I didn't like it.

"Oh, don't blame her," Grady snapped. "She did the one thing we were all trying to do. You're just jealous."

I was surprised that he'd chosen to stand up for me. Normally he preferred messing with me, seeing how far he could push things before I melted down.

"I don't get jealous of other people," Annabelle shot back. "I'm simply saying what everybody else is thinking. We're in trouble now. Any story that doesn't get the same number of clicks will be considered a failure."

Was that true? "I...."

"You what?" Annabelle feigned concern. "You're sorry?"

"She has nothing to be sorry about," Grady fired back. "She wrote a piece that went viral. She should be congratulated. It's not like the rest of us wouldn't be partying it up if we received that many views."

"Grady, I don't believe anybody was talking to you," Annabelle said, faux sweetness dripping from her tongue. "We're talking to Shay. She set the impossible curve for us. Now we all need to work together to correct that mistake."

I was instantly alert. "Why was it a mistake? And how do you think that's going to work?"

"Yeah, Annabelle, how is that going to work?" There was an edge to Grady's tone, one I hadn't heard before. The animosity between them was off the charts. Perhaps one of them was still holding a grudge over their breakup. It appeared Grady had specific feelings, none of them good.

"We need to strategize." Annabelle's tone was prim. "We need to put our heads together and come up with a plan."

"Yes," Grady said dryly. "I believe that's what the word strategize means."

Annabelle ignored him and kept her focus on me. "A group of us—the more savory members of the staff—are going to hot yoga and bandy ideas during morning workouts. You should join us."

The invitation threw me for a loop...for more reasons than one. "You want me to go to yoga with you?" That sounded like zero fun.

"It's good for you. The heat helps work your muscles."

"I've heard it's like physical torture," Grady offered. "Like you'll want to kill yourself before you're finished."

"It's not for the weak of heart," Annabelle clarified. "You'd fit in well with the group, Shay."

She'd never invited me to anything before. Heck, she hadn't even invited me to lunch even though we were eating at the same restaurant and I happened to be alone. I wasn't naive enough to think she didn't have ulterior motives. I was at a loss how I was supposed to replicate my success, but Edith had said I was the one to watch.

I couldn't see myself making it through a single hot yoga class. "Um...."

"Don't do it," Grady said in a low voice. "She's offering you candy. Don't get into the van."

I was caught and I knew it. "I can probably make it," I said finally, immediately hating myself for caving. "Give me a time and place and I'll see what I can do."

Annabelle beamed at me...and then shot a haughty look toward Grady. "Absolutely. The more the merrier."

I WAS READY TO HEAD OUT THIRTY minutes later. The rest of my group showed no signs of leaving, but I'd had enough commiserating over liquor and needed to find another idea. The one to watch couldn't fall flat on her face the second day.

"Hold up." Grady caught me outside the bar.

"You don't have to walk me home or anything," I said. "I mean...it's the middle of the afternoon. I'm fine."

Grady smirked. "I wasn't offering to walk you home."

"Oh."

"If you need me to, I will."

"Of course I don't need you to." I straightened. "I'm a big girl. I can take care of myself. I just thought...um...why did you follow me out?"

"I feel the need to offer you a friendly piece of advice." His smile disappeared. "You need to be careful about Annabelle."

"Why?"

"She doesn't have your best interests at heart."

"No offense, but I don't think anybody in there has my best interests at heart. Edith said I'm the one to watch. That means I'm the one to beat."

Grady suddenly looked uncomfortable.

"Don't pretend you haven't been thinking it," I said. "At least do me the courtesy of telling the truth."

"I like to win," he conceded after a few seconds. "That doesn't necessarily mean I want you to lose in the process."

"Somebody has to lose."

"Or maybe multiple people can win." He held up his hands when I opened my mouth to argue further. "That's really not why I came out. I want you to understand exactly what Annabelle is offering you."

"According to you, it's candy."

"And not the good kind," he confirmed. "You're going to get a bowl full of stale Good and Plenty if you're not careful."

I made a face.

"Or candy corn," he added.

"Hey, I might not like the candy, but there's nothing better than a candy corn cocktail. I had one at the Carousel Bar at Halloween last year and it was delicious."

His lips quirked. "I'll file that away. I'm serious. Annabelle sees you as a threat. She doesn't try to make friends with her enemies. She tries to crush them. That's what she wants to do to you."

"Well, believe it or not, I've already come to the same conclusion. I don't trust her."

"But...you agreed to go with her to hot yoga."

"That doesn't mean I trust her. I'm not an idiot."

"No, you're not." He chuckled. "Well, okay. I just wanted to warn you. Constant sabotage is the name of her game. I guess I've done my due diligence."

"Totally," I agreed, moving to step off the curb. "Just out of curiosity, um, do you still have feelings for her?"

Grady made an incredulous face. "Why would you ask that?"

I shrugged. "I don't know. Things between you seemed intense."

"She's a psycho. You don't let your guard down around a psycho."

That seemed to be all he was going to say, so I nodded. "Okay, I guess I'll see you around."

He winked. "Have fun for the rest of the day, superstar."

"Ugh. Must you call me that?"

"Now that I know it bugs you, absolutely."

Seven

The Quarter never lacked for fun. The trick was finding something that would make a good story. Annabelle was right. The pressure was on. I needed to come up with something good. Matching my previous numbers didn't seem possible. I couldn't come in last, but I didn't need to be at the top again.

"I'll have an iced tea," I said to the woman with the beverage cart on Decatur Street.

"Sure." She didn't bother smiling. I couldn't blame her. It was hot. Walking with to-go cups was ubiquitous, but smiles were superfluous.

While waiting for her to fill my cup, I let my attention drift to Jackson Square. A huge group of people had amassed there—much larger than normal—and they seemed to be watching something. "What's going on over there?" I asked as I accepted the iced tea.

"Oh, *that*." Now the woman did smile. "They're having a fashion show."

"In Jackson Square?"

"Yeah, the Rainbow Confederacy set it up."

"The Rainbow Confederacy?" I was familiar with the local group's work. They did outreach for at-risk street people. New Orleans had a lot of street people, and while all were considered at-risk, there were some in significant danger due to their sexuality. "I didn't realize they did fashion shows." I was intrigued.

"They partnered with that underground podcast," the woman explained. "You know the one for gay and transgender people? They're doing a drag queen fashion show to raise money."

"Oh, well that sounds fun." I meant it. I also wondered if it would make a good story.

"I guess the gimmick is that they had all the local women turn in their ugly bridesmaid dresses for the show."

That was an absolutely delightful idea. "Why haven't I heard about this? It seems the local newspapers and radio stations would be promoting it."

The woman shrugged. "You know how people get. I'm a live-and-let-live person. I say as long as you don't hurt anybody else, you know, do whatcha wanna."

I felt the same way. "Yeah. I'll check it out."

"Have fun."

THE CROWD IN THE SQUARE WAS HOPPING, and I arrived just as the music started. They hadn't bothered with a catwalk—which seemed a bummer—but they'd cleared room on the sidewalks and blocked them off so the drag queens could strut.

Several hundred people had gathered for the show, all of them having a marvelous time.

I pulled out my phone and took some crowd shots, smirking when the music switched to something with a pounding beat. I couldn't remember the name of the song, but I recognized it as something by Madonna. I wasn't good with music. If it was something from a movie soundtrack, I could usually name it. If not, I was at a loss. It hardly mattered in this case. All that mattered was that a story was beginning to take shape.

"Fun, huh?" a smoky voice asked to my left.

I nodded as I turned, my mouth dropping open as I took in the fantastical six-foot-tall presence at my left. All I saw at first was the canary yellow dress. Then I noticed the frosted blue wig with sparkles. Then I saw a pair of eyelashes that were so long I was surprised they didn't get tangled.

The laugh that exploded around me was warm and gregarious.

"Bebe Beignet."

"What?" I was confused as a hand jutted out toward me.

"That's my name. Bebe Beignet."

I nodded. "You're one of the models."

"Yes." He bobbed his head. There was sympathy in his eyes. "Do you need me to explain things?"

A cooler person would've said no. I was not cool. "Oh, please. I don't want to say the wrong thing."

"It's all for fun, girl," he said with a laugh. "You can't say the wrong thing."

I decided to go for broke. "Do you identify as a man or a woman? Because, and I'm being honest here, in my head I said 'he' when thinking about you, but I'm terrified that was wrong and I don't want to be *that* person."

Bebe's laugh was so loud it would've echoed...if hundreds of people weren't screaming and clapping around us. "The fact that you're worried means nobody can take offense. In general, drag queens exaggerate female characteristics, but most—not all, mind you, most—still identify as men."

"Okay." I absorbed the information. "Do you identify as a man?"

"Definitely. I'm an accountant four days a week and I wear a suit."

"Wow." I had trouble picturing that. "Do you...wear those eyelashes when you're an accountant?"

Bebe snorted. "No. These are just for fun."

"Is it like Halloween?" I didn't want to be ignorant, but I was curious.

"Kind of. It's a lifestyle. Today we're having fun with the lifestyle because we want to give to those who might not yet know what sort of lifestyle they'll ultimately be drawn to."

I smiled. "It's really nice."

"It is." Bebe was quiet for a moment. "We have an extra dress. It's too small for all of us."

At first, I didn't understand, but then it dawned on me. "Oh, no." I vigorously shook my head.

"Come on." Bebe's tone turned pleading. "It's a very small dress and it would fit you perfectly. It has a big sequined cat on it."

My mouth fell open. "Who has a bridesmaid dress with a sequin cat?"

"A masochist?" Bebe laughed yet again at my horror. "Supposedly it was from some Garden District kook who wanted her five cats to be bridesmaids along with her sister. The sister was horrified and couldn't wait to give the dress to us. Unfortunately, none of us can fit into it. We need you because it will be a travesty if people don't see that dress."

I felt put on the spot. "Won't I stand out?"

"Girl, you were born to stand out. Come on." Bebe extended his hand. "I promise not to go overboard with the makeup. You don't have the sort of face that can take too much mascara. A wig might be fun, though."

. . .

IT TOOK BEBE TWENTY MINUTES TO fix my face. He picked a purple wig for me, and when I slid into the silver cat dress behind the curtained dressing room they'd erected in the corner of the park, I got my first gander at the new me. I had to say...I looked kind of interesting.

"Marigold took about fifty videos," Bebe said as he returned my phone. That was part of the trade-off for me agreeing to do the show. I needed video of the crowd and strutters for my story. "You have no memory left. You have to delete something so we can film you."

I stared at the phone. "Maybe it's best I don't become part of the story."

"Oh, no." Bebe was adamant as he shook his head. "You need to be the star of your own story, girl. You're a headliner. That's why I approached you. I could tell."

Okay, that was a step too far. "Yeah, I'm thinking you approached me because I fit the dress and looked a little lost."

"I approached you for multiple reasons. The dress was only part of it."

"Well, I think you've pegged me wrong. I don't want to be the star of my own story. I have plenty of stuff for my piece. I think I'll just have a good time walking. Is that okay?"

Bebe looked like he wanted to push things further, but he nodded. "Okay. It's your show. Do what you want. You get to be the queen in your world."

"Thank you."

"As long as you do it now." Bebe collected my phone and gave me a firm push toward the opening. "Strut that dress, girl."

"Now?" The question came out as a squeak. "I don't think I'm ready."

"You're ready." He was firm. "Show me what you've got." Our size difference meant he had no problem pushing me out. The crowd erupted in gales of laughter when they saw the dress, and even though I initially stumbled, I recovered quickly.

It wasn't just that I needed this to be a feel-good story so I could get plenty of hits. I needed it to be good for the people the Rainbow Confederacy was trying to help. I believed in the cause.

I found the beat of the music after a split-second pause to collect myself. Then I did my best Tyra Banks impression and headed down the walkway. The applause was thunderous, although I had no illusions that it was for me. The dress was a monstrosity. It was like a train wreck: You simply couldn't look away.

With each step, my heart thundered. My smile felt frozen, but I kept walking. I started giggling. It turned into raucous laughter as I reached the end of the sidewalk. This really was fun, and I was sad I wouldn't have video of my walk.

And then I saw him.

Grady stood at the end of the pavement, phone raised as he taped me. He was smiling for my strut, but there was something else in his expression when he met my gaze. I didn't know him well enough to identify the emotion, but when I passed, we stared at each other.

Time stopped for one brief instant, then the music shifted, and Daphne Dauphine ushered me behind another curtain. I'd done what I set out to do, and now that I was finished my knees were shaking.

"My clothes are in the other curtained area," I realized, feeling like an idiot.

Daphne laughed and pointed to a stack in the corner. "Bebe brought them — and your phone. Don't worry, girlfriend, we would never hang you out to dry that way."

I was unbelievably relieved. "This dress should really be burned."

"Totally."

. . .

IT TOOK TWENTY MINUTES TO GET back in my clothes and hit the spot at the end of the runway. I wanted to get a few more videos if I could, even though I had no space left on my phone. I would have to delete something.

I found Grady standing in the exact spot he'd been in when I'd walked the runway, and he was grinning when I reached his side.

"Let me have it," I said, bracing for the worst. "How bad did I look?"

"Are you serious?" Grady studied my face. "You were the hit of the ball, princess."

"Don't be ridiculous."

"You were. You got the loudest cheers."

"The dress got the loudest cheers."

"No. It was you." He was silent a beat. "I've never seen you smile that wide."

I was taken aback. "I smile."

"This was different. You were having a good time."

"I have a good time." I was feeling defensive but couldn't pinpoint why.

"Oh, geez." He held up his hands in surrender. "It wasn't an insult, Shay. You looked beautiful. Just accept the compliment."

My cheeks heated under his plaintive demand. "I...." Words escaped me, and then something occurred to me. "What are you doing here?"

His smile turned rueful. "Well, up until I saw you on that runway, I imagine I was doing the same thing you were. I happened upon the show when I was passing the Square. I didn't realize you were here."

"I was at the other end." Disappointment raced through me. "I guess you want to keep the story."

"No." He shook his head. "This is your story, Shay. You were part of the show."

"You're the only one who has footage of me. It doesn't have to be my story."

"No, it's your story. I'll give you my video."

That didn't seem fair. "You spent at least an hour filming."

"I did, but I don't think two of us turning in the same story will work out well for either of us. It's yours."

I felt horrible for him. "I'm sorry."

"It's not your fault. You were probably here before me because you left the bar first. Fair is fair."

"I had no idea you were such a proponent of fair play."

"What can I say? Winning is only fun if the playing field is even. This is your day, Shay."

I was grateful, but that gratitude was tinged with guilt...and then I had an idea. "Wait." My eyes drifted to the people watching the show. It was a mix of both men and women, and everybody seemed to be having a good time. "What if we both cover it?"

Grady was exasperated when I looked back at him. "We've already talked about that. We'll split the hits."

"Not necessarily." I shook my head. "What if we turn it into a man and woman thing?"

His face was blank. "You've lost me."

"Like a battle of the sexes thing — without the battle. You can gear your coverage to a man's point of view, and I can do the female point of view. People will want to read it from both angles if we tell them what we're doing...and make sure it's funny. We can make a game out of it. Sort of a Hepburn-and-Tracy thing. Readers will enjoy it."

He hesitated, his tongue drifting over his teeth, and then he slowly nodded. "I think you might be on to something."

"I'm a veritable genius," I agreed.

"People like the 'he said, she said' stuff. Like...remember

that episode of *The X-Files* when they took turns showing Mulder's and Scully's points-of-view?"

I shook my head.

"It was that vampire episode."

"I'm not disagreeing with you. *The X-Files* was a little before my time."

"My mom loved the show. She watched it all the time when I was a kid. Don't give me grief."

I held up my hands in mock surrender. "I wasn't giving you grief. I was just stating a fact."

"Well, it was a great episode. *Supernatural* did one too. Dean and Sam were fighting the whole episode and telling their version of events to Bobby. It was hilarious."

I brightened. "Oh, I saw that. I know what you're getting at."

"What if we did that on purpose?" His eyes gleamed with unreadable intent. "We don't insult each other or anything, but we film each other with the crowd." He gestured vaguely at the people surrounding us. "And then we do a commentary from dueling perspectives. You're right. People love that stuff."

I nodded, a plan taking shape. "We'll have to share footage," I cautioned. "We can't hold back from one another...and we have to make sure we don't use the same footage."

"I think we're good. We were at opposite ends for most of it."

For the first time that day, I was feeling better about things. "Okay, we need to get interviews. We have to separate for that. Where do you want to meet when we're done?"

He glanced around. "At the brewery." He pointed.

"Cool." I checked my phone screen. "So, we head over there when the show is done?"

"Yeah. See you then."

"I'm looking forward to it." The words escaped before I

could think better of them. I felt like a bit of a dolt when I realized what I'd said.

Then he extended an olive branch and ignored the comment. "Me too. I'll buy you a drink while we sort footage."

It wasn't the worst offer I'd had all day. That honor went to the hot yoga. "You're on."

Eight

We spent two hours sharing footage in the brewery. When we finished, we had two pieces...and we were proud of both.

"What do you think?" I asked as we used Grady's laptop to load them.

He smiled. "I think we're going to be okay."

"Yeah?" I couldn't help being nervous. "I bet we don't get twenty-five-thousand hits."

"We don't need twenty-five-thousand hits. We just need to start a buzz. That's all they're looking for, and the dueling nature of our pieces has appeal."

"Too bad you didn't get dressed up for the show," I mused.

"Next time." He winked as he closed his laptop and then gave me a quizzical look. "What are you doing for the rest of the night?"

I was caught off guard by the question. "Oh, um, I don't know." Was he about to ask me out?

He checked the clock on the wall. "Do you need me to walk you home?"

"Not last time I checked. I only live a few blocks away." I found I didn't want to say goodbye to him. That had never happened before...at least where he was concerned. "What are your plans? Do you have a hot date?"

"Yes." He bobbed his head.

I wanted to stab my stupid heart for dropping the way it did. "Well, have fun." I moved to hop off the stool. We'd picked a spot at the far end of the bar so we wouldn't get distracted by the other customers. "It was...um...nice working with you."

His eyebrows shifted, reflecting confusion. "What just happened there?"

I was the picture of innocence. "I have no idea what you're talking about."

He didn't look convinced. "Shay...."

"I really should be going. I have a hot date too." That was a total lie. Not only had it been forever and an age—okay, real time seven months—since I'd had a date, but I had no intention of dating anytime soon. I was far too frazzled about my work situation to even consider dating. That would be torture for the poor soul who attempted to take me on.

"Oh, yeah?" Grady's smile was back, although it seemed somehow strained. "Who is the guy?"

"Oh, you don't know him."

"I didn't ask if I knew him." He seemed a bit intense as he eyed me. "He must have a name."

I thought fast on my feet. "Greg."

"Greg?" Grady didn't bother to hide his eye roll. "What a mundane name."

"I happen to like it." Actually he was right. Greg was not the sort of name that just rolled off your tongue. It was so...Greg. It was all I could come up with as Greg Banks, a local newscaster, was on the television above us. "He's a very nice guy."

"A nice guy? Is that what you like?"

Now it was my turn to be confused. "Who doesn't want a nice guy?"

He held his hands palms out and shrugged. "Just a question."

"And your date?" I found even asking about her irksome. "Did you pick her up hanging from some pole?"

"Oh, jealousy isn't becoming." He tapped the end of my nose, causing me to rear back. "My date is much more casual. I'm sure Greg will take you somewhere great."

"That's the plan." I was going for breezy but feared I came off as mildly deranged.

"Well, I hope everything goes as planned." He hesitated. "Are you sure you don't need me to walk you home?"

I was exasperated. "It's the middle of the day."

"Right." He bobbed his head. "So, that's a no?"

"That's a no."

We continued to stare at each other.

"I should probably be going," I said finally. This would drag on forever if I wasn't careful. "Um...thanks a lot for giving me the footage you took." I was back to feeling awkward. "You could've kept it and had the better story."

"No, I really couldn't have done that." The right side of his mouth tipped up in a lopsided smile. "It worked out. Now we have a strong package. That's better for both of us."

"They never mentioned anything about strong packages," I pointed out.

"No, but this could be a case of them not knowing what they want until it's right in front of them."

"That's something to hope for."

"Absolutely." He shifted his hand, and for a second I thought he was going to cup my face. Instead, he moved it to my shoulder and gave me an awkward squeeze. "Don't spend the whole night worrying about work. There's nothing we can do now but wait. Go out and have some fun with Greg."

"Right. Greg." I forced a smile. "You have fun too."

"I will do my best."

BECAUSE I FIGURED SITTING AT HOME alone and watching the hit counters on the pieces we filed was too pathetic even for me, I collected Cally for a night out. I was feeling better. Not only had I stopped saying "I'm never drinking again," I was actually ready to drink again.

"Nothing too strong," I warned Cally as she reviewed the drink menu at Moxie's Cantina. "I cannot have a repeat of this morning. I need to go to bed early and start hunting for a story before noon like a good girl."

Cally's response was a snort.

I waited for something more. When I didn't get it, I lightly kicked her under the table. "What was that snort?"

"I didn't say anything." She refused to meet my gaze.

"But you're clearly thinking something."

"I'm thinking that your profound meltdown about me pressing the publish button on that piece you did last night was all for nothing. Not only did it turn out well, but you're also now the one to watch. Where is my 'Thank you, Cally?'"

A bigger person would've thanked her. "You gave me a heart attack. It's only by some fluke that I wasn't fired today."

"You're a media darling," Cally corrected. "You weren't even close to being fired."

"Says you. What would've happened if those college kids hadn't picked up on my piece?"

"It doesn't matter what *might* have happened. It only matters what *did* happen. And guess what, Shay? You were a hit. I always knew you could do it."

Her confidence felt misplaced. "I don't feel as if I did anything."

"Well, you did. You wrote a strangely poignant piece about shoes. Very few people can do that."

"If you say so." I rubbed my head as Moxie came to take our orders.

"We've got those Witch's Brew drinks with the dry ice you love so much," she offered. "Gus just got back with the dry ice."

I perked up. Those were my favorite. "I'll have one."

"Me too," Cally said as she handed Moxie the cocktail menu. "While you're here, tell Shay to stop being a pill. There will be a little extra something in your tip." She let loose an exaggerated wink that would've looked ridiculous on anybody else.

"Stop being a pill," Moxie ordered.

"I'm not being a pill," I said. "I'm simply telling it like it is."

"And what are you telling?"

"It's not important." I waved off the question.

"Oh, no." Cally made a tsking sound. "We need an impartial third party to judge."

I had trouble believing that Moxie was indeed impartial, but I smiled all the same. "Sure. Let's let Moxie decide."

Cally laid everything out for her—including a lengthy recital of my viral piece—and when she finished Moxie bent at the waist laughing.

"I told you it was a fluke," I said.

"It's not that," Moxie said as she waved a hand in front of her face to stifle the giggles. "That sounds like an amazing piece. I love my Converse."

"I'm right, right?" Cally demanded.

"You might be," Moxie conceded after a few seconds of contemplation. "Even if it was an accident, Shay, you should take the win. You did good work. People responded. Now you're in a better place for keeping your job."

My cheeks colored under the faint praise. "Thank you."

"Don't mention it. While we're at it, that stuff you did on the ugly bridesmaid fashion show was amazing too."

I was taken aback. "How did you know about that?"

"What ugly bridesmaid fashion show?" Cally demanded.

"It's this thing I did this afternoon," I said. I'd yet to tell her about my adventure. I figured it would be funnier after two – or maybe three – cocktails. "I stumbled across it in Jackson Square."

"I heard people at the bar talking about it." Moxie tilted her head toward two women who looked to be trying to flirt with Gus if I was reading their body language correctly.

"They already know about it?" I did the math in my head. "They must've pushed our stuff through faster than normal."

"I especially like how you worked with that guy on the dueling pieces," Moxie added. "That gave it an extra bit of pizzazz." She wiggled her fingers. "And, yes, those two over there are gushing about the dude—when they're not trying to get Gus to look down their shirts, that is. But they like your piece too. They totally want that cat dress. They said they're going to go shopping tomorrow to find it."

"Cat dress?" Cally's eyebrows looked as if they were trying to make a break for it. "Show me these videos right now."

I couldn't acquiesce fast enough, so Moxie pulled her phone out of her apron, cued up the videos, and then started back for the bar. "I'll reclaim my phone when I bring your drinks," she called back.

"Thank you," Cally said absently as she studied the screen. She watched my video first, laughing when she saw me in the wig and dress. "That is amazing." She slapped her knee. "I can't believe you did that without me. That looks right up my alley."

"The queens were amazing," I admitted. "I met quite a few of them. I had a lot of fun." It was only after I said it that I realized it was true. Work hadn't felt like work this afternoon, even when cutting the videos with Grady, because I was having so much fun.

"And this other video?" Her eyes were inquisitive when she lifted them to study my face. "This is that guy you work with. Grayson, right?"

"Grady," I corrected. "Grady Dalton."

"But he's the guy in the office you hate," she said.

"I hate him," I said, trying to tamp down the quick flash of guilt that rolled through me. Did I really hate him? The lines had become blurred, and fast. Now we were simply co-workers who occasionally helped one another. Yeah, that was it.

"You don't look like you hate him," Cally noted.

"He helped me today." It wasn't easy to admit. "I was out of room on my phone and there wouldn't have been footage of me if he didn't take it."

"The footage made your piece."

"I know. I thought maybe he would try to keep it for himself and beat me to the story. But we worked together and came up with the dueling takes on the event."

"A smart move." She went back to watching the coverage, switching back to my video. "So, he took this footage of you?"

"Yeah, why?" Had she noticed something I hadn't? "I didn't actually flash the camera or something, did I?" That would be even more mortifying than the cat dress.

She chuckled. "No. It's just...he caught your good angles. He didn't get underneath you to film, which would've made it look like you had a double chin."

My hand automatically flew to my neck.

"You don't have a double chin," she said. "But filming is

tricky. He caught all your good angles." She handed the phone back to Moxie when the bar owner returned.

"Did you see how many hits those videos are getting?" Moxie asked as she placed my smoking drink in front of me.

My heart skipped. "They're already getting hits?"

"Half the bar has already watched them. The girls up there were giggling about them. Then they watched them again when the guy came in."

Multiple viewings were good, but I still had questions. "What guy?"

"The guy from the video." Moxie tilted her blond head.

When I looked over, my mouth fell open as I recognized the shoulder-length dark hair on the guy sitting on one of the stools. I'd been close enough to run my fingers through it two hours earlier. "Oh, my...."

"Is that him?" Cally sat straighter in her chair. She seemed enamored with the idea. "It is!" She pumped her fist, causing me to frown. "Sorry. I just got ahead of myself there. It won't happen again."

"You won't pump your fist again?" I had no idea what was happening.

"We should invite him over." Cally's smile went from triumphant to suspiciously benign in the blink of an eye.

"No, we should not." In fact, I was trying to figure out how we could escape the bar without him seeing us.

"Yeah, we should." Before I could stop her, Cally raised her hand in the air and started waving like a madwoman. "Oh, Grayson," she called out.

"Grady," I barked, slapping my face an instant later for being so stupid as to correct her.

"Right. Grady." Cally made a face. "I like the name Grayson better. Maybe he'll be willing to change his name."

"I seriously doubt it." I reached for her hand to stop her. All it did was make her wave her other hand. "Don't!"

"Grady," Cally called out, sending me a smug smile when I sank back in my chair. It was too late to stop her now and we both knew it.

For his part, Grady seemed confused at having his name yelled across a bar. When he looked in our direction, he did the biggest double-take ever. He froze for a moment, and then leaned in to whisper to the person sitting directly to his left...who happened to be a guy. With more than a little curiosity, I watched him ignore the woman on his right and head in our direction.

Wait...were they not together?

"Hello." Grady's smile was warm and wide when he fixed it on Cally. "Did you call me over?"

"I did." Cally was used to men falling at her feet. She didn't appear to want Grady to fall at them, but her charm was on full display. "You know my friend Shay?"

"I do." Grady's eyes briefly drifted to me before returning to Cally. "Is your name Greg by any chance?"

Ugh. I wanted to find a hole to crawl in and die.

"Greg?" Cally's lips curled. "Why would my name be Greg?"

"Oh, I don't know," Grady drawled. I felt his eyes on the side of my face, but I refused to look in his direction.

"I don't even know a Greg," Cally lamented. "That's one of those names that always pops up on a television show about college hazing, but you never actually meet a Greg."

"Is that so?" Grady was clearly figuring things out. "How well do you know Shay? Are you recent acquaintances?"

"Oh, no." Cally fervently shook her head. "I've known Shay practically since she got here. We're best friends. We don't do anything without one another." She seemed to rethink that statement quickly. "I wasn't talking threesome stuff if that's where your head just went. We don't do that."

Grady barked out a laugh. "You're safe. I just find it interesting that you're Shay's best friend but you don't know a Greg."

Well, this conversation was clearly slipping away from me. I had to turn things around. "Is she your date?" I pointed to the blonde sitting next to his empty stool. "You should bring her over so I can meet her."

"That is not my date."

Something occurred to me. He hadn't talked to the woman before heading over, only the man. "Oh." I lowered my voice. "Is he your date?" I felt like an idiot. I was mildly disappointed too—although I couldn't dwell on that now—but mostly I felt stupid. "I'm so sorry."

Grady shot me a quelling look. "I'm here with my friend."

"I thought you had a date."

"And I thought you had a date."

Obviously we'd both lied. That was weird, right?

"Bring your friend over," Cally said pointedly. "That way nobody will be on a date. We'll just be four friends having a good time."

Grady briefly looked as if he was going to turn her down, but he ultimately nodded. "I'll be right back."

Cally was all smiles as she watched his back.

"What are you doing?" I demanded when he was out of earshot, horrified.

"I'm going to meet your friend who isn't a friend but who also isn't an enemy," she replied. "What do you think I'm doing?"

The answer was nothing good. There was no way this would end well.

Ugh, and the day had taken such a marvelous turn earlier.

Ah, well, I guess it was too good to last.

Nine

Grady introduced his friend as David Parsons. They'd grown up together in Marigny and were still tight. They had the type of relationship that involved constantly insulting one another, and yet you knew they'd both take a bullet for the other.

"You should've seen this one when we were in high school," David said, jerking a thumb at Grady as we waited for Moxie to bring the bill. "Once he figured out that growing his hair out meant the chicks would throw themselves at him, he was a monster. He spent all his time looking up hair care products. He was a total pain."

I slid my eyes to Grady, who had settled in at my right. "Is that true?"

He shrugged. "What can I say? I like my hair."

His hair was beautiful. It was so shiny I wanted to run my fingers through it. In fact, I'd caught myself considering just that more than once. Thankfully I caught myself before looking like a real idiot. "Do you ever put it in a man bun?" The question escaped before I could think better of it.

Grady scalded me with a dark look. "Only morons wear man buns."

"I think they're kind of cool," Cally countered. She snagged the bill from Moxie before anybody else could jump on it. She had oodles of money thanks to her father and was generous to a fault. "Like...Jason Momoa wears a man bun. How can you find fault with Jason Momoa?"

"I would never find fault with him to his face," Grady reassured me. "He's way too big and manly. He's one of the rare guys who can pull off a man bun. I cannot."

"Here." I threw a twenty at Cally, but she pushed it back. "You can't pay for all of us," I complained.

"Of course, I can." Cally was firm. "You and Grady are fighting to keep your jobs. I'm more than capable of picking up a bar tab."

Grady didn't look convinced. "That doesn't seem fair."

"It's perfectly fine," Cally reassured him. "But I do need to be going."

I was about to tell her I would walk her to her place before Cally did the unthinkable.

"David, would you like to walk me home?" she asked.

David looked confused. He'd had a great time with Cally —they'd laughed really hard—but it had been in a friendly way. There had been no flirty vibes. "Oh, um...."

"I'm not asking what you think I'm asking," Cally said bluntly. "I just want to force Grady to walk Shay home."

"Oh." David's eyes lit with amusement, and he bobbed his head. "I'd love to walk you home."

"Thank you." Cally's smile was demure when she fixed it on Grady. "You'll make sure my best friend makes it home safely?"

I was mortified. "You don't have to," I said.

Grady was already shaking his head. "I want to." The smile

he shot me didn't look forced. "I have no problem walking you home. In fact, after three cocktails, a walk sounds nice."

I glared at Cally as I stood. "We're going to talk about this tomorrow," I warned as Grady lightly placed his hand at the small of my back and prodded me toward the door.

"I have no idea what you're talking about," Cally drawled. "I just wanted to spend time alone with David. You shouldn't give me grief over it. A woman has urges."

"Yes, we're both looking forward to the walk," David agreed as he held his fist out for Grady to bump. Apparently, he'd decided to ignore the "urges" comment. "It's going to be a magical conversation."

"I have no doubt what you guys are going to talk about." Grady was calm as we shuffled through the crowd toward the exit. "You're not fooling anybody."

"I should hope not," Cally said when we'd made it outside. "We weren't exactly subtle." She sent me a sunny wave. "Have fun!"

I opened my mouth to tell her where she could shove the fun, but she was already gone.

"Shall we?" Grady held out his arm in chivalrous fashion as we crossed Bourbon Street.

"We can walk together, but we don't need to make a big show of it," I hedged. "Cally is obvious, but you don't have to play the game by her rules."

Grady studied me for a moment, his expression unreadable, and then lowered his arm. "Let's walk."

I fell into step next to him. By unspoken agreement, we crossed Bourbon Street and stuck to the nearest side street rather than risk picking our way through the crowd. We were on Governor Nicholls Street within two minutes, crossing in front of the LaLaurie Mansion before I could really wrap my head around what Cally had done.

"Do you know what that is?" Grady asked as we looked up at the patio balcony that overlooked the street.

I nodded. "This was one of the first places I visited when I moved here."

"Really?" He made a face. "That's a little creepy."

"I've always been fascinated by the story. Not in a gross way or anything. I've always been fascinated with murder stories."

"New Orleans is full of those."

"Oh, I don't doubt it. The LaLaurie Mansion story has been adapted for a lot of movies and television shows. When I moved here from Florida, I wanted to embrace everything the city had to offer. That included the darkness."

I could feel Grady's eyes on me, but I didn't meet his gaze. "You're a morbid little thing, aren't you?"

I shrugged. "I've always liked horror stories. Scary books are my favorite. Ooh, I really love slasher movies, like the ones with Freddy and Jason."

He chuckled. "I like a good horror movie too. Heck, I even like the bad ones."

"Yeah, as long as I know what I'm facing when I go in, I don't care if a horror movie is good or bad."

"I'm kind of the same way. Some of those Shudder horror movies? They're terrible. I know going in they're going to be terrible, but I'm okay with that because my expectations are always low."

"Yeah." I bobbed my head. "Did you see that one about the group of kids trapped on a boat in the middle of a lake? There's a giant mutant fish trying to kill them. One of those kids from that old show *Seventh Heaven* was in it. It was the worst thing I've ever seen...and yet I couldn't stop watching."

His laughter was warm and light. "I did see that one. It was...not good."

"What's your favorite bad horror movie?"

"Hmm. Good question." He took a moment to think, and his expression told me he was really considering his answer. "Did you ever see *The Happening*?"

I was convinced I'd misheard him. "No way."

"It's not that bad," he said, reading my expression.

"The trees are trying to kill them," I argued. "That movie makes no sense. On top of that, Mark Wahlberg actually tries to reason with a houseplant. The whole thing is terrible."

"I thought there was some interesting stuff in it."

"Ugh, and here I was starting to like you."

His lips quirked. "What's your favorite bad horror movie?"

"It's from about seventeen years ago."

"I was alive seventeen years ago. In fact, I was probably just getting into horror movies, because I would've been about twelve years old. I'm guessing I saw it."

"It was the *House of Wax* remake," I admitted.

He mock-clutched at his heart. "Oh, no! You can't be serious."

"I am." I bobbed my head. "It had great ambiance. The hot guy was waxed when he was still alive. The end, when the house of wax melts in the fire, is creepy and weird. Plus, well, Paris Hilton gets a rod shoved through her head. What's not to like about that?"

"The story is bad."

"All horror movie stories are bad."

"Not *all* of them." He fervently shook his head. "Take *The Shining*. That's a really good story."

"It is, but Stephen King famously didn't like the Kubrick movie."

"I get that the story was changed, but I liked both the book and the movie. I also really liked *Dr. Sleep* with Ewan McGregor. I like both of those movies."

"Seriously?" I whipped my head to look at his profile. "I love both of those too."

His eyes glinted when they locked with mine. "Well, I guess we have more in common than you thought."

"Maybe just a little," I admitted reluctantly. "We need to cut over once we reach Decatur. I mean...unless...." Something occurred to me. "Where do you live?"

"Why? Do you want to come home with me?"

The question threw me. "No, I just didn't want you to feel obliged to walk me home because of Cally. I can walk myself."

"Where is your place?"

"Near St. Louis Street."

He nodded. "That's on my way."

"Are you sure?"

"I'm sure." He flashed a quick smile. "Don't get all...you. I have no problem walking you home. It's a nice night and it's still early."

I checked the time on my phone. "It's almost eleven. It's probably good we left the bar when we did. Otherwise, I wouldn't want to get up tomorrow morning."

"Okay, Grandma," he teased as we turned right onto Decatur Street.

"We both have work tomorrow," I reminded him. "We need to check the numbers on those videos."

"I think we'll be fine. The way Moxie was talking, everybody in the bar loved them."

"Yeah, but that just adds to the pressure." Why was I giving voice to my fears in front of him? For some reason, the darkness and quiet propelled me to run my mouth. "Once you get something good, you need to fight to keep it. Everybody will be coming for us if we're not careful."

"Everybody is going to be gunning for everybody else no matter what," he said. "They set up the transition in as cutthroat a way as possible. We're all fighting over limited jobs. They knew what they were doing."

"Meaning?"

"Meaning that they want us to rip each other's throats out to win."

It was a sobering thought. "Who do you think will win?"

He held out his hands and shrugged. "I guess we'll find out in a month."

"I guess so."

We spent the rest of the walk talking about horror movies, sharing our favorite scenes, and laughing ourselves silly over the most ridiculous kills. By the time we reached my place, we were feeling comfortable with one another, which seemed both odd and nice at the same time.

"This is me." I gestured toward my small creole cottage. It had been updated and was beautiful inside. Outside, it looked a bit of a mess. That was normal for New Orleans. Historical guidelines wouldn't allow you to update the outside of a home without jumping through a multitude of hoops.

"How can you afford this place?" Grady looked intrigued as he studied it. "I bet it's nice inside."

Was he bucking for an invitation in? Unfortunately, he wasn't going to get his wish this time.

"Cally's father owns it. He owns a lot of property in the area. He rents to me, and I'm betting at less than he could get from someone else. Cally has him wrapped around her finger, so he's always been generous with me."

"That's cool." Grady's smile was quick and flirty. "Are you going to invite me in so I can see it?"

One of the things I liked best about him was his directness. Unfortunately, it was one of the things that also irritated me. "Um...no."

"No?" He was incredulous as he barked out a hollow

laugh. "I can't believe you're saying no to inviting me inside. What are you afraid of?"

"I'm not afraid of anything," I said hurriedly. "I just...don't think it's a good idea."

His eyes narrowed. "Why? I thought we were, if not friends now, at least friendly."

"We are, but I have an early morning and it feels weird to think about having you in my house."

"It feels weird?"

"That's what I said."

He didn't look convinced but nodded. "Fine. What are you doing tomorrow morning?"

Apparently, he was willing to drag out the conversation on the street if I wouldn't invite him inside.

"I'm going to hot yoga with Annabelle." Even saying it out loud left me with an uncomfortable hitch in my side. "I don't even like regular yoga. All I know about hot yoga is that it will make me want to die."

"Then why did you agree to go?"

That was a good question. "She put me on the spot. She never invited me to anything before—I mean, we've eaten in the same restaurant more times than I can count and even when she knew I was alone she didn't invite me over. I didn't think to say no."

Grady was quiet. The lighting was limited, but his gaze was intense as it roamed my face. "You know she's going to try to use you," he said. "You're on top and she wants to be on top. She's going to try to figure out whatever 'trick' you used and steal it from you." He used air quotes and matched them with a rueful grimace.

"I know I can't trust her," I reassured him. "I'm not an idiot."

"I know you're not."

"I shouldn't have said yes. It's too late to say no. I'll just go and that will be the end of it."

"You could call and cancel." He managed a roguish grin. "You could use me as an excuse, invite me in for a drink, and conveniently forget her in the morning."

He hadn't come right out and asked to sleep over, and yet it was almost implied. He hadn't said the words, so I had no intention of calling him on it.

"I agreed to go." I was firm. "I'll have a rotten time, but maybe I can turn hot yoga into something funny."

"I don't see how."

"I happen to be hilarious."

He cracked a smile. "You're pretty funny," he conceded. "When you loosen up, like you did at the fashion show today, you're very funny." He hesitated and then continued. "You should loosen up more often."

He likely hadn't meant it as an insult, and yet I couldn't help taking it that way. "I think I'm plenty loose," I blurted.

Grady held it together for a full three seconds before bursting out laughing at my unintended double entendre.

"Oh, shut it." I pushed open the gate to my place. "Thank you for walking me home. You don't have to worry about me hanging out with Annabelle. I know she doesn't have my best interests at heart."

"She doesn't have anybody's best interests at heart but her own," Grady said as he sobered. "Just be careful." He turned to go, and suddenly I felt desperate for him to stay...even if only for a few more minutes.

"Are you okay to walk home?" I asked, cringing when I realized how stupid I sounded.

The amusement was back on his face when he glanced over his shoulder. "I'm fine. It's a fifteen-minute walk. It will be good for me. I should be sober by the time I get to my place."

"Fifteen minutes." I was confused. "Do you live in the Central Business District?"

"No, I live over on the edge of Marigny."

My mouth dropped open. "Then we walked by your place."

"Not exactly, but close," he confirmed.

"You said my place was on your way." I felt horrible. "You didn't need to go out of your way for me. I could've walked on my own."

"I wouldn't have let you walk alone, and I enjoy walking at night. An extra fifteen minutes won't kill me."

"It's more than that."

"And yet the horror movie conversation was totally worth it." He shot me a winning smile. "Don't sweat the small stuff, Shay. There are bigger things to worry about. The little things will kill you, so steer clear of them."

With that, he turned and started back down the street. He was halfway down the block when he saluted without looking back. "See you on the battlefield," he called out.

"You bet your ass you will."

His laugh rolled through the street. "I love that competitive spirit of yours."

Oddly, that was one of the things I was learning to love about him. I could never admit that, though. "I'm going to crush you tomorrow."

"Looking forward to it."

Ten

I felt hung-over the next morning, which shouldn't have been possible because I was completely sober by the time I got home. When the phone on the nightstand rang, I automatically answered it.

"Brunch." That was all the individual on the other end of the call said.

"Good morning, Cally," I drawled, memories from the previous evening popping up. "How was your date with David?"

I didn't expect her to admit what she'd done. I thought for sure she would offer a half-hearted apology, but she decided to embrace the lie — whole hog.

"Well, it was a very nice walk," she said. "There's nothing better than a NOLA night when the humidity dips below fifty percent. Am I right?"

Oh, well, two could play this game. "Yes, but how was the walk specifically? Did you hold hands?"

"Did you hold hands with Grady?"

"Of course not. We're not romantically involved."

"Yet. You're not romantically involved *yet*. It's coming."

She might've been my best friend, but there were times she drove me insane. "It's never going to happen. Tell me about your walk with David."

"Well, we had a beautiful time commenting on the moon. It was a pretty silver last night. Full and lovely."

"It was a waxing moon, and it was three-quarters."

"Oh, really?" Cally's tone shifted. "Did you spend much time staring at the moon during your walk last night?"

Yup. I'd walked right into that one. "You're not fooling anybody," I complained. "I know exactly what you were trying to do last night. For the record, it didn't work."

"I wasn't trying to do anything, so I have to state the obvious. You're imagining things."

"If you say so. Just keep in mind...it won't work no matter how hard you push it. Grady and I are co-workers. That's it. In another month, the odds of us both still being employed are slim. One of us will be out of a job." Likely me. "Nobody has time for a relationship."

"But do you want a relationship?"

"No." I was firm on that. "I don't even like him. We had to cover a story together yesterday and it worked out. It was a fluke. We're not friends and we're definitely nothing more than that."

"You guys have a spark."

"You're mistaken." Cally often let her imagination run away. I refused to let that be a thing today. "I'm glad we're not at each other's throats, but we're not going to be whatever it is you're imagining."

"Fine." Cally sounded annoyingly blasé. "If that's how you want things."

"It is."

"So...where did we land on brunch?"

I was about to suggest we head to one of the restaurants by Jackson Square when I remembered where I was supposed to be. "Son of a—" I viciously swore under my breath and rolled to look at the clock on the nightstand.

"What's wrong?" Cally asked. "Did you accidentally elbow Grady in his gumdrops because you guys were trying to be slick and not let your good friend Cally know you had hot and sweaty sex last night?"

"Let it go," I snapped. "Good grief."

"I just want you to be happy."

"Then you should definitely let it go." I was grim as I debated how to inform her of the bad news. "So, um, about brunch...."

"The acceptable reason for not accepting is because you're playing *Chutes and Ladders* with Grady. I will accept no other excuse."

"I forgot I told Annabelle Chalmers that I would go to hot yoga with her." I was rueful right up until the moment Cally broke out in gales of laughter.

"You did not," she sputtered. I could practically imagine her swiping tears from her eyes.

"I did."

"You don't even like that chick."

"I definitely don't like her." Actually that was the understatement of the year. "But she invited me."

"So?" Irritation flashed hot in Cally's voice. "Just because someone invites you to something doesn't require you to go. If Jeffrey Dahmer invited you to a barbecue, would you accept?"

"Well, not now. Maybe back in the day."

She snorted. "Just blow her off. It's not as if she wants to be your friend."

I knew that. No, really I did. This wasn't a case of me wanting her to suddenly like me. I had no interest in getting chicory and beignets with her at Cafe du Monde—I was betting she wasn't a beignets girl anyway—but I was interested in getting close enough to see if I could figure out her end game.

"So, you know that saying about keeping your enemies close?" I hedged.

"Is that what you're doing?" Cally didn't sound convinced. "She's diabolical. She can out manipulate you. If she figures out what you're up to, she'll eat you for lunch with a side of gumbo."

I had no doubt she was right. "I just want to see how she is. If I feel it's a dangerous situation, I'll leave. It's not as if I believe she's suddenly going to turn into a good friend. She might let something slip regarding her plans for keeping her job."

"She might," Cally agreed. "Or she might try to sabotage you. Whatever she says, you can't believe her."

"You don't have to worry. You'll always be my best friend. I'll love you best forever."

"Oh, stuff it." Cally snorted. "Just remember, when you're sweating so badly you think you might pass out, I'll be eating biscuits and gravy at Oceana and enjoying the air conditioning."

I frowned. "You can't get the big pasta bowl of biscuits and gravy without me. That's not allowed."

"Since when?"

"It's in the Best Friend's Handbook."

"So is not dumping your friend for hot yoga with your frenemy. I guess we're both going to be disappointed today."

I opened my mouth to argue further, but she'd already hung up. I knew she wasn't really mad—that's not how Cally rolled—but I couldn't help feeling a little guilty.

Just how bad of an idea was this?

. . .

ANNABELLE WAS ALREADY AT THE yoga studio. I'd opted for loose capri sweats and a ribbed tank top that showed off my bra strap. She was dressed in what could only be described as designer leggings—they had rhinestones glittering around the pockets—and one of those bra tank tops that put all her assets on display. There was no uni-boob to be found. No, she'd gone for sexy when picking her outfit.

"Do men go to hot yoga?" I asked stupidly as I took in the full scope of her ensemble.

"Only the smart ones." She offered me a tight smile and I felt her eyes roaming over me, head to toe and back again. "You don't work out often, do you?" She didn't wait for me to answer. "I know it's easy to gloss over things like muscle tone when you're in your twenties, but if you aren't careful, you'll find you're too far behind to catch up when you're in your thirties."

That was such an Annabelle thing to say. "Okay, well...thanks for the tip." I hoped the smile I offered her came across as legitimate, because if she grasped what I was really thinking about her things would go downhill fast. "Where do we go?"

Obviously, Annabelle was familiar with the studio because she turned on her heel without uttering another word and led me into the facility.

"I already paid for you," she said as she pointed to a door.

I pulled up short. "Um...you didn't have to do that."

"Don't worry." She gave a haphazard wave. "I had coupons."

Oh, well, coupons. And here I thought I was special. "Lead the way."

In theory, I knew what hot yoga was — a series of stretching exercises in a hot room. Supposedly it made you more bend-y or something. At least that's what I read in an article once. Nothing prepared me for the wall of heat that I walked into when we joined the others in the room.

"Holy Satan's sweaty ball sack," I exclaimed as I waved my hand in front of my face.

Annabelle shot me a horrified look. "What did you just say?"

I was instantly sheepish...and a bit upset. Cally would've found the comment hilarious. We'd gone to a yoga class once, six months ago, when we'd both decided we needed to be healthier. Well, and Cally had read an article about how men preferred flexible women and was determined to find out if it was true. This was clearly going to be worse than that outing, which shouldn't have been possible.

Between the odd names for the poses and the immense pain we found ourselves in—seriously, nothing hurts more than stretching muscles you didn't even know you had—we lasted twenty minutes before the instructor asked us to leave. We could barely hear the request over our giggling and moans.

Now, standing in the world's hottest room with a person I knew I couldn't trust, I had never wanted Cally more.

Why had I agreed to this?

"There's a mat for you there." Annabelle pointed.

I obediently went to the mat, thankful that Annabelle had picked spots for us in the rear. I had no doubt that she'd selected them for a strategic reason, but because I preferred the back of the class, I saw no reason to complain.

"So how long have you been doing this?" I asked as the instructor began to lead us through a series of light stretching exercises.

"Five years now." Annabelle didn't even have to look at the instructor to see what was coming next. She already knew.

"Why is it so hot in here?"

The look she shot me was initially withering. She tried to

cover quickly...but failed. "Because it's better for your muscles."

If I had to guess, I would say it was a solid one-hundred degrees. And the humidity felt like a solid eighty percent. It wasn't like that dry heat I heard people from Arizona talk about. I'd often thought that sounded like a version of Heaven...especially when it was ninety-eight degrees with ninety-eight percent humidity at midnight in August.

"So, tell me how you got those girls to promote your video," Annabelle asked. She appeared to be balancing her entire body on one hand and one toe, contorting in such a way that I had to wonder how her spine didn't snap.

"I already told you that I don't know how that happened." I'm generally an affable person, even when I don't like someone. Unfortunately for Annabelle, the one thing that could make me mean was heat. Well, that and a haughty expert. So, putting them together? Yeah, it wasn't going to end well for either of us.

"I just have trouble understanding how a bunch of college kids magically managed to stumble over your shoe video."

"If I had an answer to that I would've tapped them for the second video." I pressed my hands to the mat and tried to straighten my legs as the instructor demonstrated but couldn't quite manage it. I really did need to work out more.

"Didn't you?"

I was distracted by the move the instructor was making so I almost missed the way Annabelle's lip curved. "Didn't I what?"

"Didn't you use them again? How else did you get thirty-thousand hits?"

I froze in place. "What are you talking about?" I asked.

"Your video from yesterday—the one you did with Grady Dalton—it went viral."

Was she joking? "Define viral."

"Thirty-thousand hits!" She practically screamed.

I glanced up, pressing my lips together as the instructor shot us a quelling look. I tried for a smile, but it was almost impossible to muster. "I didn't realize we'd gotten that many hits. I mean...it was two videos, so that's fifteen thousand each. It's not as good as the first piece."

"No, you got thirty-thousand hits and Grady got almost that many. It was almost sixty-thousand combined. They sent out an email congratulating the two of you this morning and said we should all be thinking outside the box like the two of you."

I was flabbergasted. "Um...." What was I supposed to say here? I'd gotten such a late start there hadn't been time to check my email. I figured I could do it after, when I was stuffing my face with beignets and hating myself for falling victim to Annabelle's machinations.

"Oh, don't pretend you didn't know." Annabelle's lip curled. "You were probably sitting with Grady all night watching the numbers climb."

I had been with Grady, but we'd spent very little time talking about work. "I...didn't...know. I got up late this morning because I was out with friends last night. I didn't check my email before coming here."

"Uh-huh. Are you really going to tell me you weren't with Grady last night?"

I could've lied. That was my first instinct. Instead, I said nothing.

"Just so you know, he's using you. He wants to keep his job, and he's decided you're the one to help him do it."

"I don't see how I'm going to help him keep his job." I kept my eyes averted because I was afraid she would somehow see into my soul and turn into the sort of beast who could suck it out through my nose or something.

"Obviously it's already working." Annabelle paused what

she was doing and fixed me with a serious look. "He and I were together for months. I thought we were the real deal. Turns out, he had a bet with the other guys in the office to see who could sleep with the most women. That's all he wanted me for."

That made very little sense. "But...if he had a bet, wouldn't he have taken off after one date?"

"You would think, but he's diabolical with the hurt he likes to dish out. He's a user, and he's using you. He'll figure out how you're getting the hits, steal your contacts, maybe give you one roll in the hay for the points, and then call it a day."

"I'm not really interested in rolling in anything with Grady," I said. "Yesterday was a fluke."

"If you say so." She clearly didn't believe me. "But I've seen the way you look at him when you think nobody is watching. He'll never be what you want him to be. I should know. He hurt me, but only after using me for a few months. That made it worse.

"He's a player, and if you think he won't play with your feelings you're more naive than I thought," she continued. "You need to wake up and see who your friends really are."

"And you are?"

"I'm your co-worker, not your friend. That doesn't mean we can't work together to build something great."

I wasn't a moron. She clearly wanted me to help her. If she had anything to offer me, it was very little. But the information about Grady did sting a little. No matter what I told Cally, there was indeed a spark. Unfortunately, I'd already had my doubts about exploring that spark before Annabelle had weighed in.

Now it seemed like a lost cause all the way around.

"Well, thanks for the info about Grady." I tried to stretch

again but my heart wasn't in it. "I think I'm just going to work on my own from here on out."

"If you think that's best." Annabelle's voice was prim. "Just remember, teams are strong. Individuals are weak."

I didn't necessarily disagree, but who exactly was I supposed to trust?

Eleven

I was pretty sure I was dying when I left the yoga studio. Annabelle made a series of faces right out of an old *Sex and the City* episode when I informed her I was going to shower at home rather than stripping at the gym and hosing off there.

She was less than impressed.

I didn't care. I needed to get away from her and the demonic torture that was hot yoga. I couldn't get out of the building fast enough. It took everything I had to keep my back straight and not walk like a bow-legged cowboy when I made it to the street.

I held it together for a block…and then I threw myself on the steps of the Supreme Court building to have myself a proper cry.

It wasn't exactly comfortable, but nothing about my life was comfortable these days. I stretched out on my back, threw an arm over my face, and closed my eyes so I could listen to the street musician play his saxophone. He was very talented.

"Hey, lady?" an unfamiliar voice asked after several minutes.

"I'm not dead," I replied, refusing to uncover my face. "I just wish I were."

"That's because you have a curse hanging over you."

"Oh, yeah?" That was enough to get me to move my arm. The guy I found standing over me was tall, thin, and wearing ragged clothing. I knew right away he was one of the street people who made constant rounds in the French Quarter. Not everybody in the city had money to throw around. A lot of people struggling to make it day to day ended up in New Orleans because even in the winter it was warm enough to sleep outside. "I'm sorry, dude, but I don't have any money."

When I first moved here, I tried to help every individual I crossed paths with. I realized quickly I would blow through all the money I had put away if I didn't stop. I was more than willing to buy a meal for those who approached me—there were plenty of places to choose from—but that was rarely what they wanted.

"Oh, come on," the guy complained. "I know you have something."

"I don't," I replied. "I'm sorry. I didn't even bring my purse when I left the house."

He didn't look convinced. "Is that why you're out here? Are you looking for coin too?"

"I have no idea what I'm looking for," I replied. "I'm thinking of day drinking. I mean...it couldn't possibly hurt at this point."

The guy's brown eyes narrowed. "How are you going to day drink if you don't have no money?"

"I haven't figured that out yet."

"How are you going to day drink if you're suffering from a curse?"

"I...what?" Now I was confused. That was the second time he'd mentioned a curse.

"You've got one hanging over your head," he insisted. "I can see it."

"You can see a curse hanging over my head?" This was a new approach. "I didn't know that was a thing."

"My Grandma was a bruja. She taught me how to recognize curses."

"That's a handy ability to have in New Orleans."

"Yeah." He bobbed his head. "You'll never be happy unless you get rid of that curse. You need to get it together."

"I'm guessing you know how to get rid of the curse," I surmised.

"Yup, and it will only cost you five bucks."

I had to bite back a sigh. "I'm not messing with you. I don't have any money."

"You must have money. White girls like you can't make it without money...but those pants don't fit, so maybe you don't have money and I read you wrong."

I glanced down at my jogging pants. "These are workout pants. I just came from hot yoga."

"Is that why you wet them?"

"What?" I propped myself up on my elbows and frowned when I saw the stain that had spread through the crotch of my jogging pants. "Oh, geez. No wonder she wanted me to shower so bad."

The beggar held up his hands. "Hey, I'm a God-fearing man. I don't like to judge, but God don't like nasty...and showering with another woman is nasty. Well, unless you let me watch."

Under different circumstances I might've laughed. This time I merely smiled and shook my head. "I'll take that under advisement."

"Uh-huh." I'd very clearly dismissed him, but he didn't move on. "Where did we land on those five bucks?" he asked after a few seconds.

"I don't have five bucks. I don't have anything. I don't even have my wits. All I want to do is die."

"I need five bucks."

He was persistent. I had to give him that. "I don't have any money. I'm sorry."

"Well, then I hope you keep peeing your pants in public thanks to that curse." He was huffy when he turned to leave, pulling up short when he realized someone was standing behind him. "Don't go near that one." His tone was grave. "She's nasty, pees her pants, and showers with other women. God is going to smite her."

"Good to know." I recognized the new voice that had me squinting into the sun. Sure enough, I found Grady standing there when the curse exterminator slid to the right. He had two cups of coffee and what looked to be a takeout bag in his hands. "I think I'll take it from here," he said when my new friend didn't make a move to leave.

"I need five dollars," the stranger insisted. "I cannot remove that curse without payment."

"Curse, huh?" Amusement lit Grady's features as he placed the coffees near my feet and dug in his pocket. He returned with a ten but didn't immediately hand it over. "Use half of this for eggs," he said, never moving his eyes from the man's face. "I know you're going to buy brew—and it's not my place to tell you what you can and can't do—but I would appreciate it if you would get some eggs to go with your brew."

"I don't like eggs," the man replied.

"Then pancakes."

"Fine." He threw up his hands. "I hate when y'all get bossy."

"I'm sure it's irritating," Grady readily agreed. "Don't forget to remove the curse before you go. I can't have her peeing herself twice in one morning."

"I didn't pee myself!" I snapped as the stranger began waving his hands in some elaborate pattern in front of my face. He looked like he was doing interpretive dance or something.

"All gone." The beggar snagged the ten from Grady's hand. "I'm going to eat my pancakes. It was a pleasure doing business with you."

Grady's lips curved in amusement as he watched the man go. Then he turned his full attention to me. "You really shouldn't pee yourself in public." He was blasé as he picked up the coffees and then sat near my feet.

"Oh, I can't deal with you," I complained. It was obvious I hadn't peed myself...well, mostly. "That's not pee. It's sweat."

"I'm not sure that's better." Grady waited until I rolled to a sitting position before he handed me one of the coffees. "Sugar-free vanilla latte with almond milk."

My mouth fell open. "How did you know that?"

"You look like a vanilla latte girl."

I wasn't certain that was a compliment. "Whatever." I was torn on two levels as I accepted the latte. On one hand, I was mortified that he would actually think I'd peed myself in public. On the other, I needed the caffeine badly. "How did you find me?"

"You mentioned you were hanging out with Annabelle today." He sipped his own coffee before resting the cup on the step and opening the bag of food. "I happen to know she goes to the yoga studio about a block from here."

"How do you know that?"

"She's written articles about it."

"Oh." I assumed he was going to tell me they'd gone together when they'd been dating. "You're not...like...stalking her, are you?"

"Definitely not." He opened a takeout container and propped it between us. It was filled with beignets, and I almost started salivating. "You smell really bad," he noted after a second.

"Hey, you try stretching your body in ways it's not meant to be stretched for an hour in a room that's a hundred degrees and see how you smell."

"I always smell like powdered sugar and coffee beans."

"How do you manage that?"

"I don't go to hot yoga, and I eat beignets for breakfast as often as possible."

"That's way better than how I spent my morning." I snagged one of the beignets and sniffed it. "Cafe Beignet. Nice choice, but Cafe du Monde is better."

"You identify beignets by scent?" Grady looked impressed.

"I love Cafe du Monde beignets."

"How do you feel about chicory?"

Now it was my turn to make a face. "Not as good."

"That's why I got Cafe Beignet lattes."

I didn't want to laugh—it would only encourage him—but I couldn't help myself. "You're not the first person who has told me that."

"I'm sure I'm not." We fell into amiable silence for a few minutes, the only sounds chewing and sipping. He was the first to speak. "Did you see our numbers this morning?"

"No, but Annabelle did." I wrinkled my nose as he leaned over to wipe powdered sugar from my cheek. "She's not happy."

"I told you she wouldn't be."

"No, you told me not to trust her."

"And I stand by that."

I couldn't argue the point, so I reached for another beignet. "What do you think we should do about it?"

"That's why I tracked you down. We need to come up with a plan."

"We?"

"Yeah. People love the package we put together. Have you been reading the comments?"

"No." It hadn't even occurred to me to look for comments. "What are they saying?"

Grady pulled his phone out of his pocket and tapped the screen a few times. He then handed it over so I could look. I was dumbfounded.

"There are more than a thousand comments on my piece," I said.

"Yup. I have almost the same number. We can't just let this go. We have to move ahead with it."

"And how do you suggest we do that?"

"I'm glad you asked." The smile he bestowed upon me was smug. "How do you feel about joining together to do an entire series?"

"I don't think I'm following."

"It wasn't just the event, Shay," he insisted. "It was that we took different tacks covering it. We can do that all over town. This is the sort of thing that people love...and we can both be funny."

I forced myself not to react as I handed his phone back to him. "I'm funny," I said finally. "I don't think you're very funny, but I'm hilarious."

"That's why the pieces will be funny. I feel the same about you."

I understood what he was getting at. "Do you think we can do the same thing twice?" I honestly wasn't certain. "It could've been a fluke."

"If it was a fluke, we'll figure that out soon enough. If it's a wave we can ride, we have to catch it now."

"Did you just lay a surfing metaphor on me? You can't do that in New Orleans. It's sacrilegious."

He smirked. "Does that mean you're in?"

"It means I'm intrigued." I was. I had questions, however. "What are we going to do?"

He nodded. "I can always rely on you to be practical, can't I?"

"Is that code for boring?"

"You're never boring, even when you're trying to be practical."

"I'm simply trying to figure out how we're going to do this," I said. "I mean...I get that we're going to have to hit up events and cover them from opposing angles. We lucked out with the ugly bridesmaid fashion show. How are we going to find events?"

Grady shot me an incredulous look. "Are you serious? This is New Orleans. The entire city is full of events...the sort that will bring in advertisers."

"How so?"

"We can take tours together and make them funny. We can hit up art shows and festivals. Heck, we can head to Uptown and make fun of those wine painting parties. It's not about what we cover, Shay. It's that we do it together...and make it funny."

I hated to admit I didn't dislike the idea, but I was uncomfortable relying on him. "No offense, but how do I know I can trust you not to walk out on me if things start getting good? If we're going to do this, we need to commit."

"I get that it's not easy for you to trust me," he said.

"I barely know you, and what I do know doesn't paint you in the best light."

"What is that supposed to mean?" he demanded.

"Oh, come on." I wasn't going to let him be evasive. "Everybody knows you're a ladies' man. I don't need that sort of hassle. This has to be strictly platonic...and you can't just abandon me if something better comes along. This is a partnership."

"I don't abandon people simply because something better comes along." He looked frustrated with my reaction. "That's not who I am. If I say we're going to work together, I mean it. I'm a loyal guy."

Part of me wanted to believe him. The other part wasn't so sure. "Well, we are the ones to watch, right?" I didn't see that I had a choice. We needed to work together if we were going to keep this up. Besides, I liked the idea of having someone else to bounce ideas off. "We have to keep at this. It's best for both of us."

"There you go." Grady flashed a smile, but it didn't make it all the way to his eyes. There was something else lurking there as he looked me up and down. "So...are you up to sitting down and making a list? I figure we'll make things easier on ourselves if we can talk through some of this stuff."

"Sure." I wiped my hands on my jogging pants, leaving powdered sugar behind. "Did you bring a notepad and pen? We can do it here."

His eyebrows migrated toward his hairline. "Or we could go to your place, you could take a shower so I don't have to smell you, and then we could make the list."

I balked. "Why do we have to do it at my place?"

"Because I'm assuming that you don't want to shower at my place...especially because none of my clothes will fit you."

I hadn't considered that. "I guess that makes sense." My legs were still shaky when I stood, and I was convinced I was going to be in unbearable pain about three hours from now. "Just for the record, I don't want any funny business. I will be showering alone."

That was enough to have him rolling his eyes. He balled up the bag and tossed it into a nearby trash receptacle. "Baby, you need to get over yourself. I don't care what you do in the shower."

"Don't call me baby."

"Our readers might like it."

"I very much doubt that."

"I guess we'll have to see."

I couldn't decide if this was the best or worst idea I'd ever had. I mean...opening myself to Grady Dalton? That couldn't end well.

Unfortunately, I had no other ideas. I had no choice but to join with him, because otherwise the suffering would start all over again.

"Let's head to my place. I'll get changed and then we'll start making that list. You can do some heavy brainstorming as I shower."

"I believe I suggested that plan of action first."

"Are you going to turn this into a thing? Winning isn't everything, you know."

"Says the woman who has been on top two days in a row."

"Let's just go."

"Sure." Grady let me get three paces ahead before following.

"What are you doing?" I demanded, confused. "Why are you walking behind me?"

"I can't walk next to the woman who peed her pants. Even in the French Quarter, that's frowned upon. I have a reputation to uphold."

"I didn't pee my pants!"

"Me either," someone yelled from across the street. "But that's the goal for this afternoon."

"Right on!" someone else yelled as I strode down the street with as much dignity as I could muster.

"This is the worst," I muttered.

From behind me, I heard Grady chuckling. "At least

nobody will remember your face because all they'll see when they try to pull up this memory is your soiled jogging pants."

"You're not helping."

"I didn't realize I was supposed to be helping. I guess I'll know for next time."

"Yeah, yeah, yeah."

Twelve

It was weird having Grady in my place while I showered. He obediently sat at the small kitchen table and started making a list while I excused myself. Most of the time I didn't bother shutting the door even if I wasn't alone – Cally didn't care about seeing me naked—but I made sure to not only shut it but lock it this time. Why? I had no idea. It wasn't as if I thought Grady would just wander into the bathroom and start chatting...or anything else. It was instinctive.

Rather than one of my patented twenty-minute showers, I washed quickly. I practically doused myself in lime coconut shower gel to make sure the sweaty smell didn't cling to me. Then I changed into comfortable shorts and a T-shirt before joining Grady in the kitchen. He was still in the same spot, and he offered up a small smile when I sat across from him.

"You smell nice," he said as I dragged my fingers through my damp hair.

An absurd bolt of pleasure rolled through me. "Um...thanks."

"I wouldn't have thought that was possible given the fact that you peed yourself, but good on you."

My scowl was back in an instant. "You're a real pain in the ass. Has anybody ever told you that?"

"Only anybody I've ever met." Grady flashed an impish smile. "Now, come on. I have some ideas."

I was almost afraid to ask what they were. "Do any of them involve strip clubs?"

"I didn't think you would be up for that. But if I can include them, I think things are looking up."

I rolled my eyes hard enough it was a miracle I didn't topple out of my chair. "Just tell me what you have."

"Well, for starters, I was thinking we could hit the Natchez tomorrow."

I was caught off guard. "The steamboat?" I'd heard the name before, but I'd never been on it.

"Oh, and people say you're not smart."

I refused to smile at him. "Nobody says I'm not smart. I might not be the prettiest woman in the room...or the sexiest...or the best dressed, but I'm always one of the smartest."

"And humble, too."

"I'm...you know what? Let's talk about your idea."

Rather than agree and shove the uncomfortable conversation to the background, Grady shook his head. "You are smart. That's one of the first things I noticed about you. You're also pretty, though I tend to prefer women who don't realize they're beautiful."

My cheeks felt as if they were on fire. I desperately needed to find a way to shift this conversation. "I notice you didn't mention my wardrobe."

"Your wardrobe is a travesty. It is, however, what makes you you. Those stupid Converse fit." He waved his hands in front of my face, as if that would somehow anchor what he was saying.

"I guess that's a compliment," I said after a beat.

"It is," he confirmed. "Now, let's talk about the Natchez.

It's the last authentic steamboat on the Mississippi. It's a huge draw for tourists. Even the locals find it cute...but they never go out on it because it's full of tourists."

"And the locals hate tourists," I mused. It was something I'd realized not long after I'd arrived in New Orleans. The locals played games with the tourists, always nice outwardly because they knew the money was important, but they didn't like temporary guests in their town.

"You're not a tourist," Grady noted. "I mean...if that's what you're worried about."

"I know," I said hurriedly. "I wasn't feeling sorry for myself or anything."

"That's good."

"It's just...I might not be a tourist any longer. But I'm not a local. I live in that in-between."

"I don't think you can be a local unless you've put at least ten years in. I don't make the rules. That's just what people believe."

"Yeah, I think you have to be born here to be considered a local. Or I guess you can marry a local and be grandfathered in. You'll always be an outsider otherwise."

"Does that make you sad?"

I shrugged. "I guess, in a way. But I get it."

"Well, maybe you'll luck out and find some poor schmuck who is already considered a local to marry you one day. That will cement things for you."

I shot him a sarcastic thumbs-up. "Here's hoping."

He laughed.

"What's the deal with the Natchez?" I was determined to keep the conversation from devolving into something that it shouldn't become. "I mean...I know what it is in theory." Even as I said it, I wondered if that was true. "I mostly understand."

Grady snorted. "You're hilarious."

I didn't think he meant it as a compliment. "I'm just trying to understand the angle."

"We need to draw attention to things tourists will like because that's where the money comes from." Grady was all business now. "The people who win at this game, the people who keep their jobs, will bring in the advertising. Tourist draws, however annoying, will bring in the advertising."

I bobbed my head. "That makes sense, but why the Natchez?"

"It's a symbol of the city. The current boat has been in operation since 1975. There were other Natchez boats, all operated in the 19th century. They're a mainstay of the city. When people think about New Orleans, what's the first thing they think of?"

"Bourbon Street."

Grady scowled. "After Bourbon Street."

"The cemeteries...and Cafe du Monde...and the voodoo shops."

"You're making me tired."

Now I couldn't stop from smiling. "I get it. People picture the boat. What are we going to do on it?"

"They have a jazz brunch tomorrow morning."

I ran the idea through my head. In truth, I wasn't opposed to his suggestion. "What sort of food are we talking about?"

"I love how your mind immediately surrenders to your stomach."

"Like you're not interested in the food."

"Fair point. It's standard stuff: gumbo, grits, crescent city eggs, potatoes, croissants, Bananas Foster, and bread pudding."

"I don't like grits."

"You don't have to eat them."

"They taste like lumpy glue."

"Eat a lot of glue, do you?"

"I might've partaken back in the day." I shot him a sunny smile. "I was a daring kindergartener."

His laugh was so light it shot a jolt of warmth through me. "Well, like I said, you don't have to eat grits. There will be plenty else to eat."

"How long is the trip?"

"A couple hours."

"And then we just write up pieces about our experience?"

"Yes, but it's important to make them funny. That's what you and I do best."

"I don't particularly think you're very funny."

"Says the girl who peed herself."

"I didn't pee myself!" I snapped out the words just as the front door pushed open. My eyes were wide and full of venom when they locked with Cally's confused orbs.

"Well, that's quite the greeting," she drawled as she made her way to us. "I'm certainly happy to know you didn't pee yourself, hon, but why are you screaming?"

"Because he's annoying," I replied, crossing my arms over my chest and slumping in my chair. "Tell him to be nice to me."

Cally lightly cuffed Grady's head. "Be nice to her."

"I wasn't being mean," Grady countered as he rubbed the spot she'd smacked. "She's just being sensitive."

"He keeps saying I peed myself," I insisted. "I didn't. He's being a jack-off."

"Uh-huh." Cally, who was carrying a bag of groceries, glanced between us. Then she continued to the counter to unload the bag. "You two are clearly boning up for some weird sexual stuff. I don't want to participate, so you'll have to take a breather."

"We're not boning up for anything," I shot back.

"Speak for yourself," Grady replied. "I'm always boning

up for something. I'm a guy. It's impossible not to bone up for things."

"You're adorable." Cally tossed an apple at his head, which he easily plucked out of the air. "Seriously, what are you guys doing? I thought for sure you'd be in bed the rest of the day after your hot yoga thing, Shay."

"That was the plan," I said. "I ran into Grady and we decided to put together a list of things to cover as a team."

"Kind of like 'he said, she said,'" Grady explained. "We got a lot of hits on our ugly bridesmaid coverage, and we want to build on it."

"Huh." Cally looked to be genuinely absorbing the information. "That's a fabulous idea," she said. "I want to help you guys pick outings."

"We're hitting up the Natchez tomorrow," Grady said.

Cally wrinkled her nose. "Why?"

Grady didn't look bothered by the question. "It's a New Orleans mainstay, and if we do it right the advertising will kick in early for us."

"That's probably smart." Cally bobbed her head. "You should totally write about hot yoga today, Shay. I bet you could make it funny."

"It was like stretching in Satan's armpit," I complained.

"See, that's funny." Cally's smile was bright. "Then, Grady, you can talk about how she smelled after hot yoga, and how you think it's weird women do all these things to make themselves pretty for men."

I made a disdainful snort. "He's not going to write about how I smelled."

"Of course not," Grady readily agreed. "I find scent to be difficult to convey in writing. I am going to explain how you peed yourself, however."

My mouth fell open. If flies had been buzzing around, I

would be in danger of swallowing one. "You. Wouldn't. Dare."

"I've already written half of it in my head." He winked, which had my stomach and heart twisting at the same time...and for completely different reasons. "It'll be glorious."

"I didn't pee!" I shrieked so loudly I was surprised the glass light fixtures didn't shatter.

The room fell into uncomfortable silence before Cally and Grady burst into gales of laughter.

"I hate you guys." I was morose when I folded my arms over my chest. "Like...I completely and totally hate both of you and never want to see you again."

"Oh, my poor girl," Cally cooed as she moved behind me, her hands landing on my shoulders as she kissed the top of my head. "Stop agitating her, Grady. She doesn't take well to public humiliation."

"She'll learn to live with it."

I wanted to tell him where he could stuff his pithy comment, but Cally was already taking control of the conversation.

"So, who wants to hear about my day?"

"I do," Grady replied. "I'd love to talk about anything other than your best friend's bodily functions."

"I'll kill you," I warned him in a low voice.

Apparently he didn't believe the threat, because his laugh was instantaneous.

"What's up with you, Cally?" I asked. I needed to focus on something—anything really—other than myself. "How can you have already had some sort of crisis? We spoke on the phone three hours ago."

"You've already had a life crisis in that time," Cally pointed out. "As for me, I think I met my soulmate."

Grady looked impressed. "That was fast work in one morning."

"Right?" Cally beamed at him. "He was in the Square when I was drinking my chicory and he stared at me the whole time."

A sinking sensation started to fill my stomach. "Jackson Square?"

"Do you know any other Square?"

"Lafayette Square."

"Well, aren't you quick this morning?" Cally made a derisive sound in the base of her throat. "Anyway, he stared at me the entire time I was drinking my coffee."

"He didn't say anything?" Grady prodded.

"Oh, he couldn't. You know they have to be quiet when they're doing the statue thing."

It took me a moment to realize what she was talking about. "Wait...you're going to date one of the human statues?"

"Absolutely." Cally clapped her hands and did a little dance. "You know how those guys turn me on. I finally nabbed me one today."

I was almost afraid to ask how.

"Is she talking about the guys who paint themselves silver and bronze and stand on those pedestals for hours on end in the hot sun?" Grady demanded.

I briefly closed my eyes and tilted my chin.

"That's exactly who I'm talking about," Cally confirmed. "They're hot."

Grady worked his jaw, seemingly at a loss as to how to respond. He was always quick with a joke. Perhaps there were too many fighting for supremacy in his head to throw one out now.

"Of course they're hot," Cally insisted. "Can you imagine the stamina those guys have? They stand there motionless for hours on end."

I'd had to listen to Cally go on and on about the statue guys for two years. She was determined to nab one, even though they never responded to her...and she put on a full-court press when she was determined. Still, I had a few questions...and the opportunity to ask one of them was upon me. "Just out of curiosity, how does the not moving thing benefit you in bed?"

"I'll move for us. He just needs to remain *rigid*." A shudder went up my spine as she posed to show us what she meant.

I pressed my lips together and looked at Grady.

"My turn?" he asked.

I nodded.

"Right." He scratched his chin. "Those guys are notorious for not saying anything."

"They are." Cally's eyes sparkled. "I like the strong but silent type."

"Who doesn't?" Grady's tone was far too enthusiastic. "Just out of curiosity, if they don't talk, how did you manage to arrange a date?"

"We did it with our eyes."

My heart sank. "Oh, you didn't make up a date in your head with one of the human statues, did you?" It wouldn't be the first time. I still felt sorry for her.

"Of course not. I waited for him to take a break—even statues have to tinkle—and then I started talking to him."

Oh, well, that was better. "Where are you guys going?"

"We're having dinner at August later tonight."

Alarm bells immediately went off in my head. "That's pretty expensive. I wouldn't think a human statue could afford that."

"I'm paying." Cally let loose a dismissive hand wave. "I love a good meal. And French food? Amore!" She kissed her fingers in dramatic fashion, apparently not caring that she was using an Italian word to describe French food. "There's no reason he can't love a good meal too. I brought you lunch and luckily I got enough for all three of us even though I didn't know Grady was going to be here."

"That is lucky," I agreed in a flat voice.

"I'll dish everything out after hitting the bathroom." Cally was a flurry of movement and giggles as she took off down the hallway. "Isn't this going to be fun?"

"Fun," I automatically agreed.

Grady waited until he heard the bathroom door shut to speak. "You're not having fun, are you?"

"Not even a little," I agreed. "She does this all the time. She falls for losers and convinces herself they'll be great just because they're artists."

"I don't think the human statues are artists."

"She does, and you can't talk her out of it."

"That's too bad. She seems nice."

"She has bleeding tragic taste in men." This day just kept getting worse and worse, I mused. First hot yoga, and now this? The universe had it in for me.

"Well, maybe she'll learn her lesson this time," Grady noted. "Eventually she has to grow out of this phase."

"One would think." I blew out a sigh. "So...Natchez for brunch tomorrow?"

"Yeah." Grady was silent for what felt like a long time. When he spoke again, his tone was soft. "You're a good friend. She's lucky to have you worrying about her so much."

"She's a better friend."

"She's...amazing."

I shot him a dirty look. "Oh, don't you go trying to break her of her Bohemian phase. I don't think dating love-them-and-leave-them types is a better option."

A momentary flash of annoyance crossed Grady's face, but he recovered quickly. "You shouldn't believe everything you hear."

"What should I believe?"

"Maybe try embracing what you feel."

"I'll give it some thought."

"Good." He tapped the pad of paper. "Now, come on. We'll be much better at this if we have a list to work from."

I didn't disagree. I couldn't forget what he'd said earlier, however. "You're not really going to write a piece that says I peed my jogging pants, are you?"

"Yup. People will love it."

"I'll make you pay."

"I look forward to the attempt."

Sadly, his expression told me he felt just that.

Thirteen

I spent an hour scanning photos of previous jazz brunch cruises on the Natchez to determine an appropriate outfit. I went with khaki capris and a basic black shirt with a V-neck. It didn't plunge so low as to offer a glimpse of the goods, but it was flattering...although why that was important was beyond me.

I walked to the Natchez the next morning, stopping at Cafe Beignet long enough to grab some coffee. Grady was already on a bench, reading his phone.

"Nice job on the hot yoga," he said when my shadow landed on him. He didn't bother looking up.

"How did you know it was me?" I asked.

"Maybe I'm psychic." His smile was cheeky when he glanced up. "Or maybe I recognized your lime coconut body spray."

"Is it too much?" I lifted my arm and sniffed.

"You smell delightful." He slipped his phone into his pocket as he stood. "Of course, I had the misfortune of smelling you yesterday before you showered. Anything is an improvement over that."

I shot him a dirty look. "If you tell anyone I peed myself...." I trailed off, leaving the threat hanging.

"Would I do that?"

"Yes."

"You're right. But not today. You're safe."

I was thankful I had my sunglasses on, which allowed me to scan him without his knowledge. He'd opted for a pair of knee-length khaki shorts and a black T-shirt, tight enough to display his impressive arms and broad chest. He looked good.

Damn him.

"Why didn't you write the hot yoga piece from your perspective like you threatened?" That was the first thing I'd checked when I woke this morning. Thankfully, he'd gone with a piece on dressing for the gym, which had only gotten a thousand hits. Compared to my piece on hot yoga, which hadn't been a grand slam by any stretch of the imagination with ten-thousand hits, it was a staid attempt.

"I didn't think writing what I wanted to would allow us to start off on solid footing, and that's what I'm most interested in."

"Yeah, but you could've embarrassed me."

"Believe it or not, that's not my main goal." He flashed a small smile. "That was your story. You did a bang-up job. I laughed throughout the entire thing, especially the part where you wrote your girl parts were threatening to go on strike after you stretched them."

"That wasn't an exaggeration. They're totally on strike."

"Well, that's sad...but maybe they'll feel better in a few days." He held his arm out to me in chivalrous fashion. "Shall we?"

I was taken aback by his gallant showing. "We need to buy tickets."

He reached into his pocket with his free hand and flashed two. "Already taken care of."

"Seriously?"

"I was here early. I wanted to make sure we were good to go."

"How much do I owe you?" I reached for my small purse.

"It's fine. I've got it."

There was no way I could let that slide. "No. This is a work thing, not a date. I need to buy my own."

Exasperation momentarily flitted across his eyes. "They were thirty-eight bucks."

I sorted through my wallet, coming back with two twenties. "Here you go."

He grudgingly took my money. "Are you ready?"

"Absolutely. Let's eat like tourists."

That earned a legitimate smile. "I was thinking the same thing. We should probably try everything, even if we don't like it. Some of the funniest stories stem from gross foods."

I fell into step with him, perplexed. "Maybe I'm in the minority here, but I don't find vomiting stories amusing."

"Nobody says you have to vomit."

"I know but...I don't like eating gross stuff. I have a weak stomach. It's going to be hard enough to eat on a boat."

Grady slowed his pace. "Are you telling me you're going to get seasick?"

I shrugged. "I don't think it's likely, but nothing is impossible."

"Well, thankfully I can make anything funny. If you throw up, I'll save us both."

I shook my head. "You can't write about it if I throw up."

"I didn't agree to that."

"Don't make me hurt you."

He belted out a laugh. "And here I thought this was going to be a boring cruise."

"Nothing with me is ever boring."

He arched an eyebrow, his expression unreadable. "I'm starting to come to that same conclusion."

I'D NEVER BEEN ON A STEAMBOAT. THEY obviously weren't prevalent in Florida. I'd been on other boats—and there was an ill-fated cruise my mother insisted on when I was fourteen that I still wasn't over—but the Natchez was a new experience for me.

I found I liked it.

"Look at the view." I stood on the deck next to Grady and pointed, lifting my phone so I could take photos of the New Orleans skyline. "It's beautiful."

Grady smiled but was focused on me rather than the view. "It's cute that you're so worked up for this."

"What?" I reined in my enthusiasm. "I like pretty things."

"Who doesn't?" He leaned in close for a moment—and I swear he looked as if he was going to kiss me—but then pulled back. "Get your photos and video. Then we should head inside. We don't want to miss the food and music."

"I'm still not going to vomit," I warned as I snapped photos. "You might want to make me try, but it's not going to happen."

"Like I said, the end goal here isn't to get you to throw up."

"Is it to get you to throw up?" I asked.

He shook his head. "I would honestly rather not."

"That's good because I'm a sympathetic puker. If I'm around someone who throws up, inevitably I do the same."

"Then it became a Puke-o-Rama."

"Yup." I solemnly bobbed my head.

"Yeah, let's make sure that doesn't happen." His grin was electric, to the point I momentarily forgot what I was doing.

After a few seconds, I recovered. I had all the photos I

needed, but I took three more for good measure. Then we headed inside.

I don't know what I expected. It was a steamboat, so I had no basis for comparison. What I found didn't scream "steamboat." It was more like a middle-class restaurant with a chandelier and a great view.

"The carpet is...interesting." Grady watched the floor as we went to find a seat.

I glanced down to see what had garnered his attention. The carpet was indeed interesting. It was red, pink, green, and tan, in a vague floral pattern. It was far too busy to help with my potential stomach issues, so I forced my attention away.

"You would think that ceramic tile would be easier to clean," I mused. "I mean...it's a boat. There are bound to be spills."

"Yeah, but broken tiles might be an issue and keeping someone on staff to fix them would likely be a pain." Grady led me to a table. The band was at the far end of the room, tuning up. "Is this okay?" He gestured toward a square table pushed together with three other square tables, couples spread all around us.

"Um, yeah." I nodded. Honestly, I wasn't picky about where we sat.

He moved to the other side of the table and sat across from me. Then we looked around to get the lay of the land.

"Do we just take our plates up and start filling them?" I asked after a few moments.

"That would be my guess." Grady craned his neck to get a look at the people in the room. "Do you want to eat now, or wait for a few minutes? I don't want to risk you puking on these nice people." He smiled at the couple to our right, but the expression slipped quickly when they glared at him. "That was an inside joke," he offered lamely.

"Puke stories aren't funny," the blonde shot back. She had

on way too much makeup for my comfort, but her face was expressive, and her glare had me hiding a smile behind my hand.

"Duly noted," Grady said as he stood. He absently held out a hand for me. "Let's get some food."

I took his hand without thinking. We were already in the buffet line when I realized what I'd done, and I instantly released him. "I hate to say, 'I told you so' when you're already feeling down," I started.

"Then don't." Grady shot me a pointed look.

"Okay." He was in line in front of me and I tried to keep my attention on the food as we reached the steam tables. I couldn't stop from messing with him though. The opening was too wide not to step through. "I told you so." I nudged him lightly with my hip.

I expected him to be frowning when he turned back to me, but there was a light in his eyes. "Is that out of your system now?" he asked.

"Pretty much."

"Awesome. Let's focus on the food."

Because he was right—we had a job to do, after all—I moved closer. "I don't really like brunch foods," I said.

"No?" Grady already had a plate in one hand and a spatula in the other as he dished frittata. "I thought you liked all foods."

"I'm not overly picky," I agreed. "Well, except for grits. Grits are gross."

"Grits were sent from the heavens to fill us all with joy."

"That's a load of crap."

He barked out a laugh. "Tell me how you really feel."

"That is how I really feel. Grits have no taste."

"That's what makes them good. You load them with cheese and shrimp and they provide the taste."

"Why not just eat the shrimp and cheese?"

He looked puzzled by the question. "Because...you need a conduit for the cheese and shrimp," he said. "Think of it as a delivery system."

"I'm not going to think of it at all." I bypassed the grits, though I did indulge in the frittata. "What I meant about brunch food is that it's a mixture of lunch and breakfast fare. I'm a big proponent of keeping meals separate."

"Are you telling me you've never had breakfast for dinner?" He looked as if he was trying to lay a "gotcha" question on me.

I answered honestly. "No. Well, I guess I ate cereal a few times, but not by choice."

Grady remained rooted to his spot. "You've never had eggs and hash browns for dinner?"

"You act as if that's weird."

"It *is* weird."

"It just wasn't done in our house. My mom was a stickler for rules. You can't eat breakfast after ten-thirty."

"I think those are McDonald's rules."

Now that he mentioned it, I had to wonder if he was right. "Huh."

"Huh what?"

"We did eat a lot of McDonald's for breakfast. My mother worked sixty hours a week to keep food on the table. It just now occurred to me that maybe that wasn't her rule."

Grady chuckled. "I love how you're just figuring this out."

"Yeah, it's not my finest moment." I nudged him with my hip again. "Keep going. They have some really good-looking bacon down there."

"Are you a big fan of bacon?"

"Who doesn't love bacon?"

"Sociopaths."

I choked on a laugh. "I wonder if the Behavioral Analysis Unit at Quantico uses that technique."

His forehead crinkled. "The Behavioral Analysis Unit?"

"That's what I said."

"How do you know the formal name?"

"I read things."

He paused a beat. "Or you watch a lot of *Criminal Minds* reruns."

My cheeks burned under his light scrutiny. "I...don't...watch a lot of television." Even as the lie slipped from my tongue, I felt like a moron. "I watch news shows and stuff, but not much else."

Grady shook his head, clearly enjoying my discomfort. "I bet you thought Reid was hot."

I responded without thinking. "No way. Derek was the hot one."

"Ha!" He jabbed a finger at me. "You totally watch *Criminal Minds*. You just want to pretend you're above it all."

I was caught and we both knew it. "Fine. I watch *Criminal Minds*. Sue me."

"Don't feel bad. I watch it too."

"Because you think JJ is hot?"

"No, I'm all about Derek too. I'm straight, don't get me wrong, but I can admire a hot dude as much as the next person."

The next sentence slipped out of my mouth before I could stop it. "I like that you're so comfortable with yourself."

He was quizzical. "Aren't you comfortable with yourself?"

The question threw me for a loop. I'd opened myself to the topic, however, so I felt the need to finish it. "Not always."

"Why? You seem pretty great to me."

My cheeks, which had just started cooling after the *Criminal Minds* faux pas, started blazing again. "You're one of the only people who thinks so."

"That's not even remotely true."

"It is. People don't notice me. I'm just Shay, the work drone. I don't have a life outside of other people's perception."

"I don't believe that."

"Well, I know it's true. I'm not the life of the party. I'm comfortable being me, but I understand that I won't be considered the fun one in a group."

"I don't think you have a very clear view of yourself."

"No? What do you see when you look at me?"

"Someone coming out of her shell."

I snorted. "Like a turtle?"

"If you like. You're more than you think, Shay. You just need to open yourself and see it."

He was so earnest it made me uncomfortable. "This conversation took a weird turn," I said.

His impish smile returned. "Let's fill up and head back to the table. Then we'll make fun of the food and music for two hours before docking. No muss, no fuss."

"Sounds fabulous."

TWO HOURS LATER I WANTED TO curse my weak stomach...and him in the process.

"Oh, thank God." I dropped to my knees on the riverwalk and rolled to the shade. I didn't care that the pavement was hard under my back. I was just happy that the ground beneath me was solid.

I closed my eyes, sucked in gaping mouthfuls of oxygen, and tried to forget the last two hours of rocking.

"Hey." Grady appeared above me. He looked concerned, but not as if he was ready to call the paramedics. "Do you think water would help?"

My brain wasn't firing on all cylinders, so it took me a moment to compute what he was saying. "I don't think so," I said finally. "If I add a single thing to my stomach I will definitely heave. I just need a few minutes to collect myself."

"Are you sure?" He didn't look convinced. "You're so white you're almost transparent."

"I'm sure."

He leaned over, and in a move so tender it caused my heart to stutter, brushed my hair from my face. "You're clammy but not feverish."

"Why would I be feverish?"

"I don't know. You could've picked up a bug."

"I get motion sickness if I'm not careful. I'll be fine in a few minutes."

"Why didn't you mention that yesterday?"

Was he really blaming this on me? He was unbelievable. "Because I didn't want you thinking I was shooting down your idea simply because it was your idea."

"I wouldn't have thought that."

"Oh, I can't even." I pinched the bridge of my nose and closed my eyes again. I could no longer see him, but I could feel him. His worry felt like a wave that kept knocking me over. "You don't have to stay with me," I said when it became apparent he wasn't going to abandon me.

"I'm not going to leave you here when you're sick."

"I'll be fine. Just...go. You don't have to act as my babysitter."

"What did I just say?" A muscle worked in his jaw. "I get that you can take care of yourself and don't need a man to take care of you."

"You've got that right," I muttered.

"That doesn't mean I'm leaving you here. I'll be walking you home...or to a restaurant so you can take advantage of the air conditioning and iced tea. Those are your choices."

He was really starting to bug me. "I think I'll go home."

"Because you're going to throw up?"

"Because we just ate and the last thing I want to think about is food."

He rolled back on his heels, as if considering what I'd said, and then nodded. "Okay, that makes sense." He extended his hand. "You need to get up. You're freaking me out."

I didn't want to get up. It was too soon to risk my newfound comfort, but the determined look on his face told me I didn't have a choice. "Fine." I slapped my hand in his and braced myself as he pulled.

For one glorious moment the world remained sharp and warm. I was going to be okay.

Then reality set in and the ground beneath my feet began to rock.

"Oh, crap!" I tried to cover my mouth, but it was too late. When I lost my stomach contents, that expensive brunch we'd gone out of our way to enjoy, it was all over Grady. It wasn't just on his shoes. It was on his shirt...and shorts...and in his hair. It was everywhere.

He stood there a moment, seemingly shocked, and then he leaned to the side and added to the mess. He'd eaten the grits, so his offering was even grosser.

"I'm so sorry," I said through tears, afraid that this was only the beginning. "I tried to tell you."

Grady looked haggard as he rested his hands on his knees. "Do you really think this is the time to drop another 'I told you so' on me?"

He had a point. "Do you want me to get you a bottle of water?"

"No, Shay, I don't want a bottle of water. Just... be quiet. I need to collect myself."

"Okay. I think I'm going to rest on the pavement. If you don't mind, I mean."

"Just...stop talking."

"Okay. Tell me when you're feeling better."
"You'll be the first to know."

Fourteen

Unsurprisingly, Grady wasn't keen on hanging out after the puke fest. I felt sorry for him—and myself—but it wasn't as if I hadn't warned him.

It took me twenty minutes to peel myself off the pavement and I made sure to avoid people on my way home and immediately hit the shower. Then I raided my limited bar goodies and found a lone can of ginger ale. It was two hours before I felt better.

Then it was time to write.

I was convinced I would leave out the puking—really, who would want to read about that?—but ultimately, when it came time to put everything together, the story didn't feel complete without mentioning it. I included it in what I hoped was a tasteful way, crossed my fingers, and pressed publish. Then I forced myself not to log on and check viewership numbers the rest of the day.

There was no containing me when I woke the next morning, however, and I held my breath when I logged on at the dining room table.

"What are you doing?" Cally chirped from behind me.

I screamed and practically jumped out of my chair. "What are you doing here?" I clutched at my chest like an old lady looking for her angina medication.

"I brought you breakfast." She held up a box of doughnuts.

I sucked in a calming breath and adjusted my tone. I mean...she got the doughnuts from my favorite bakery. They were the real deal, fried in grease and covered with chocolate frosting and sprinkles. "Don't you think you should knock?"

If Cally was bothered by the question, she didn't show it. Instead, she dropped the box on the table and meandered into the kitchen. "Where's the coffee?"

"Um...in the Keurig pods." Was she serious with that question?

"You know how I feel about the Keurig. That's not real coffee. When are you going to get a real coffee machine?"

"That's as real as I'm going to get." I meant it. "When I want real coffee, I go out to get it."

"Ugh. You're such a pain." She smiled despite the words. "So, I'm here for a reason."

Of course she was. She wouldn't be Cally if she wasn't. "Let me guess: Your plan to snag a statue man has fallen into disarray."

"Of course it has. Those dudes are weird. I went out with my statue last night and he dropped his pants when we were standing outside my place to say goodbye. He just unsnapped them and let them fall. Dude apparently goes commando in case you were wondering."

That was a lot to take in. "I guess I can see him wanting to go commando. He probably has to with all that paint."

"I think underwear would be a necessity in that situation, but what do I know?"

I often asked myself that question. "Well, better luck next time."

"He was hung like an infant anyway." Cally didn't look overly bothered by the turn of events. "I mean...we're talking the bottom sixteenth of a hot dog."

"Maybe he was cold."

"It was ninety-five degrees. I'm not here to talk about him. We both knew that date was going to end poorly, but I do appreciate the fact that you didn't go all out and tell me it was going to end poorly this time." She cocked her thumb and winked.

"I'm fairly certain you knew it was going to end poorly," I said. "You just like to flip your own stomach. It's what you do."

"You could be right."

"Oh, I'm right."

"Which is why I'm here to talk about your date."

Confusion pulled my eyebrows together. "Excuse me? I haven't had a date in...a bit."

"Months," Cally corrected, "but you had one yesterday."

It took me a moment to realize what she was referring to. "Oh, no." I made a tsking sound with my tongue and shook my head. "That was not a date. Grady and I are not dating."

"Girl, he's warm for your form."

I shot her a dirty look. "Did you steal that saying from your grandmother?"

"Clara is much too cool to use that. Heck, I was never even allowed to call her Grandma. She's way cooler than me. I came up with that myself."

"Or you were watching old episodes of *Full House* again."

"Hey!" She jabbed a finger in my direction. "That was a house full of love and laughter."

My lips inadvertently curved. Cally's adoration of old television shows was one of my favorite things about her, but I wasn't going to indulge her delusion regarding my association with Grady. "We had a work thing yesterday. Nothing more."

"Yeah, I read about that work thing online. Congrats on the twenty-thousand hits, by the way. I think you guys are on the right track. If you continue publishing funny stuff like that your audience will grow by leaps and bounds."

"We got twenty-thousand hits?" I hadn't gotten that far yet. My heart did a happy jig. "That's awesome."

"So were the articles. I even liked the vomit part."

I stilled. "Did you read both of them?"

"I did."

"I don't suppose you noticed if he mentioned the vomit?" I almost didn't want to hear her answer.

"He did. His rendition of you lying on the pavement was pretty funny. I preferred your take on him insisting on being a man, therefore he knew better, and that's why he tried to pull you up even though you told him you weren't ready, resulting in the projectile vomit. Either way, when read together, both takes were delightful. There are hundreds of comments."

"Really?" I couldn't stop myself from scrolling. I loved reading comments on my stuff.

Cally sat across from me and opened the doughnut box. She seemed amused by the cackling noises I made as I read. I barely noticed when she slipped a doughnut into my hand. Then I practically tripped over a comment that had my eyes going wide.

"Wait...."

"I got you sprinkles, girl."

My eyes were narrow slits when I slid them to Cally. "Did you post this comment about what a cute couple we make?"

"No. Why would you say that?" Cally was suddenly the picture of innocence.

"Because you said we're cuter than Uncle Jesse and Aunt Becky."

"I also said you were funnier than Alex P. Keaton and

Ellen. That right there is a compliment, my friend." She extended her arm for a fist bump.

I ignored her. "You need to take it down."

"No way." Cally vigorously shook her head. "I've got a hundred and twenty-five likes on that thing. You know I can't help but be thrilled when I'm loved."

"Cally." I was exasperated. "You're going to get all these people worked up if they think there's something going on between us. This is man-versus-woman, not man-loves-woman."

"Why can't it be both?"

"It can't. He doesn't even like me."

"Oh, please." Cally's eye roll was fierce. "That guy totally has the hots for you."

"That's your imagination. It's just like the statue guy. You see sparks that aren't there."

"Hey, the statue guy and I had sparks. I just don't happen to be into nudists."

"Especially if you need a magnifying glass to see their junk," I muttered.

"That is true, but it doesn't change the fact that I'm right about you and Grady. There's a spark. Even vomit and you peeing your pants can't extinguish it."

"I didn't pee my pants!" I was sick to death of that story.

"Aw, you're so cute when you get worked up." She beamed at me. "What's the plan for today with your non-boyfriend?"

I was glum as I went back to staring at my computer screen. The views on my story kept increasing. "We're going to a Cajun cooking class."

"Seriously?"

I bobbed my head. "We agreed. It's something we can make funny with very little effort."

"It's also something couples do."

"I picture huge groups of women drinking wine and

burning their gumbo. It's one class. Don't read too much into it."

"Sure. I'll let it go."

I was hopeful. "Really?"

"Sure. I've got your back."

"Thank you." I blew out a sigh and glanced at the clock on the wall. "I should get in the shower. I need to be there in a little more than an hour."

"Make sure you look good for your boyfriend," she called out as I started down the hallway with my doughnut.

"You said you'd let it go."

"Yeah, I lied. I'm never going to let it go."

GRADY WAS OUTSIDE THE CULINARY SCHOOL when I arrived. When he'd told me where the facility was located—prime property on Royal Street—I'd been convinced he was lying. Apparently not.

"Hey." I was suddenly shy as I approached him. It was a hot day, but I was used to the temperature by now. There was no way the sun was causing my cheeks to combust the way they were. "How are you?"

I expected him to be angry, convinced he would unload on me. I had puked on him, after all. Instead of scowling, however, he grinned.

"That was going to be my opening line."

His welcoming smile calmed me a bit. "So, you're okay?"

"I was fine not long after we separated," he reassured me. "I went home, threw out my clothes, and took a shower. After that, I felt pretty normal."

"You threw out your clothes? Why not just wash them?"

"Because then there would've been puke in my washing machine."

"Yeah, but...."

"It's best we don't talk about it again." He was firm. "Talking about it makes me think about it. When I think about it, I picture it. When I picture it, I remember the odor. When that happens...." He trailed off.

"I really am sorry." We made our way into the building. "I tried to warn you."

"I thought you were being dramatic."

"Just for the record, when puke is involved, I'm never dramatic."

"Good to know." He shot me an impish grin as we followed the arrows on the wall to the classroom. "Are you ready to become a professional chef?"

"If you would've asked me that yesterday I would've said no. I mean...I didn't even want to think about food the rest of the day. I guess that was good for my thighs, in retrospect."

"Your thighs are nice. Don't worry about your thighs."

That burning feeling in my cheeks was back in an instant. "Um...."

"Here we are." We made our way to one of the open kitchens. He clearly understood he'd taken it to a weird place and was ready to pretend he hadn't. "Oh, look, there's a list of ingredients and steps to follow right here in our station." He held up a laminated sheet of paper.

I took it from him, studied it a bit, and then handed it back. "Seems easy enough." I scanned the room, convinced that Grady would be the only man in attendance...right up until I started looking at the cooking stations. "Huh."

"What?" Grady was focused on the ingredients.

"It's just...I thought this was a girls' outing sort of thing." I chewed my bottom lip.

"As compared to what?" He looked puzzled.

"It's all couples."

"Yeah, this is a big date night thing. That's what it said in the reviews. I told you."

He most certainly hadn't. I would remember that. "I...um...."

"What's the problem?" Grady fixed me with a serious look. "You seem upset."

I made up my mind on the spot. If he didn't think this was a bad idea, there was no way I would voice that particular concern. It would be worse if I said that people would think we were dating if we weren't careful and he thought I was actually pressuring him to date. "I'm fine. I'm glad we're going with gumbo. I love a good gumbo."

"I do too. Can you cook?"

That seemed like a loaded question. "Of course I can cook. I'm still alive, right? I would be dead if I couldn't cook."

He licked his thumb and moved it to my cheek, causing me to hop and glare.

"You have frosting on your cheek," he said. "Do you make your own frosting?"

"Cally surprised me with doughnuts this morning. This is not normal." It happened twice a week tops.

"Okay, well...it looks like the instructor is going to do an introduction. Then it will be up to us to cook. We need to remember to take videos of the entire process. We'll split the footage when we're done."

"Sounds good." I flashed a smile I didn't feel. "I can't wait to cook you under the table."

He snorted. "Are you really going to turn this into a competition?"

"Yup, and I'm going to win."

He studied me a moment and then smirked. "I have news for you. I'm going to be way better at this."

I didn't believe him for a second. "Bring it on."

"Right back at you."

. . .

IT TURNED OUT I WASN'T NEARLY AS GOOD at cooking as I thought. I mean...we had to follow a recipe card. They spelled things out for us as if we were idiots. How hard could it be?

Pretty hard. It was way harder than should've been allowed under the Geneva Convention.

"How do people not starve?" I demanded as I glared into the pot in front of me. I was convinced the contents had been possessed by some sort of demon and a creature would crawl out at any moment. "I mean...this is crap."

"It's total crap," Grady agreed. He had his phone in his hand, filming me as I worked. "You're the one who wanted to handle the roux. Keep going."

"I didn't say I wanted to handle the roux." He was remembering it wrong.

"You said, and I quote, 'I've got this. It says right in the recipe that it's the most important part. That means I need to do it.'" He used a high-pitch voice that was clearly supposed to suggest an imitation of mine.

"I sound nothing like that," I groused, my bad mood causing me to bump him with my hip. "Also, did you know that roux isn't supposed to be lumpy? Seems to me, if it wasn't supposed to be lumpy there should be a better way to get out the lumps. I mean...what in the hell?" I glared into the pot again — all I saw were lumps.

Grady was silent so long I had to look over to make sure he was still there. The good news is that he was no longer filming. He'd lowered his phone and seemed to be taking a break. The bad news was that he was bent over at the waist, his shoulders shaking with silent laughter.

"This is not funny." I folded my arms over my chest.

"Of course it's not." His face was red as he straightened. "Not funny at all."

"Roux is clearly the devil's thickening agent."

He snorted again. "Yeah." He reached over and swiped at my cheek with his thumb. "Can you do anything without getting dirty?"

"Oh, don't bring up the puke again."

"I wasn't going to."

"Or the pee, because you've been getting a lot of mileage from a story that didn't really happen."

"I apologize."

He almost looked sincere. "As for cooking, clearly I've been misled. I was told it was something all adults not only *could* learn but *should* learn. It's like the Santa Claus thing all over again."

"You mean when our parents told us Santa Claus was real?"

"Oh, my parents never told me that." I shook my head. "My mother was a hippie. She didn't believe in lying to children. She told me Santa Claus wasn't real at a young age. Imagine my surprise in kindergarten when I ruined it for all the other kids."

Grady's lips twitched. "I...um...how is this like the Santa Claus thing again?"

"My mother told me that adults lie to children because it's comforting for the adult," I explained. "That's what we're dealing with. It's the Cooking Lie, which is apparently something everybody knows about but never comments on."

Grady's grin widened. "I think you just nailed the headline for our series."

"Right?" I grinned back.

He stared for a moment longer and I thought he was going to go back to messing with me. Instead, he turned serious. "Do you want to have dinner with me?"

It was the last thing I expected. In fact, I almost choked. Then I made a sort of whirring to clear my throat. He swooped in before I had the grace to respond.

"You know what? You're not ready yet. How about we just focus on the cooking today and leave the other stuff for later?"

Was he serious? How was I supposed to ignore what he'd said? I had to give it a try. "Sure. Let's cook. What's next?"

"We have to use the provided seafood stock," Grady replied. "Apparently, if we were going to make it ourselves, we would have to use seafood shells."

And I thought I was annoyed before. "It's the Santa thing all over again. Cooking is not fun."

"Definitely not, but we're stuck seeing it through to the end."

"Yeah, yeah, yeah. Let's finish this up. Just know, I'm not eating anything I cooked."

"Don't trust yourself?"

"Not even a little."

"I'll give it a try."

"What if there's puke involved in our outings two days in a row?"

He shrugged. "I'm willing to risk it."

Oddly enough, so was I.

Fifteen

I was still bothered by Grady's statement—*you're not ready*—hours later. What did he mean? Ready for what? Did he really think I would ever be ready for whatever he meant? Was that what he was banking on?

The most insecure part of myself, the part I buried and kept hidden from others, had to wonder if his plan was to make me fall for him so he could use it to his advantage for the pieces we were writing. It didn't matter that I had no idea how he planned to do it. The mere possibility had me buzzing with nervous energy. Despite that, I edited the video I'd put together—it really was cute with all the banter about who was the better cook—and then filed my piece. It came together quickly, almost as if it wasn't work at all. I was proud of the end product.

I was also still full of questions.

When Cally texted to see if I wanted to go out, I jumped at the chance. If I stayed home, I would spend the entire night obsessing about Grady. The way he'd looked at me when asking me to dinner was seared into my mind. Was he really that good of an actor? What was his end game? If I went out with Cally, I could keep my mind busy with other things. If I showed interest in Grady, however minor, she would use it against me...and I couldn't handle any more pressure right now.

We went to Moxie's Cantina—our new favorite hangout—and ordered Witch's Brew drinks. Moxie delivered them, and then flopped down in one of our open chairs.

"What's new in the life of our resident media darling?"

I was mid-sip when I realized she was referring to me. "What?" My eyebrows moved toward one another like magnets. "I'm not a media darling."

Moxie snorted as she wiped her hands with her apron. I noted the beautiful diamond engagement ring from Gus. She wasn't the fussy sort, and yet occasionally I'd noticed her staring at the ring when she was secluded in the corner or had a quiet moment behind the bar. She always had a goofy expression on her face when she eyed the ring. Even as I told myself she was acting ridiculous, it filled me with a sense of yearning I couldn't explain.

It wasn't just having a fiancé, or a wedding to plan, I ultimately realized. It was that she had someone who understood her. Not only that, but Gus also wanted to make her life better. He put her first whenever possible. She did the same for him. It was appealing to think about...even as I chastised myself for being such a sap.

"I'm serious," I insisted. "I'm hardly a media darling. That's the sort of thing you say about the Kardashians...or those Real Housewives of Pompous City. I'm not a media darling."

"You keep telling yourself that." Moxie awkwardly patted my shoulder. "Don't you realize that everybody in town is talking about you?"

I certainly didn't realize that. I also didn't want to think about it too hard. "I think you just believe that because I'm a regular here and people recognize me. I very much doubt it's like that in the other corners of the Quarter."

"That's not true." Cally solemnly shook her head. "I heard people talking about you on the riverwalk this morning."

"You're making that up," I insisted.

"They might not have mentioned you by name, Shay, but they certainly were talking about you," Cally argued. "They mentioned the ugly bridesmaid fashion show and how they wished they would've known it was a thing so they could've seen it in person. They were also laughing themselves silly over the puke story on the Natchez."

"Technically that didn't happen *on* the Natchez," I reminded her. "It happened on the pavement in front of the Natchez."

"Well, I'm glad you clarified that for me," Cally said drily. "I have no idea what I would've done if I wasn't clear on the details." She shot me a dirty look. "People are responding to you. Why can't you just take your accolades and enjoy it?"

Oh, if only it were that easy. "You're blowing things out of proportion." I was adamant. "I mean...I'm hardly the belle of the Bourbon Street ball."

Moxie's forehead creased at the declaration.

"It could be a thing," I said defensively. "I know it's not, but it was supposed to be funny."

"We got it," Cally said.

"And it's a great idea." Moxie shifted on her chair. She'd looked like she needed a rest when she sat down, but now she bubbled with energy. "Where is Gus?"

"What are you doing?"

"Were you looking for me, my little beignet bottom?" Gus said as he appeared behind Moxie, an empty tray in hand. He looked amused by her dour expression.

"How many times have I told you not to call me that?" she demanded.

If Gus was bothered by her bad mood, he didn't show it. "So many times I've lost count."

"It bugs me," she growled.

"That's why I keep calling you that. I like when you're feisty." He dropped a kiss on top of her head. He was clearly an expert dealing with her moods, and I couldn't help but smile at the way they played off each other. They bantered with the best of them but the love they shared was rock-solid. "Did you need something, baby? As much as I love spending time with you—there's nothing I love more than fighting until you're frothing at the mouth—I figure one of us should work if we want to keep the bar operational."

Moxie looked as if she was caught between wanting to laugh or to throttle him. "I'm just taking a break."

"I didn't say anything."

"I can get up and help."

"No, I want you to rest." He grinned. "If you want something, just tell me. I'm more than willing to wait on you. I figure that's my lot in life going forward."

"Ha, ha, ha. You're so very funny."

"I think so." His expression didn't change. "Tell me what you've got going on in that busy brain of yours."

"I was thinking that we should do a thing." Moxie might've been irritated with the turn of events, but her eyes were sparkling when she fixed them on Gus. "The Bourbon Street Ball."

"I'm not sure I understand."

"We can turn it into a Southern thing," she insisted. "Like a *Divine Secrets of the Ya-Ya Sisterhood* bar night or something. People can dress up and throw out a bunch of drunken 'Bless your hearts' whenever the mood strikes. We can do theme drinks. You know people love theme drinks."

Gus looked intrigued. "You know, that's not a bad idea.

We might be able to work with some of the other bar owners and turn it into a really big event."

"And you and Grady can hype it and help," Moxie insisted when she turned back to me. "You can write dueling POVs on the bar ball, make it really funny. People will come from the other parishes. The tourists will eat it up. This could really be fun."

I was taken aback. Was she really asking me to participate in this with her? "I don't...I mean, it sounds fun, but I'm not sure what I can do."

Moxie let loose a haphazard wave. "We'll figure that out down the line. This will take weeks to plan. It will be good for the business community and for you."

I glanced at Cally to see what she thought of it. She was already nodding her head and wriggling in her chair. "I want to help. It sounds amazing. We should pick a charity for part of the proceeds."

"That's a great idea," Moxie enthused. "You can definitely help."

They were so primed at the idea all I could do was nod. "I'm in." Honestly, I figured why not. It could turn into a huge thing, and if I was involved from the start it was bound to draw attention. "I'll talk to Grady tomorrow when we figure out what our next piece is going to be."

"Oh, I don't think that will be necessary," Cally drawled.

"Why?"

"Because Grady just walked in the door. I think it's best we talk to him about it now." Before I could stop her from calling him over, she hopped to her feet and started waving like a maniac. "Yoo-hoo! Grady! We're over here!"

I. Was. Mortified.

Every head in the bar swiveled in our direction. Cally didn't seem to care. She was too excited to see my workmate to worry about my reaction.

Grady was all smiles as he approached us. He didn't seem nervous, and he didn't come out and remind me that he'd suggested I wasn't ready for some mysterious *something* earlier. He was his normal gregarious self. "I was hoping you were here. I took a chance when you didn't answer my call."

I made a face. "I didn't get a call." When I pulled out my phone, I realized I'd missed three calls...all from Grady. "Oh."

He smirked at my discomfort. "Oh," he said. "It's fine. We still have time."

If I was baffled before, I was in the Twilight Zone now. "Time for what?"

"I got us in for a haunted ghost tour." He said it as if I was supposed to applaud.

"I don't understand. We already did our assignments for the day."

"Yes, and the pieces are already blowing up." He grinned at me. "You said you wanted to do a ghost tour. The one you wanted was booked, and you put our names on a waiting list."

"I remember." It had come up during our plotting session.

"Well, I called and asked if we could fill in if anyone canceled," he explained. "The tour starts in an hour."

I glanced at Cally, unsure. "I can't just abandon my friend."

"It's fine." Cally waved her hand. "I like being abandoned. I've found some of my best dates when left to survive on my own."

"Are you sure?" The question should've been internalized. *Was I sure?* After what he'd said this afternoon, the meaning behind the words I'd yet to suss out, I couldn't decide if I was ready to go out with him again so soon.

"Absolutely positively."

"If it's not for an hour, you have time for a drink," Moxie offered as she stood. "I'll get you something. Shay has something she wants to talk to you about anyway."

"Is that a fact?" Grady's expression was difficult to decipher as he took the chair Moxie pulled out for him. "What's on your mind, Shay?" He seemed tense.

"I made an offhand comment," I started. I felt backstory was necessary.

"About me? Is this about what I said this afternoon? We don't have to talk about that. I meant what I said. You're not ready. It's fine. I can be patient."

My cheeks heated at his words, and I was glad for the muted lighting in the bar. Otherwise, Cally would've picked up on my blushing and needled me endlessly. "That's not what we were talking about," I hissed.

Grady took a moment, perhaps thinking, and then smiled. "Okay. What were you talking about?"

"Hold up." Cally lifted her hand and glanced between us. She was much more observant than most people gave her credit for. "What were you talking about, Grady?"

Ugh. "Nothing." I was the first to respond. "We just had an interesting conversation at our cooking class."

"It was definitely interesting," Grady agreed. He glanced at Moxie. "I'll take whatever you have on tap. Thank you."

"Sure." Moxie nodded as she darted her eyes between Grady and me. "Whatever is going on, don't say anything good until I get back." She was off like a shot, sliding around Gus—who had moved to a neighboring table to take orders—and practically hopped over the bar to get to the glasses.

Gus watched her move with fondness. His lips curved into a smile, and he shook his head before returning to his customers.

I decided to fill the now uncomfortable silence. "So, Moxie wants to do a Bourbon Street Ball with costumes and a theme, and she thinks it will be good for us to cover with dueling POVs," I explained.

"Yeah?" Grady lifted an eyebrow. "Sounds like fun. And we'll be in on the ground floor."

"That's what I was thinking."

"Yes, yes, yes." Cally made a tsking sound with her tongue. "We're all excited about the ball. I want to know what you were talking about when you said Shay wasn't ready."

"Oh, good!" Moxie appeared with a flourish, a Pilsner glass in hand. She smoothly slid the glass in front of Grady. "I didn't miss anything. I'm ready." She folded her arms across her chest and waited.

I couldn't help thinking that I'd somehow been tapped for a hidden camera show. "It's nothing," I said. "It was just cooking stuff."

"I asked her to dinner," Grady countered. Apparently, he'd yet to grasp the divine magic that was the white lie. Not everybody needed to know every tidbit of our private business.

"You did?" Cally's smile was wide for him, but it shrank to a bland scowl when she turned it to me. "How interesting. Don't you find that interesting, Shay?"

"Not really." I felt put on the spot. "I have no idea why you find it so interesting."

"It's interesting enough that you would think my best friend would've told me about it when she first saw me...what with the other things we've been discussing of late."

"What have you guys been discussing?" Despite the awkward conversation, Grady seemed to be in a good mood. He sipped his beer and happily glanced between us. "Am I right in assuming that I'm part of this discussion?"

"Don't flatter yourself," I warned. "We don't talk about you when you're not around."

"She's lying." Cally lifted a challenging eyebrow when my mouth dropped open. "We talk about you all the time. Most of it revolves around the fact that I want her to date you, but she says absolutely not."

"Really?" I didn't think it was possible, but Grady's smile widened. "Why do you think she doesn't want to go out with me?"

"She's afraid."

"Can you guys not talk about me like I'm not here?" I growled.

"Shh," Moxie admonished, waving a hand in my face. "I want to hear what they have to say."

Oh, this was just too much.

"What is she afraid of?" Grady asked, that easygoing nature he always seemed to have in spades on full display.

"Word is you're a ladies' man," Cally replied.

"One shouldn't believe everything one hears on the street," Grady said.

"Is that you saying you're not a ladies' man?" She looked hopeful.

"I don't believe I am." Grady was choosing his words carefully. "I don't want to mislead anyone." Even though he was clearly saying it for my benefit, he kept his gaze on Cally. "I have dated. I think I'm a nice guy. I try to be respectful and loyal to everybody I date."

"Annabelle?" I challenged. The name slipped out of my mouth before I realized it.

"That was...not one of my better relationships," he acknowledged. "I should point out that it was barely a relationship."

"That's not what she says."

"Yes, well, she and I see things differently."

"Hmm." Cally pursed her lips as she regarded him. "You should ask her out again. Maybe wait a few days. You're right about her being a Nervous Nellie, but you'll get what you want eventually."

"Is that so?" Grady looked downright tickled. "Thank you for the tip."

"Don't mention it." Cally went back to her cocktail with a blasé shrug. "If you hurt her, though, I'm going to hack off your franks and beans and serve them as the main course at a picnic."

Grady choked on his drink. She'd delivered the threat in her sunniest voice. "I'll keep that in mind," he said when he'd recovered.

"You do that." Cally turned her attention to me. "We're going to have a talk about keeping secrets from your best friend tomorrow. Don't bother claiming you're busy. I'll handle the food. You get your story straight."

Crap. I should've seen this coming. I narrowed my eyes and slid them to Grady. "I can't help but feel like this is your fault," I said.

He merely shrugged. "I can live with that."

He looked perfectly contented. I believed him. "So, a haunted tour?" I forced myself to look to the future. "I've always wanted to go on one. Cally never let me because she said they were tourist traps."

"Oh, sure, blame it on me," Cally lamented. "We're going to talk about that too."

"I can't wait."

"You say that now, but we both know you're going to feel differently tomorrow."

Was I that transparent?

Sixteen

The first thing our tour guide Dexter did was compare himself to the serial killer from the books and movies.

"I have a code," he intoned, his ridiculous tricornered hat —boasting a peacock feather—tilted to one side. "I research death. I revere those who have died. I only kill those who deserve it."

I slid my eyes to Grady, who seemingly couldn't stop smiling. "This guy is the king of corny," I whispered.

"Isn't that what we're looking for?" Grady asked. "The cornier the better, right?"

"I guess." Honestly, he wasn't wrong. "I guess we should start filming." I started rummaging for my phone, but Grady stilled me by grabbing my hand. "What?"

"Let's get a feel for him first." The tour lasts an hour and a half. It has six stops, including at a bar. I asked why. "Let's listen to the first stop so we can decide how best to cover him."

"Okay." I stood there like an idiot for a moment. Then I looked down. Grady's hand was still wrapped around my fingers. He showed no signs of releasing me. "Do you get scared about these things?" I asked.

He shrugged. "I don't know. Do you?"

"I asked you first."

"Is your answer contingent upon my answer?"

"No. I just...no." The truth was things that were designed to scare me rarely frightened me. "I love horror movies."

"Me too, but this is different."

"How?"

He'd been avoiding eye contact up to that point. When he turned back to me, there was a hint of mischief reflected back. There was also a hint of something I couldn't put a name to. "This is a murder and mayhem tour. There will be ghost stuff, but the city has a rich history of sick bastards."

"Okay." I had no idea where he was going with this.

"Sick bastards are different from movie killers. Take John Wayne Gacy. That guy was a total freak. He was a real monster. He frightens the crap out me, but I can laugh at the absurdity of Jason Voorhees."

"Ah." I bobbed my head. "I get it. Jason Voorhees is one of my favorite slasher killers. He's the most frightening."

"Oh, no way." Grady made a face as we began following Dexter. There were fifteen people in our group—mostly couples—and we were toward the tail end of the line. "Michael Myers is way scarier."

"How do you figure?"

"He was a real man. He started as a boy who killed his sister for no reason and then went on a rampage as an adult. He wasn't supernatural."

"I've seen some of those movies," I hedged. "They played him as indestructible at a certain point. And in one of those movies there was a doomsday cult."

"That doesn't count. Only the first movie counts. They

retconned everything between that and the most recent trilogy with Jamie Lee Curtis."

"Just because they retconned it doesn't mean they didn't try to sell us on it. I didn't mind the second *Halloween*...or the fourth one...or the one set at the boarding school. There were quite a few duds in there otherwise, but those weren't bad."

"You're going completely off script."

It was only then that I realized Grady was still holding my hand. Had he forgotten? Was he purposely holding me close because he was afraid? Was it something else? I searched his profile for an answer but came up empty.

I didn't pull my hand away. I couldn't seem to make myself. I let him continue holding it.

"I didn't know we were following a script," I said.

His smile was soft. "I like going off script. Keep at it."

"If you insist."

Our first stop was a parking lot. Dexter drew us to the far end and started talking in his hokey manner. I did my best to listen—I really was interested, I told myself—but I couldn't stop focusing on the fact that Grady and I were holding hands. In public no less. It felt strange...and somehow right.

"New Orleans's most infamous serial killer is the Axeman," Dexter said. "The most important thing to know about him is that he was never caught. He left a bloody trail through the city, death and destruction in his wake – and he could still be out there."

I made a face. "Wouldn't he be at least a hundred and twenty years old?" I asked, cringing when I realized I'd interrupted his flow.

"Fine." Dexter gave a tight smile. "His ghost could still be out there."

I pressed my lips together to keep my mouth shut and forced myself to listen.

"The first victims were Joseph Maggio and his wife

Catherine. They were killed May 23rd, 1918, while sleeping in their house on the corner of Upperline and Magnolia streets. The killer broke into their home and cut their throats with a straight razor before he bashed their heads with an axe.

"When police arrived on the scene, they found bloody clothing belonging to an outside individual," he continued. "Meaning the killer changed his clothes before he left so as not to be noticed on the street. That points to premeditation. Joseph's brother was considered a suspect for a long time, but they could never break his alibi.

"About a month later, Louis Besumer and his mistress Harriet Lowe were attacked in the back of his grocery store. They both survived but could not identify their attacker."

Dexter paused for dramatic effect, raising his nose in the air and inhaling deeply.

When I glanced at Grady, I found him smirking. He was obviously enjoying the story.

Dexter continued running through the tale, periodically dishing out theatrical pauses. I had to admit, he was good at building tension. When he got to the end, to the part where the Axeman supposedly wrote a letter claiming that he would spare victims who played jazz in their homes, a genuine chill ran up my spine.

"Are you okay?" Grady clearly noticed my reaction because he dropped my hand and slipped his arm around me. "Are you cold?"

That was a ridiculous question on the face of it. The sun might've fallen, but it was still in the high seventies...and humid as hell. I was used to sweating profusely daily and rarely noticed any longer, but Grady's proximity was making me flash hot all over.

"I'm fine." I told myself to shrug off his arm. This wasn't a date, after all. Did I? Of course not. That would've been the smart thing to do but apparently, I'd fried all my brain cells when trying to be cool earlier. That was the only explanation.

Grady kept me close until Dexter finished with the Axeman story and we'd started walking again. His fingers trailed over my arm, and when he dropped his hand, he immediately reached for mine. I choreographed what he was going to do and told myself to shift so we wouldn't be touching. Instead, I met him halfway. This time he twined his fingers with mine...and neither of us said a single word.

Next on our tour was the Omni Royal Orleans, where Dexter told a brief—but terrible—story about a war hero who jumped from the hotel roof. The suicide note in his pocket led police back to his apartment, where they found his girlfriend's head, hands, and feet in pots on the stove. Her arms and legs were in roasting pans.

"I'm kind of glad I didn't eat meat for dinner," I said as we resumed walking.

Grady chuckled. "What did you eat?"

"A salad. I didn't have much of an appetite after our cooking class. I mean...if you can call it that."

"It was definitely a cooking class. Whether or not we were good students is up for debate."

"Not really."

"No, we both bit the big one in that class."

I laughed, earning a dark look from the couple in front of us. Grady shot them an apologetic smile.

Through all this, we continued holding hands as if it were the most normal thing in the world.

"Here we go," I noted when we turned left onto Governor Nichols Street from Chartres. I recognized where we were.

"The LaLaurie Mansion," Grady noted in a low voice.

"You seem fascinated by it."

His smile was instantaneous. "I'm a local boy, Shay. I know about the LaLaurie Mansion because everybody in this town knows about it. Every single kid in the Quarter was terrified of that place. We had to learn about it in school. Of course, all the kids made up stories to go with the real ones. That doesn't make the truth any less terrifying."

"Did you ever get to see it? Inside, I mean."

"No. I wish, but unless I somehow win the lottery and convince the owners to sell, I don't think that's going to happen."

I realized then that everyone around us had fallen silent, and when I glanced up, I found fourteen sets of eyes on me.

"If you're done, I would like to take over now," Dexter said.

"Sorry, dude." Grady let his oodles of charm out to play. "I'm just trying to ramp up the 'Oh, hell no' factor for my girl so I can get lucky tonight."

My mouth dropped open, and I slowly extricated my hand from his.

Dexter grinned. "Got it. Can't say I blame you." He winked at Grady and then launched into a true tale of murder and mayhem.

Because I didn't want to be tempted to hold Grady's hand again, I pulled out my phone and began filming. It was the only thing I could think to do if I didn't want to fall over from embarrassment...or some other feeling I couldn't name.

"Marie Delphine LaLaurie built this mansion in 1832," he started. "She lived here with her third husband and two daughters. She was known to have slaves, and when her kitchen caught fire in 1834, neighbors who were trying to help found one of the slaves chained to the stove." He proceeded with a tale of murder and mutilation of other slaves.

"A further search of the house resulted in the discovery of several other slaves who were bound in the attic. They showed signs of cruel abuse that was apparently long running," he continued. "Madame LaLaurie herself was not captured that day. She escaped to France with her family.

"An outraged mob of citizens burned the house down, but it was subsequently rebuilt. As for Madame LaLaurie, her son wrote to a friend that she was serious about returning to New Orleans in 1842. It doesn't appear that happened, however, because her family disapproved. As for the circumstances of her death, they're murky. Some people believed she died in a boar-hunting accident in France—no joke—but others believe she somehow returned to New Orleans and is interred in St. Louis Cemetery."

He paused for dramatic effect. That was part of his schtick, and he was good at it.

"Now let's talk about what really happened in the house," he intoned.

I filmed him for a long time. The information he provided was interesting, but I had to wonder how much of it was embellishment. I'd read up on the LaLaurie Mansion and the atrocities that happened there, but most records were incomplete. Some of the stories had been adopted as legend.

When we finished at the LaLaurie Mansion I stopped filming for the continued walk. There was nothing of note to cover, and I found myself watching Grady. His gaze was on the ground, which was uneven. New Orleans sidewalks were notoriously uneven. When you're navigating a city known for drinking, that's not necessarily a good thing.

Because he'd been silent for so long, I was desperate to get him to talk. About what, though? I didn't think asking him why he held my hand for so long was a safe topic, and yet I could think of nothing else.

"What are you thinking?" I blurted out.

"Hmm." Grady's expression was inquisitive when he lifted his head. "What are you thinking?" His voice was low and husky.

"Nothing." That wasn't true in the slightest.

"No?" He cocked an eyebrow. "You look like you're having some intense thoughts."

"I'm just enjoying the tour." That was true. I was having a good time, loath as I was to admit it to him and myself.

"Hmm." He inhaled deeply through his nose and then exhaled through his mouth. He'd moved close enough to me that I felt his breath on my face. I was already hot. "I've been thinking about the same thing for the past few days."

"How Cafe du Monde should serve lattes?"

Grady chuckled and shook his head. "No, but I'm not opposed to that if it would make you happy. I've been thinking about something else."

I didn't want to know what he'd been thinking and believed I would die if I didn't hear him say it. "What?"

He moved closer to me. My instinct was to take a step back, and that's when I realized there was nowhere to go. We'd somehow maneuvered ourselves into one of the street doors, alone in a shallow alcove.

"I want to kiss you, Shay."

I felt like a guppy gulping for oxygen. I moved my lips, dumbfounded, and racked my brain for a response. Any response would do.

"Can I kiss you?" he prodded.

I didn't know how to respond. He leaned close, his lips practically brushing mine. "I'm not going to kiss you unless you say it's okay," he whispered.

My heart hammered so hard it reminded me of those old Bugs Bunny cartoons when his heart practically leaped out of his chest.

"Can I kiss you?" he repeated.

I had to tell him no. No matter what my hormones wanted—and they were lodging a firm opinion—this wasn't a good idea. "Sure."

Who said that? I was shocked the single word had escaped my mouth. I didn't have time to think about it, though, because he was moving in.

His lips were soft against mine. The initial touch of lips was tentative, as if he were testing me. All I could think was, "Oh, this is nice."

Then things got frantic. It was as if some unseen force pushed us together, and before I realized it our tongues were tangled. He was pressed so close I could feel his heart galloping next to mine.

His arms went around me. Someone was groaning. I think it might've been me. We were both panting.

We stood wrapped up so long in each other I thought time might've stood still.

One of us finally pulled away. It could've been him, but I wasn't certain. When we finally separated, my lips felt swollen and my mouth was dry.

"Thank you," he said. His voice sounded as if it had been dragged over a cheese grater.

"For what?" I asked dumbly.

He smiled. "I needed to know."

"Know what?" Apparently, I was a complete moron this evening. I couldn't keep my head from spinning.

"I needed to know if what I've been feeling for you is a result of you saying I couldn't possibly be feeling something for you."

"Was it?"

"Not even a little." He sighed as he pushed my sweaty bangs from my forehead. "I want you to take a chance on me."

Panic licked at my insides. "I...don't...."

"Shh." He pressed his finger to my lips. "Don't answer right now. You're too worked up. Hell, I'm too worked up. I just want you to think about it."

"I thought you said I wasn't ready." It was a stupid thing to say and yet it slipped out.

His lips curved into a crooked grin. "I'm ready. I desperately want you to be ready. I won't force you. I need you to think about it. I don't want you making a knee-jerk reaction either way."

"What if I think this is a bad idea?"

He shrugged. "I guess I'll have to live with it."

"What if I think it's a good idea?"

"Then I'll be happy to live with it." He leaned in close, inhaling deeply—as if scenting me—and then pulled back. He was all smiles when he extended his hand. "We need to catch up with the rest of the group. We don't have enough for our pieces yet."

I slid my hand into his because I didn't know what else to do. "Right. Work comes first."

"Not necessarily, but we need to focus right now."

My mind was too muddled to think about anything of substance. "You fuzzed my brain," I complained as we briskly walked the sidewalk. "I think you did it on purpose."

He laughed, as I'd intended. "I'll try to do better next time."

Did that mean there would be a next time? Lord help me, I was certainly hoping that was the case.

Seventeen

I woke the next morning to something hard hitting me on the head.

"Ow!" I bolted upright, prepared to fight an intruder, only to find Cally watching me from the end of the bed. "What the hell?" I demanded. "I'm taking that key away from you."

"I thought you needed a gift," she replied, ignoring my outrage. Cally never thought other people's anger applied to her. "Open it."

I narrowed my eyes, sensing a trap. "You woke me up to give me a gift?" That wasn't like her. Not that she wasn't generous, she simply didn't play Santa Claus before noon.

"You're getting up in one minute anyway."

I refused to look at my phone on the nightstand to see if she was right out of spite. "You don't know that."

As if on cue, my phone started playing a Cat Stevens song. I reached over to switch off the alarm. "You did that on purpose," I grumbled.

Her smirk was impish. "Open your gift."

She was far too gung-ho about this. "It had better not be

body paint," I grumbled as I reached into the gift bag on the bed next to me. "I'm not going to feed your fetish and become a human statue."

"Of course you're not," she said in her most reasonable voice. "You don't have the patience to sit still that long."

I grumbled and pulled out a rectangular black box devoid of lettering. "Thanks...I guess."

"You have to look inside the box," she insisted.

"I'm afraid to."

"Just look."

"I'm thinking no."

"Look in the box!" Her eyes flashed with annoyance.

For some reason, it reminded me of that scene in the movie *Se7en*. I'd caught it on television about a week earlier and had found myself sucked in all over again even though I'd seen it years before. "What's in the box?" I demanded in my best Brad Pitt voice.

Her lips quirked. "It's a special gift for you."

Because I knew she wouldn't leave until I acquiesced to her demand and I had exactly one hour to get showered and dressed before I had to leave to head into what would soon be our old office, I acquiesced. "Fine."

I carefully opened the box, opting to dump the contents on my bedspread rather than risk sticking my hand inside. I wouldn't put it past Cally to teach me a painful lesson if the opportunity arose. What slid out had to be one of the brightest—and biggest—vibrators I'd ever seen.

"What the...?" I was flabbergasted.

"That's the Greedy Girl," Cally said. "A friend told me about it. She needs to have sex with machines because she has terrible taste in men and she's on a man fast. I decided you needed to give it a go because you're trying to keep the world's prettiest piece of candy at arm's length and it's a freaking travesty."

Cally's mind didn't often work like that of a normal person, and it took me a moment to sort through what she said. "Oh, this is about what I texted you last night," I groused, using the comforter to push away the offending piece of machinery. It had testicles and everything. It didn't exactly look normal of course—Cally didn't do normal—but having a big pink peen on my bed was going to give me nightmares.

"It *is* about what you texted me last night." Cally sat on the edge of my bed without invitation and plucked the vibrator from the comforter. She tipped it left and right, let the sun glint off the glitter, and grinned. "It's kind of pretty, huh?"

"No, it's not pretty." I vigorously shook my head. "That's the worst gift I've ever received."

"Oh, please. Your mother sent you a blow-up boyfriend in a box last Christmas because she was worried about your serial killer ways."

Even I couldn't decipher that one. "Serial killer ways?"

"You know. People always say 'He was quiet and kept to himself' when talking about serial killers. I don't want that to be you, Shay. That's why you need to jump on the man candy and see what his Twixt looks like."

I wanted to die. No, I wanted to find a hole to crawl into and then die. "Cally...."

She barreled forward as if she hadn't heard me. "He likes you, Shay. It's obvious when he looks at you. Why can't you give him a chance?"

"He has a certain reputation."

"Don't we all?"

"Yes, but his reputation includes romancing women in the office and then breaking their hearts before leaving them in a crying puddle on the floor. I don't think I could take a broken heart on top of the job thing. One catastrophe is all I'm allowed every six-month period. That's my limit."

"You kissed him." She wasn't going to let it go. I knew that when I told her about the kiss. I should've kept it to myself. That ultimately wasn't an option because I was so flummoxed after we parted ways that I couldn't think of anything but him and needed to talk to someone. That's why I called her...and this was my payback.

"Cally, I know you're afraid that I'm going to end up husband-less and poor and have to move back to Florida..." I started.

"I'm not worried about you being poor," she countered. "You've been hitting it out of the park with your pieces. You're turning into an actual NOLA celebrity. In six months, people will be begging you to cover them. You're set for your job."

She was the only one who believed that.

"The other part is only partially true," she continued, barely taking a breath. "I'm not worried about you being husband-less. I don't think you need a man to be happy."

"Then why are you pushing Grady so hard?"

"Because you light up around him. He pushes your buttons. He gets you hot. Just because you don't need a man doesn't mean you shouldn't embrace the right one when he comes along."

"How can you possibly know he's the right one?"

"I have a feeling."

I had to bite back a sigh. "Two months ago, you had a feeling that the guy who dressed like the clown from that horror movie and performed interpretive mime in Jackson Square was your soulmate," I reminded her.

"Hey, it's not my fault that he had so many issues. He hid them well."

"He dressed as a clown. That's not a sign of sanity."

"I happen to like clowns...and mimes...and people who dress as statues. That's my kink. Your kink is a nice guy who gets you. I'm telling you, that's this guy."

"But he has a horrible reputation."

"Not all reputations are earned." Callie was prim as she got up from the bed. "Now, I have a tea to go to with my father. He insists that I learn more about his business if I plan to take over for him. I don't have the heart to tell him that the last thing I want is to work in corporate America. For now, I'm just going to placate him."

"That's probably smart. Take your...gift...when you go."

"No way." She shook her head and moved toward the door. "That's for you. I want you to know your options if you let this guy go."

"Cally." I was exasperated. "It was just a kiss. We both like horror stuff. We were hopped up on stories."

"Yeah, you keep telling yourself that." She disappeared through the door.

"We're not going to get together," I called out. "It's not going to happen."

"Oh, it's going to happen."

"How can you possibly know that?"

"I can see your life more clearly than my own. He's your destiny."

"I'm not sure I believe in destiny."

"That doesn't mean destiny doesn't believe in you."

THERE WAS AN OPEN CHAIR NEXT TO Grady when I arrived in the newsroom for the meeting. The desks we'd used for the past several years were gone. All that was left were folding chairs and seeing the stripped-down office had my heart sinking.

"Hey." Grady shot me a smile and handed me a coffee. "I thought you might need something to do with your hands."

I was caught off guard. "Is this for me?"

He looked amused at my response. "Who else would drink a sugar-free vanilla latte with almond milk?"

The fact that he knew my drink was both exhilarating and annoying. "A lot of people drink it." I took the cup from him. "Did you buy this for me?"

He blinked twice. "Who else?"

"I...don't...know."

"I saved the seat for you too."

"Oh, well...." I had no idea what I was supposed to say.

"Geez." He blew out a sigh. "You're going to need some hand-holding I see."

I shifted on my chair, afraid he would actually try holding my hand at a work meeting. I could just imagine the fallout from that. Thankfully I didn't have to give voice to my concerns because Annabelle picked that moment to join us. She flopped down in a chair one row in front of us and then turned to face us. "You two are certainly sitting pretty, aren't you?"

Because I didn't know what to say, I sipped my coffee and let Grady handle our rebuttal.

"I'm always pretty when I'm sitting," Grady replied. "Depending on how flattering the lighting is, some people actually refer to me as beautiful."

Annabelle narrowed her eyes. "I don't know anybody who has ever spent time talking to you who says that. Only morons who spy you from afar who haven't yet had time to pick up on your personality defaults might say that."

Rather than respond, Grady pulled his phone out of his pocket and pretended to answer it. "Hello, Pot? Yeah, this is Kettle. You're black."

Annabelle scowled. "I don't know why I even talk to you."

"That makes two of us."

She shifted her eyes to me. "As for you, I warned you what would happen if you let this grifter get around your defenses.

Do you really want to risk your entire future on this guy?" She jerked a thumb toward Grady. "You know he's going to drop you the second something better comes along. And something better *will* come along. Something with a low-cut top and long legs. He's only sticking with you because you drive traffic right now."

"Don't say that," Grady snapped.

"Because you don't want her knowing the truth?" Annabelle challenged.

"Because you're delusional and I hate when you target her with your nonsense."

"Oh, whatever. I—" Annabelle didn't have a chance to complete her sentence because Edith had taken center stage and was staring at the group of us with feigned patience.

"Thank you all for coming." Edith's tone was grave, but she managed a smile, although it resembled a grimace more than anything else and made me decidedly uncomfortable.

"So, we've managed to make it a full week." She sat in one of the chairs, a cup of coffee clutched in her hands. "We've learned a lot. I'm guessing you guys have learned a lot. We don't want these meetings to be a source of stress. That's why we're not going to focus on what people are doing wrong. With that in mind, let's talk about what people are doing right."

I wasn't surprised when Annabelle's hand shot in the air. She didn't wait for Edith to call on her before speaking. "Did you see my piece on the new glow-in-the-dark shoelaces that are becoming a thing on Bourbon Street?" she asked. "They're practical and fun, and everybody is wearing them. I got six-thousand hits on that piece."

"You did," Edith agreed. "Several hundred of them were from the same IP address, but it was still an interesting take. Unfortunately, I don't know many customers who will advertise on a shoelace story."

Annabelle frowned. "Um...the people selling the shoelaces will advertise."

"The people selling the shoelaces are street folk," Grady replied, his voice dripping with disdain. "They're getting them from a wholesaler and unloading them on drunks. They won't take the time to set up an advertising account on our platform because they don't need it."

"Grady brings up a good point," Edith noted. "The focus should be on the sort of thing that can sustain advertising. As much as I liked your video, Annabelle—and I did because it was colorful and fun—it won't appeal to advertisers."

Annabelle huffed as she folded her arms across her chest and sank lower in her chair. It was obvious the meeting wasn't going as she hoped.

"This isn't a meeting about what's going wrong," Edith reiterated. "Let's talk about what's going right." Her eyes landed on me, and my cheeks suddenly felt as if they were catching fire. "Let's start with Shay and Grady. Shay hit the ground running with her material and although her ode to shoes came out of left field—and likely wouldn't draw in advertisers—it was a massive hit with the younger set. They're now tuning in with encouraging regularity at Tulane to see what she writes."

"You just said that piece couldn't attract advertisers," Annabelle growled. "Why are you pretending it's good if all we care about is advertising?"

"Because it increased our readership exponentially," Edith replied. "We need to focus on that as well as the advertising. Besides, her second story—the one on the fashion show—works on both fronts. Joining with Grady and doing his and her takes was a stroke of genius. People are reacting...and they're loving it."

"Well, bully for them," Annabelle muttered. Her petulance was off the charts.

"You two are magical," Edith continued, pretending she hadn't heard Annabelle's frustrated lament. "I want you to keep at it. People freaking loved the Natchez thing—and they've already contacted us about advertising. Not a single person complained about the vomiting. I expected some complaints, but there were none, and it was fantastic."

I pressed my lips together. I could feel multiple sets of eyes boring into me.

"Thank you," Grady replied. "I want to thank Shay for the vomit. She made it all possible."

That elicited laughter from the group.

"I loved the cooking class too," Edith enthused. "They want to advertise as well. Apparently, the bickering is igniting romantics everywhere. We're bombarded with messages asking if you guys are involved."

"We're not," I blurted out.

Grady kept his face impassive, but I saw the muscle work in his jaw. "We're just having fun," he said.

"Well, keep it up." Edith bobbed her head encouragingly. "You don't have to be romantically involved to make people laugh. In fact, it's best you don't cross that line. Just keep the readers on their toes. Do you have something for today?"

"We went on a murder and mayhem tour last night," Grady volunteered. "It was very...stimulating. We already have our footage. We just have to edit it and write the pieces. It didn't end until late last night, so that's on the agenda for today."

"Sounds amazing," Edith said. "I can't wait to see what you guys come up with. As for the rest of you, keep working at it. We've seen some flashes of interest and some of you are learning." Her eyes drifted back to Annabelle. "Some of you need more work. With that in mind, I need to see five of you in my office before you go." She rattled off five names in quick succession.

"The rest of you are free to go," she said as she shuffled toward her office. "Keep up the good work. For those I asked to stay, come this way."

The Human Resources lady Lacey—I could never remember her last name—suddenly appeared. She was going into the office with the group, and she had five folders with her.

"You don't think they're being cut loose, do you?" I asked Grady, my stomach constricting.

He shot me a sympathetic look. "Don't get worked up. You're killing it these days. That won't be you."

I really wanted to believe that. "I need to get out of here."

"Come on." Grady stood, making sure to show Annabelle his ass as he prodded me toward the exit. "I'll buy you some beignets. I have an idea I want to run by you, and I think you're going to like it."

Anything to distract me was a win. "Sure. That sounds good."

Eighteen

"How did you find this?"

Grady's idea for the day's activity wasn't on the list we'd come up with days ago. He'd been sly when we were eating—he ended up taking me to lunch instead of a late breakfast—and insisted it would be better if it was a surprise.

I'd been suspicious—who wouldn't be after our outing the previous evening resulted in a make-out session?—but he'd been on the up-and-up and I was flabbergasted.

"My friend David told me about it," Grady replied. He looked smug. "You remember him?"

"Yes, Cally went on a fake date with him."

Grady smirked. "I think David might go on a real date with her if she can get past that human statue fetish."

"I thought he didn't like her."

"He likes everybody. I figured she wasn't his type, but he had no problem walking her home. He's brought her up three times since, so I think I might've been wrong."

"Really?" I considered what that could mean for all of us. "I really wish Cally would start considering appropriate guys, but I'm not sure she's there yet. As for this...." I gestured toward the huge warehouse, filled with five floats, all in varying stages of completion, and at least fifty people working on them. "I can't believe you actually thought of this."

"I didn't. David did. It's for a special charity, one close to his heart."

I slid my eyes to him and found him staring into nothing. "What charity?"

"Breast cancer." Grady flashed a flat smile. "His mother died of it."

"That's sad."

"It is, but he donates a lot of his time to fundraisers. He keeps his ear to the ground. He knows what we've been working on and thought a parade—working on the floats and participating in the actual event this afternoon—would be good for the cause and for us."

"It's a great idea." I meant it. "Where do we start?"

"We're working on that one." He pointed to a huge monstrosity decked in NOLA'S trademark yellow, green, and purple, with a huge jester in a box bopping from the central focus point. Of course, because it was New Orleans, the jester had an absolutely huge rack and a shirt that read "Get abreast of it."

"What do we do?" I rubbed my hands together.

"I don't know." Grady craned his neck. "We're supposed to look for a woman named Connie. Supposedly she wears a feather boa all the time."

Oh, well, I already liked her. "There." I pointed to a woman in her forties. A scarf covered her head and a feather boa flapped around her neck.

Grady took my hand and started across the warehouse.

It was less of a surprise this time and I did my best to push the initial burst of panic out of my mind.

"Hello." The woman beamed at us. Her name tag did indeed read Connie. "May I help you?"

"My friend David should have called," Grady replied. He was good when dealing with new people and had a charming smile at the ready. "My name is Grady Dalton. This is Shay Archer."

"Oh, right." Connie perked up. "You're the ones who have been posting those delightful male-versus-female pieces highlighting area activities for *The Bugle*. I heard you were coming."

"We want to help," Grady explained. "I understand you're finishing the floats today and taking them right out. We want to help and then film the parade — if that's okay with you."

"It's better than okay," Connie said. "I'm very excited at the prospect. You'll be able to get the word out and that will help with donations. We're more than happy to have you."

"Great." Grady released my hand and glanced around. "Where do we start?"

Connie eyed him, her gaze speculative. "Have you ever worked on a float?"

Grady hesitated and then shook his head. "I wasn't much of a joiner in school."

I was surprised. I would've pegged him as a school spirit guy through and through. "I worked on a few floats when I was in high school," I offered, speaking for the first time. "I wouldn't call myself an expert, but I know my way around."

"Awesome." Connie's smile was contagious. "We have very little to do. You can work on filling in the back wall with the tissue paper." She led us to the rear of the float, which consisted of exposed chicken wire where the skirt was supposed to be. "Do you know how to fill in the holes?" she asked me.

"Absolutely." This was something I would have no trouble

with. It was in my wheelhouse, definitely more so than the cooking.

"Are you sure?" Connie didn't look convinced. "I watched your gumbo attempt."

My cheeks burned. "That was different."

"It's a good thing she's pretty, huh?" Connie said to Grady with a sly smile. "Because that gumbo was not pretty. You'll have to do the cooking if you want to keep this poor thing fed. Otherwise, you're going to be a takeout couple."

I opened my mouth to correct her – we were not a couple – but Grady spoke first.

"I happen to be a big fan of takeout." His hand landed on my back. "Shay can show me what to do."

"Awesome." Connie shot him an enthusiastic thumbs-up. "You guys will be a big help."

I wasn't certain she was right, but I wasn't all that worried about messing up the rear of a float. Even we could handle this task.

ONE OF THE FIRST THINGS I NOTICED about Grady when I started at *The Bugle* was that he could never shut up. He talked when he was in a good mood. He talked when he was nervous. Heck, when he was in a bad mood, he pouted for long stretches and then immediately started talking. He couldn't stand long silences.

"Tell me about making floats as a teenager," he insisted. He'd caught on to what he needed to do with the tissue paper relatively quickly. His hands were deft as he filled the chicken wire. "Were you a prom queen on display when you finished with these floats?"

I almost choked on a snort. "Absolutely not."

"Why not?"

"Do I look like a prom queen?"

"Um…yeah." He bobbed his head.

I stilled, unsure how to feel about that. I shook my head. "Take that back."

"Why?"

"Because…because I'm not a prom queen."

"I fail to see why that's a big deal. I didn't say you had to be a prom queen. I just said you struck me as the type who would be prom queen." He looked confused.

"Well, I wasn't." I focused on the chicken wire that needed to be filled. "I was not from the right part of town. Prom queens come from ritzy areas."

His expression was challenging to read. "I guess I don't know much about your background."

"I know about yours." Why I decided to take this tack was beyond me. It wasn't necessary…and somewhat obnoxious. "You come from a rich family."

"I come from a middle-class family," he corrected. "We weren't poor, but we were hardly rich. My father made some good investments that benefitted the family. I wasn't raised with a lot of money, though."

"To me, middle class is rich. I mean…your family isn't rich like Cally's father, but you guys live in the Garden District."

"My parents do." He looked to be treading carefully, which made me feel guilty. "It's not like they live in a mega-mansion or anything. It's a four-thousand-square-foot house — five bedrooms and a yard too small for me to ever have a dog."

"Did you want a dog?"

He nodded. "Very much. It never happened."

"I had a dog." Momentarily, I was lost in through. "Sherman. I found him on my way home from school one day. I begged my mom to keep him."

"She obviously let you."

"Yeah. I was fourteen when I brought him home. She

agreed to keep him when I went to college, but...." It was difficult to finish. I didn't like talking about my parents much. They both had issues, refused to recognize them, and kicked up a fuss when I brought them up. In the grand scheme of things, I knew I had it better than most. That didn't mean my childhood wasn't without issues.

"What happened to Sherman?" Grady asked. He steeled himself for the answer.

"I called one day from college." I hated thinking about this. It made me so angry...and sad. It wasn't something I told many people. Cally knew, and she was furious on my behalf. Nobody else in New Orleans knew about the trouble I had with my parents, my mother especially. Why I was telling Grady was a mystery. "We talked about normal stuff. My mother never said a word. Then, toward the end of the call, I asked about Sherman.

"She was quiet for a long time," I continued. "That's when I knew it was bad. She usually just said 'He's fine' and moved on to something else. She didn't want to answer at first, but I pressed her."

Grady reached over and grabbed my hand. He didn't say a word. He simply offered silent comfort.

"I thought she was going to tell me he died," I admitted. "Instead, she said he chewed up her couch, so they dropped him at a local shelter. I hung up with her right away. I called, but it was a high kill shelter. He'd been gone for days."

Fury blazed in Grady's eyes. "I'm really sorry."

"Yeah, well...there's a reason I was glad to move to a different state when I was done with college." I slid my hand out of his and grabbed more tissue paper. "Anyway, that was a downer of a story. We should start getting video."

Grady didn't move to stand. Instead, he stared at me. Then he did something I wasn't expecting and pulled me close.

For a moment I thought he was going to kiss me again. Even as I told myself I didn't want that, my heart played the role of traitor and started thumping hard. He didn't kiss me. He wrapped me tight and rested a cheek on top of my head.

"I'm sorry for whatever it is you went through as a kid," he said in a low voice. "Nobody should have to go through that."

I didn't realize I was on the verge of crying until I had to swallow the lump in my throat. "I'm okay. It was a long time ago."

"You're not okay and stop that. If you're upset about something, it's okay to admit it. You don't always have to be this ray of freaking sunshine."

I pressed my lips together. This time it was laughter I was fighting off. "I don't think anybody has ever referred to me as a ray of sunshine."

"No?" Grady shifted to stare into my eyes. "You don't have a solid vision of yourself. Whenever I look at you, all I see is the sun."

"Because I make you hot?" The question was out of my mouth before I registered how flirty it sounded.

His smile was instantaneous. "You do indeed make me hot. But it's more than that. You're bright...and warm...and my day is better when you're in it."

I'm ashamed to say I practically melted.

"On top of that, you walked into this warehouse with me and didn't once pitch a fit about building a float," he continued. "You were excited at the prospect. You're adventurous, and even when you wet yourself, you're open for a good time."

I pinned him with a glare. "I didn't wet myself!"

He choked on a laugh. "And you're always entertaining." He leaned in and pressed a quick kiss on the top of my nose. It was hardly romantic, and yet the emotion in his eyes had my blood pumping. "Come on. We need to finish. I don't want to let these people down. Then I want everybody else to see you shine when we ride the float."

I worked my jaw for a moment, conflicted. There were so many things I wanted to say to him. Ultimately, I nodded. "Let's finish, but we really do need to get footage."

He held my gaze and then increased the distance between us. "You start. Just get three minutes of me working. Then we'll switch and I'll do the same for you."

"And then I'll swoop in and get footage of both of you," Connie offered, causing me to jolt. I hadn't realized she'd been lurking behind us. "It's no fun if the viewers can't watch you bicker."

"Touché." Grady gave her a grandiose bow. "I do love me some bickering."

I'D NEVER RIDDEN ON A FLOAT. Grady never asked after the whole prom queen discussion, but I figured it was a given that he knew I'd only built the float and had never been on one. I was absurdly excited when we dressed in glittery hats, Mardi Gras beads hanging from our necks, and threw candy and strings of beads to the people lining Royal Street for the parade.

I was laughing the second we hit the parade route, and I didn't stop the entire time. My bag of goodies was empty before we reached the halfway point, when I tried to share Grady's bag with him.

"Hey." He clutched the bag to his chest and gave me a mock glare. "This is mine."

"Yeah, but I'm out." I wasn't much of an eye-batter, but I went for it today. "I want to play."

"You want to play, huh?" His voice hung heavy with innuendo. We'd managed to get most of our footage from the float when we first started out. He'd roped in David to film us from the street for the extra footage. We were covered and it was time for fun. That's what he told me after fifteen minutes of filming. It wasn't as if we could use all the footage we had taken.

"Maybe." I stared hard into his eyes. This time, there was no embarrassment to trip over for either of us. There was just endless chemistry, to the point I could've sworn the air crackled around us. "You said something yesterday," I started.

It was as if there was nobody else in the world. The twenty people on the float surrounding us ceased to exist. The hundreds of screaming people on the sidewalks went mute. It was just him and me.

"What did I say?" Grady asked. He knew. He just wanted me to say it.

"You said I wasn't ready. What did you mean?"

"What do you think I meant?" He put one hand on my waist to steady me when the float hit a bump. His eyes never moved from mine.

"You wanted to take me to dinner," I pressed. "It wasn't one of these outings. It was a different sort."

"It was."

"Why did you think I wasn't ready?"

Now he did smile. "Because you need to ease into things. I've known that about you for a long time. I had ideas about why, but now I think I understand better. You've been screwed over multiple times, including by the people who were never supposed to screw you over."

I swallowed hard at mention of my parents. He didn't refer to them directly, but I knew what he was talking about.

"It's okay. I'm willing to wait," he reassured me.

"What if I don't want you to wait?" He would have no idea how hard it was for me to ask that question. Being around him constantly and fighting this...whatever it was...was exhausting. I no longer wanted to fight it.

He was quiet a moment, searching my face. "What do you mean by that?" he asked finally. "Normally I can get a feel for what you're thinking, but this time...I just can't. I need you to say it."

"I think maybe dinner would be okay," I hedged.

He continued to stare.

"Or maybe not if you've changed your mind." I chewed my bottom lip, nervous energy running through me. "In fact, you obviously have changed your mind. I'm such an idiot." I moved to turn away from him, but he kept a firm grip on my hip.

"I haven't changed my mind." He was deadly serious. "I want to take you to dinner...very badly. I just want to make sure that you understand this isn't a work thing. If we do this, you can't hide behind videos or hits on the website."

"I don't want to hide." It was weird to say it. It was even weirder to feel it. "I want to give it a shot."

He continued to stare before breaking into a huge grin. "Good. You're moving faster than I thought. I didn't even have to dress up in mime gear and beg you for a date while pretending to be in an invisible box."

"You have mime gear?" I tried to picture that.

"I guess you'll have to wait to find out." His lips curved.

"When do you want to have this dinner?" I asked. I didn't want to leave it hanging too long. I liked a solid plan so I didn't have to wonder.

"There's no time like the present. How about we finish our float ride and then pick a restaurant?"

So soon? Wow. I thought he would put it off for at least a day. I found, just like him, that I didn't want to wait. "Do I get to pick the restaurant?"

He shook his head.

I faltered. "No?"

"You'll go for something cheap. I'm buying, so I'll pick the restaurant."

"Nothing too fancy?"

"I know just the place."

I couldn't stop the smile from taking over my face. "Does this mean I can have some of your goodies?"

His eyes lit with wicked intent.

"I meant those goodies." I pointed at the bag he carried. "I'm out."

He nodded. "It's only fair. You gave of yourself. Now I'm going to give a little."

I reached in the bag and grabbed a handful of strings of beads. I stopped myself before I threw them to slide a multi-colored strand around his neck. "Here's to giving a little of ourselves."

Nineteen

After the parade, we went to my place to edit the videos and stories, and then timed them to publish later in the evening. Our tour pieces were still racking up views, so it wasn't necessary to publish immediately. Then we separated for an hour to get ready for our date, something Grady argued about.

"You don't have to get gussied up." He lingered by the door as I shoved him out. "You already look great."

The compliment was nice, but I knew better. "I've been sweating for hours and have pit stains. I'm not going out on our first official date with pit stains."

He leaned closer, his lips only a few inches from mine. "You seem to forget I've seen you at your absolute worst. I don't care."

"If you say I peed my pants again the date is off," I warned.

He smirked. "I was talking about the vomit, but okay."

"You really have seen me at my worst."

"I don't think you have a worst. Let's just go now."

"I don't understand why you can't wait an hour." I studied his face. "Afraid you'll change your mind?"

"No. I'm afraid you will."

My cheeks warmed with pleasure. "You don't have to worry about that. Just come back in an hour."

He stared into my eyes for a moment and then blew out a sigh. "Fine. Just know, if I come back and you're gone I'll be really angry...and it won't stop me from finding you. Even if you hide, we're going on a date tonight."

"How do you know you can find me?" I was honestly curious.

He tapped the side of his head. "I'm a genius."

"How really?"

"I know all your hiding spots."

"You really don't."

"Just...get ready."

TRUE TO HIS WORD, GRADY knocked on my door exactly one hour later. Because he had seen me at my worst, I opted for a floral skirt and a black V-neck that gave me a nice silhouette. I pulled my hair back in a bun because I knew the humidity would wreck it otherwise, and then slipped into my favorite sandals. I'd barely finished dressing when he knocked.

"Ready?" I asked as I slipped my purse strap over my head.

He smiled as he looked me over. "You look pretty."

"It's just a normal outfit."

"You look pretty," he insisted. "I like your hair like that. The little sparkle things are cute."

"Oh, um, thanks." I suddenly felt awkward.

"This is the part where you're supposed to tell me that I look handsome," he prodded.

A laugh exploded out of my throat. "I love that you never suffer from self-esteem issues."

"I don't see the point." He extended his hand. "Let's go."

I didn't hesitate before taking it, and I didn't miss the

significance of what he'd done. Before, he held my hand without asking because he wanted to normalize it. Now he wanted me to meet him halfway – and I was more than willing.

Grady took the lead when we left. Conversation was light and easy for the walk. He took me to Muriel's, a delightful red-brick restaurant near Jackson Square. I'd been a few times since moving to the city, but never on a date.

In fact, if I thought about it long enough, I'd hardly been on any dates since moving to the city. It wasn't a priority. The fact that he'd managed to slide under my defenses, at a time when I was so focused on keeping my job, was fairly impressive.

"Have you been here before?" he asked as we settled at a small table on the balcony overlooking the street. It was light enough that we could easily make out the people passing below, but the noise level of the Square wasn't overwhelming, so it made for a nice ambiance.

"Cally and I have been here," I said. "She loves it. I think this is my third or fourth time. We usually go for the little gumbo and po'boy places around the Quarter."

"This is one of my favorite spots." He leaned back in his chair and regarded me. "Before you even look at that menu, know that I'll be angry if you hold back. Don't order the cheapest thing just because you think that's the right thing to do."

I balked. "What makes you think I would do that?"

"Because you're the type of woman who thinks it's necessary or I'll expect something in return," he replied. "Just for the record...I don't expect anything from you. I want you to have a good time. I want to get to know you. That's all I expect, so go big when you order."

"How big are you going?"

He narrowed his eyes and took the menu that had been

left by the hostess. "I fear you're only asking because you're determined to go lower than me on price, but I'll play your game." He pursed his lips as he surveyed the offerings. "I'm getting the wood-grilled fillet and the shrimp and goat cheese crepes. There will be dessert too...and I will eat all of it."

His enthusiasm for food made me smile. "You picked the two most expensive items," I noted.

"Yup." He leaned forward, his gaze intense. "Pick what you really want. This is a first date, not an excuse for sex."

"What if I want there to be sex?" I had no idea why I was going this route, but he always managed to catch me off guard. For once, I wanted to cause him to trip.

"Then don't get the onion tart," he replied. The way his lips curved told me he was enjoying himself. "The point of this dinner is to get to know each other outside of work."

"I can't help but feel we've already done that," I said as I went back to looking at the menu. "I mean...it's not as if everything has been work stuff. I know things about you."

"Name one."

"You don't want me to get the onion tart because, at the very least, you want to kiss me later."

"I'm going to kiss you whether you order the tart or not."

"Good to know." I chewed my bottom lip as I studied the menu. "I think I'll get the pesto linguine with shrimp and the house salad."

"Good choice." He planted his feet on either side of mine under the table and leaned back in his chair. "Save room for dessert." There was a devilish glint to his eyes.

"There's cake. I'm totally getting that."

The server picked that moment to take our orders. I ordered a drink called a Honey Child, placed my dinner order, and then waited for Grady to do the same. When he finished, his eyes returned to mine.

"Tell me what you want from life," he prodded.

Wow. Apparently, he was serious about getting to know me. "Don't you want to start out with something simpler? Like...maybe ask my favorite color."

"Your favorite color is purple, but not the one that borders on pink," he replied. "You like the purple that contains a hint of a gray. You like your blues the same way."

My mouth dropped open. "How can you possibly know that?"

"I've been watching you for a long time."

I narrowed my eyes.

"Not in a creepy way," he said on a laugh. "I'd be lying if I said I hadn't noticed you, though. You like cool colors. You're also a big fan of black. What can I say? I'm an observant person."

"If you noticed me, why were you always so obnoxious?"

"I didn't realize I was being obnoxious. I was trying to flirt with you."

I waited for him to drop another punchline. When he didn't, I lifted an eyebrow. "Was that seriously you flirting?"

He was sheepish. "I didn't say I was good at it. You always cut me off at the knees and wandered away if I didn't say something snarky. That's why I started focusing on the snark."

I rubbed my cheek, considering. "I always thought you didn't like me. It was like you purposely went out of your way to tick me off."

"I like a fiery woman."

"I didn't realize I was fiery."

"Oh, come on." He shot me his best smile. "You're the fieriest woman at *The Bugle*. You must realize that."

"Honestly? I would've given that designation to Annabelle."

Grady scowled. "Do you want to talk about her?"

Another day I might've answered differently. Tonight, I

didn't care. "No." I shook my head. "I really don't. She's...not a nice person."

"You've finally realized she's out to submarine you? You can't trust her, especially not with your career. She wants to use you to climb, and then she'll trample all over you if she gets ahead by some freaking miracle."

"I don't trust her," I promised. "I won't be overtly mean to her or anything. That will just start a war, and I'm not manipulative enough to win a war against her."

He barked out a laugh, taking me by surprise. "That's such a *you* thing to say. You analyze things like nobody I've ever met."

The observation made me distinctly uncomfortable. "Most people don't like that."

"I'm not most people. I like a smart woman. It's my kink."

For some reason, the statement made me laugh. "That's a very specific kink."

"It is," he agreed, smiling at the server as she returned with our drinks. He waited for her to leave before speaking again. "I have a theory about you. Want to hear it?"

"I...don't...know."

"I'll be gentle." He rested his hand on top of mine. "You want to please people. You can't seem to help yourself. It's why you put up with Cally's nonsense about the human statues when you really think she's nuts."

"Cally is my best friend. You can't always help who you're attracted to. Besides, it's because of her I can afford the rent on that great place. She bullied her father into helping me."

"I'm sure she did. Cally has...a specific personality. She's not afraid to be who she is. She's also incredibly loyal, which is why she latched onto you. You're incredibly loyal too."

"But you don't think I'm comfortable being me," I said. I didn't take the comment as an insult. I'd thought about it more than a few times myself.

"I think the real you is amazing," he replied, earnestness on full display. "I've seen it in the office, but only when your guard is down. I saw it on full display at the fashion show. You were...glowing. That's when I truly felt it."

"Felt what?"

"I've always had a thing for you." He flashed a flirty smile. "You're beautiful. I feel a zing when I'm around you."

"You hid it well."

"That day I saw you in the fashion show, it was as if the clouds suddenly parted and I was seeing the sun for the first time. You have this incredible spirit. You're an artist underneath it all, but you're also determined. That was the part I didn't get until earlier today."

"What part?" Now I was confused.

"You don't want to rely on anybody because your parents always let you down."

"They're not bad people," I said.

"Maybe not, but they didn't do right by you." He shook his head. "That story you told me about the dog breaks my heart. You should have seen your face." He leaned forward and lowered his voice. "You don't have to please anybody but yourself, but you work overtime to please others. So you get treated like a second-class citizen in your own life. You need to stop that."

I worked my jaw. "You think I'm weak."

"I think you're stronger than anybody I've ever met. Weak people put themselves first. That's what you saw when you were growing up. Strong people put everybody else first. I just think you need to learn balance."

"And...what? I should put myself ahead of everybody?"

"You should prioritize yourself."

"Over you?"

He shook his head. "No, I want to be a priority. I still want you to be happy. The key is finding balance."

"Isn't that what we're trying to do?"

"It is." He linked his fingers with mine and grinned. "I think it's going well so far. What about you?"

He had a way of putting me at ease that should've felt alien, but I was comfortable. I had no idea how he'd managed it. "I don't have any complaints."

"I'm glad to hear it. Let's go back to talking about favorite colors. I want to know if you know mine."

It was a test. "Your favorite color is black because you like the silhouette it creates. Sometimes you add a splash of color, though, like an accent on your shirt...or even flashy socks. You used to prefer red. The past six months or so you've been wearing more purple and blue."

He smiled. "Why do you think that is?"

"Because they're my favorite colors -- and I've been a moron."

"At least you finally see the light."

"Yeah, I definitely have that going for me."

WE ATE OUR WEIGHT IN FOOD AND THEN hit the riverwalk to digest. We spent hours telling stories and laughing, and it was almost eleven o'clock before I realized we were the only people left in the area.

"I should get you home," Grady said, his grip on my hand tightening. "I didn't realize how late it had gotten."

We continued to talk on the walk back to my place. Grady slowed his pace before we got to my house. He was clearly reluctant to end the date. I couldn't blame him. I felt the same way.

"So, I had a good time." He brushed the flyaway strands of hair that had escaped thanks to the wind coming in off the Mississippi River from my face and stared into my eyes. "I want to do this again. I'm really hoping you do too."

It wasn't a question. "I wasn't looking for a romantic relationship when we started working together," I noted.

His eyes darkened but he remained quiet.

"I'm glad, for once, I couldn't keep control of my urges." My smile was mischievous when it escaped. "I don't think I could stay away from you even if I wanted to...which I don't. I keep telling myself that I have to focus on keeping my job and not worry about what you're doing. My heart disagrees."

The smile he unleashed was devastating. "I feel the same way about you. It was a fluke finding you in Jackson Square that day, but I'm not sorry. It's not just about the work. I like the work—don't get me wrong—but I really love spending time with you."

I chewed my bottom lip. "So, we can keep working together? Just because we're...doing this...doesn't mean we have to give up the other stuff."

"We definitely don't have to give up the other stuff." He was firm. "We can do it all together. That's what I want."

"That's what I want too." I thought it would be more difficult to admit. "I had a really good time tonight."

"Me too." He leaned in close and gave me a soft kiss. It was simple, and yet breathtakingly intimate.

Before I realized it, I was gripping the front of his shirt. His tongue went from chaste to intense in an instant. We were both gasping for air when we pulled back three minutes later.

"You do something to my hormones," he growled as he pressed himself against me. "I swear I lose all control around you."

"You fuzz my brain."

He smirked.

"Just...all kinds of fuzz." I licked my lips as I studied him. Would he try to come inside? Would he be a gentleman and force himself to leave? I decided to flip the script. "I was thinking...um...I didn't have the onion tart or anything."

It took him a minute to absorb what I was saying. "Are you sure? I don't want to push you to take things too fast."

"We've really been on daily dates all week. I don't think this is the time to be shy." I pushed open the door. "Besides, if we don't give in and explore each other, that's all we'll be able to think about. I don't want the work to suffer."

"You just don't want your lady parts to suffer." His smile was sly...and then his expression softened. "I want to be with you, but not before you're ready."

"Oh, I'm ready." I meant it. "I don't want to wait. If we're going to do this, let's do it right. I'm all in."

That was all he needed to hear. He grabbed me around the waist and swept me inside the cottage. "I'm so glad you said it first though."

"Good. Now...show me what you've got."

He laughed so hard I was afraid he might choke. "We both need to work on our flirting skills."

"We'll start tomorrow."

"You read my mind."

Twenty

Waking up was difficult. It was sliding from warmth into...well, something else warm. It took me a few minutes to get my bearings, and when I turned to my right, I found Grady asleep next to me.

My stomach tensed at the sight of him. He was a beautiful specimen of a man. That long hair wasn't Motley Crue-ish as much as male model delightful. His chest, well-defined, wasn't completely bare of hair, but he obviously manscaped. In sleep, his face was soft and unguarded. He really was a sight to behold.

And then he opened his eyes.

"Hey." His voice was husky as he stretched, his lips curving at the corners as he regarded me. "You're up early."

"It's not that early," I countered. "It's nine o'clock."

"That's early."

"Not really. I mean...if you work a standard job, you're there from nine to five. They even wrote a song about it."

He chuckled, causing some of the tense feelings that had flooded me to dissipate in an instant. "Fine. It's early for New Orleans."

"I guess I can give you that." I was hesitant as I rolled closer to him. "Is this...okay?" I motioned toward his shoulder, where I wanted to rest my head.

"Is what okay?" He looked confused.

"You know...this." I mock put my head down and then immediately lifted it. I probably looked like an idiot, but I didn't want to invade his personal space. Just because we'd had sex didn't mean that he wanted a relationship...or even to cuddle. He might not be a morning person. In fact, everything he'd ever said to me suggested he hated mornings.

"Come here." He growled as he slipped his arm under my waist and tugged me practically on top of him. Once he was finished situating me, I was covering half of his body. "We need to talk."

The words sent a sense of dread cascading down my spine and goose pimples broke out on my flesh.

"Oh, don't get weird," he chided, wagging a finger in my face. He kept a firm grip on me with his other arm, anchoring me to him. "I didn't plan what happened last night," he started.

"That makes two of us." I braced for the worst. "If you think it was a mistake ...." I didn't finish. I couldn't. Even though I told myself it was best not to get attached, I was losing that battle.

"It wasn't a mistake. In fact, everything about last night was perfect. I just...don't want you to regret it."

"Me?" Was he joking? "I had like...three orgasms." I counted in my head. "Maybe more."

"It was five...over five hours, which is why I said it was early. We were up late." He shot me a smug smile when my eyebrows hiked up my forehead. "And that's not what I meant. I'm afraid that you're going to pull back. I've spent the better part of a week – actually more like six months – trying to get you to trust me and then I threw it all out the window last night when my hormones got the better of me."

"I kind of like your hormones."

"I'm glad. I like your hormones too."

"My hormones were only responding to your hormones. They're to blame."

"Basically, you're saying that your hormones are copycats and don't have an original thought of their own."

"I've never really thought about it, but that's not entirely wrong. My hormones are vulnerable to peer pressure. It's the oddest thing."

He snickered, and then gave me a soft kiss. He wasn't acting like a guy ready to bolt out of bed and pretend last night had never happened.

"I think we should talk about this," he said when he pulled back, his fingers gentle as they brushed my hair from my face. "By the way, the bedhead is spectacular. It should be filmed for its own reality show."

I instinctively reached up to comb my fingers through my hair but he stopped me, instead taking my fingers on a detour to his mouth to kiss my fingertips.

"No." He shook his head. "I like it. You look truly happy, and that's what I want for you." His face was naked with emotion and it threw me more than I expected.

"Oh, well ...."

He laughed when I couldn't come up with additional words. "Have I mentioned how much I like you?"

"Maybe not in those exact words," I hedged.

"Well, I like you." His thumb moved to my cheek and lightly brushed my skin. "I've liked you for a long time."

I balked. "You don't have to say that."

"I mean it. I try to say what I mean. To a lot of people I come off blunt and rude. That's not my intention. I prefer that there's no room for misunderstanding."

I liked that about him. "You didn't like me before we started working together on these specific projects. You didn't even notice me until that day at the fashion show."

"That is not true."

"It is."

"I've liked you for a very long time. Think back to when we were in the office together regularly. How many times a day did I stop by your desk?"

I thought hard. "I guess once or twice."

"I limited myself to three visits a day," he corrected. "I figured you would peg me for a stalker if I went over that number. I wanted to be careful that you didn't grow uncomfortable with me. Apparently I should've planned better, because you didn't even notice all of my visits."

"I noticed." I had. At the time, however, I hadn't wanted to acknowledge him because...well, for reasons.

"Did you like me?" Grady almost looked amused as he studied my features.

"I didn't know what to think of you." I opted for the truth. "You seemed nice enough, a little full of yourself, but goofily aloof at times."

"Goofily aloof? I think I'm going to add that to my business card."

"You should. It's an interesting trait." I continued as if he wasn't going the self-deprecating route to smooth things over. "I also worried that you might be a bit of a ladies' man."

He made a face. "Is this about Annabelle?"

"No, and I really would rather not talk about her."

"Good. That goes for both of us."

"It's just...you flirted with everybody. I watched you."

"How closely did you watch me? Like...were you checking out my butt, or was it more lackadaisical?"

"Ha, ha." I poked his side, and then, because his skin was so soft, I ran my hand down his chest and marveled at how warm he was. "What was I saying again?" When I glanced up, I found Grady smirking at me. "What?"

"I like how distracted you just got," he said on a laugh. "It's nice to know you're just as shallow as the rest of us. You were about to tell me why you didn't want to flirt with me in the office."

"Oh, right." I shook myself out of my reverie. "Anyway, you flirted with every woman in the office. It was your default setting."

"Flirting was my default setting? That doesn't sound right."

"Well, that's what you do. Rather than get to know someone, you reach for the flirting stick and start whacking anybody in your general vicinity with it."

"I do not whack people with a flirting stick." He looked momentarily offended. "Do I?"

"It's your way." I didn't want to hurt his feelings, but he seemed genuinely oblivious. "Once, I was trying to track you down because I had a question about a piece you wrote. I couldn't find you anywhere, even though I knew you were supposed to be in the office. One of the editorial assistants pointed me toward the advertising department. Guess why."

Grady blew out a sigh. "Because I was over there flirting."

"Yes. I believe her name was Libby Baker. She was new to the advertising carousel, and she didn't last long. People say she quit because you went out with her three times, had sex with her, and then completely lost interest. She had some sort of breakdown."

Grady made a protesting sound. "I didn't sleep with her. And I didn't cause her to have a breakdown. She left to run promotions for that new bar on Bourbon Street."

I was taken aback. "I didn't know that."

"Did you ask?"

My cheeks heated under his scrutiny. "No. I just believed the office gossip."

"Did you ever ask yourself who might've started the office gossip?"

"I'm guessing it was Annabelle."

"I'm guessing you're right. It doesn't matter. I refuse to let her hurt me. As for Libby, she was a narcissist who wanted something very specific, namely me to marry her. She wasn't even interested in dating. She just wanted a way to get her mother off her back when her cousin got married."

"She told you that?"

He nodded. "She did, although she beat around the bush a bit before she told me the truth. I thought she liked me. I've since learned—and she's not the only one who taught me this particular lesson—that I might not fully understand what women are thinking."

He looked vulnerable as he stared at the ceiling, so much so that my heart threatened to break. "I'm sorry," I said in a low voice. "I should've ignored the gossip."

"Or you could've asked." He slid his eyes to me and smiled. "I didn't even really like Libby, so it's not like I had a broken heart when she left *The Bugle*. I was just looking for a distraction."

"From what?"

Incredulity flashed in his eyes as he shook his head. "From you. Are you kidding me?"

"From me?" How could he even say that with a straight face? "Libby left *The Bugle* twelve months ago."

"Yeah, and that's how long I've been carrying a torch for you."

"Seriously?"

"Yes."

"Why?"

He angled himself so he could see the full breadth of my face. "Are you asking for a list of the reasons I like you?"

"No. Only an insecure person would want that."

"Are you an insecure person?"

I squirmed under his steady gaze. "I try to think I'm not."

"But you're not sure of me." He pursed his lips, seemingly debating. Then he nodded. "You need time to get used to me. You're not sure what to think of me. Your past perceptions are ruining future possibilities for both of us."

I blinked several times and then jabbed a finger into his chest. "That is complete and total nonsense. You're just trying to make me feel sorry for you, and you're saying things that make no sense in an effort to confuse me."

He burst out laughing as he wrapped his arms around me tighter. I could feel his heart beating beneath mine as he snuggled closer. The light in his eyes told me he was enjoying himself. "I can't help it. You're such an easy mark. As for Libby, she really did leave to handle promotions for a bar. Even if she had wanted me for something more than a wedding date, we never would've worked out."

"Because of me?" I was struggling to understand.

"It's not as creepy as it sounds," he reassured me. "I just always felt this...zing...when I was around you. I can't explain it."

"Zing?"

"Yup. Zing." He whispered the second word and then kissed me. He seemed perfectly comfortable with the conversation and the fact that we were naked in my bed.

"I don't want to freak out about this," I admitted. "I think too hard about things. I don't want to do that this time."

"I don't want you to either."

"What do you want?" I cringed before I was done asking the question. I told myself I wouldn't do this. Why demand answers regarding the future when the present was so much fun? It was too late to haul the words back into my mouth, however, so I waited.

"I want to spend time with you. I want to see what this is."

"The zing."

He grinned. "The zing. I want to explore it. I also want to keep doing what we're doing for work. That's benefitting both of us, and I'm having a great time doing it."

"I puked on you the other day," I pointed out. "How could that possibly be misconstrued as fun?"

"I'm not saying the puke was fun. Before that, the time we had on the Natchez together, that was fun. The puke I'm going to ignore until it becomes funny."

"When will that be?"

"Ninety-three days."

My forehead creased. "That's a rather specific timeframe."

"That's how puke works. You have to be specific."

"Okay, well...here's hoping you completely forget about it in ninety-three days."

"Oh, no." He shook his head. "I can't forget about it. I'm just hoping we're going to make more memories, better memories, in the next ninety-three days so the puke memory just sort of fades into the background."

"What happens at the end of ninety-three days?"

"What do you mean?"

"I'm just curious. Ninety-three days is a really specific number. Are they going to repo my pumpkin coach at the end of ninety-three days or something?"

He cocked an eyebrow. "Cinderella? Seriously? I thought of you as more of a Belle girl."

"Honestly, I'm not keen on any of the Disney princesses. I'm more of a *Scooby-Doo* girl than anything else."

"Good to know." He moved his hands up and down my bare back. He was smiling but there was seriousness in his eyes. "Just for the record, I'm not going into this with a preordained expiration date. I want to spend time with you, get to you know, and keep having fun. I can't guarantee anything. We could be completely incompatible, but I don't think so. I want the option of figuring out what this means together."

I chewed my bottom lip, letting his words wash over me. Then I nodded. "I want that option too. I just...wasn't expecting this."

"I wasn't either. I wasn't planning to get you naked so soon. The opportunity just sort of fell into my lap, and apparently I have zero self-control and couldn't stop myself from taking advantage."

"You were planning to get me naked?"

"I'm not sure I like that word. 'Planning' makes it sound like I was devious and manipulative."

"Were you?"

"No. My hormones have a mind of their own."

I laughed, as I'm sure he'd intended. "So, we're just going to keep doing this?"

"You have to be more specific."

"All of this," I said. "We're going to keep working together, and...um...playing together?"

"You're so adorable I can't stand it." He made chomping noises against my cheek as he tickled me. "Yes, we're going to do all of it."

"But...what about work?" I was serious as I propped myself on my right elbow and looked down at him. "I don't think we should include the relationship stuff in the work stuff."

"For now, I agree."

"For now?"

He shrugged. "Never say never."

What did that mean? "What's the plan for today?" I refused to focus on something too serious when I was in such a good mood. If we needed to discuss the "later" part of our relationship, we would do it then.

"I was thinking we could spend the day in bed."

"What about work?"

"We don't have to file stories every day. That's not expected. We're good for today. Why not just bask in it?"

"In the story?"

"And other things." Mischief ran rampant across his handsome face. "Come on, Shay. Play hooky with me today. You know you want to."

"Fine, but if we're going to do this, we're going to do it right. That means ordering delivery and not getting dressed all day."

"Now you're talking. That's exactly what I had planned for the day."

"And tomorrow?" I prodded.

"We'll worry about tomorrow tomorrow."

Because it was what I wanted too, I settled my head on his chest and smiled as his heart beat steadily in my ear. "We should watch bad movies...and eat junk food...oh, and we should totally play naked *Twister*."

He cocked his head. "You had me up until naked *Twister*."

"That's what I thought you'd most want to do."

"Oh, I'm not ruling it out, but I might need visuals."

"Well, I don't have photos, but I can probably describe what I have in mind."

"Ding! Ding! Ding! We have a winner." He grabbed me tight and covered my mouth with his, rolling until he was on top of me. He whispered, "I can't wait to see where this goes."

He wasn't the only one, and the realization that I was suddenly in a relationship momentarily jarred me. Then I did something I never did, I let the feeling go. It was time to enjoy the present for a change.

Twenty-One

If I thought my feelings for Grady would dissipate once we started sleeping with one another, I was mistaken. Instead, things kept rolling right along...on both the work and romance fronts.

Two weeks later, we'd yet to spend a night apart—something Cally complained about bitterly because she was having a dilemma with the new statue guy on the west side of Jackson Square and needed someone to vent to—and the numbers on the pieces we'd been filing continued to climb.

We were now officially the team to beat. I would've been lying if I said I wasn't filled with pride. That also meant the stakes were higher, something I felt keenly when realizing we were having our last employee meeting in the old Bugle headquarters before the building was shuttered and offered up at auction.

"There she is." Grady peeled away from a nearby storefront ten minutes before the meeting, catching me off guard, and grinned as he leaned in to give me a kiss.

I brought him up short with a hand to his chest. "What are you doing?" My voice sounded unnaturally screechy.

"I was hoping to get to third base in public," Grady replied dryly as he pulled back and increased the distance between us. "I guess that's not happening."

"I would never let you get to third base in public. There's no way we're getting it on with an audience so close."

He snorted. "I think I need to give you a tutorial on the bases."

I stilled. "What do you mean? Third base is tongue stuff."

"Oh, you're so cute I can't stand it." He swooped in again and gave me a quick kiss, seemingly not caring in the least that somebody from the office might see. He'd opted to meet me one street over from the building. "Tongue stuff is first base."

"First base is kissing," I argued.

"Yes, and that can involve tongues."

"That's not the sort of tongue stuff I was referring to."

"I see." Grady's eyes gleamed with lasciviousness. "I guess you're right about that being third base. I thought I just might cop a feel to see if you're wearing a bra."

"That's second base."

"Really?" He didn't look as if he believed me. "Hold on." He handed me a cup of coffee. "I got your favorite because I figured you would be running late after last night."

I darted a look around again. I did not want our co-workers figuring out what was going on. "How are you even here before me?" I tried to rein in my irritation and failed. "You left my place forty minutes ago. Somehow, you're showered, changed, and have coffee. That shouldn't be possible."

The other thing that shouldn't be possible was how good he looked. His hair was still damp enough that I could smell his shampoo and it was doing weird things to my stomach. Like...third base things.

"You're right about the bases." Grady looked flummoxed when he raised his eyes from his phone. He was apparently doing some Googling. "Copping a feel is second base. My whole outlook on life has changed."

I elbowed his stomach, causing him to laugh. "You're just trying to get me going."

"It's easy, so don't be too impressed." He sipped his own coffee and studied my face. "Why are you so red?"

"I left my place late. I had to speed-walk to get here, and it's going to be a scorcher today."

"I have an idea for an outing after the meeting."

"I'm up for whatever."

"That's exactly what I like to hear."

"Don't be you," I warned.

"Who do you want me to be? Wait...is this the start of some dirty game? Who is your celebrity crush? I can totally play a superhero named Chris—complete with an interactive hammer—if that's the way you roll."

I wanted to chastise him, at the very least shut him up. Truth be told, I didn't have the heart to stop him. He was too adorable to squelch that mouth of his. Instead, I opted for the truth. "I don't want the people at work to find out what's going on with us."

His expression didn't change but his shoulders tensed. "May I ask why?"

"There are a few reasons." This was not the time to start lying to him. "I love my job. Heck, I like it even more now than I did before things fell to shit. I don't want people looking at me as the sort of person who sleeps her way to success."

Grady's eyebrows drew together. "I'm not your boss."

"I know, but we're killing it." I glanced around, perhaps looking for karma in human form in the wake of my exaltation. "We're doing so well. If people find out we're seeing each other on top of everything else...." I trailed off.

"Are you embarrassed?"

"Of course not." I pinned him with a look. "You're way too hot to be embarrassed about."

That earned a smile, but wariness remained in his eyes.

"I want to be respected because of the work I do," I said. "This—you and me—I didn't see it coming. If people find out we're together, they might think we're doing underhanded things to stay on top. I don't want the relationship to be the thing we're known for...not that we're in a relationship or anything." My cheeks colored again when I realized what I'd said. "I'm not pushing you to say we're in a relationship," I added lamely.

"Oh, geez," Grady muttered, shaking his head. "You are a bundle of neurosis, aren't you?"

I balked. "I'm totally normal."

"Yeah, you're normal." He moved his hand to the back of my neck and started rubbing. "I'm fine with keeping this to ourselves."

Hope filled my chest. "Really?" Perhaps he wasn't going to be angry after all.

"For now," he clarified. "We haven't been in it all that long. I don't think we need to spread our personal business. But eventually we're going to have to tell people we're in a relationship." He tapped my chin to get me to look up and meet his eyes. "And, yes, we *are* in a relationship."

I let loose a pent-up breath. "We are?"

"Yes, you freak." He flicked the spot between my eyebrows, causing me to yelp. "I don't want to push things. There's no reason to move at warp speed. I want to keep having fun. Nobody watching our videos will assume we're a couple."

I cocked a challenging eyebrow.

"Okay, quite a few of them will assume that we want to become a couple," he clarified. "The sexual tension appealed to people from the start. The good news for us is that the tension remains. I don't want to mess with that either."

It was everything I wanted to hear and yet .... "Why do I sense a 'but' coming on?" I prodded.

"But I'm happy," he replied. "I like spending time with you. Eventually, that means we go out for dinners that don't revolve around editing videos on the fly. I want people to know we're together because of that happiness. I'm fine with us holding off for now, but not forever."

"For now is good," I said hurriedly. "For now is great. I mean...I expect more people to get laid off today. We're only a little more than a week from the end of the experiment portion of this transition."

"And you don't want to be the person giddy with lust because things are going well for you on both professional and personal fronts," he surmised.

"Yeah." I was sheepish. "I'm afraid I'll jinx us by acknowledging just how good things are going, but we promised to be honest with each other, and that's how I feel. I've never had this much fun."

"I am gifted in bed."

I elbowed him. Hard. "I'm talking about the professional front. That stuff is good too."

"Oh, my poor bruised ego." Grady ruefully rubbed his stomach. "It's okay, Shay. Nobody needs to know our business. In another month, things might be different. We're good for now."

"That means you can't hold my hand during the meeting," I warned.

"What about holding something else?"

I pretended I hadn't heard the question. "You can't kiss me or anything else. It has to be strictly professional in front of our co-workers."

"Got it. We can't flaunt our joy in the face of their misery."

"That's a little heavy-handed, but basically."

"I can handle this, Shay. You have absolutely nothing to worry about."

I hoped beyond hope that was true.

I RETHOUGHT WHERE I SHOULD SIT TWICE, first settling next to Grady, then thinking better of it and moving, and then thinking better about it yet again just in case not sitting next to each other made people suspicious.

Edith moved front and center twenty seconds after I ultimately settled and took control of the meeting. "I know this has been difficult for everybody," she started.

"Difficult? Try impossible." Brandon Klondike sat in the middle of the audience, flanked on both sides by former sports reporters, and glared at our boss. "This isn't a newspaper. This isn't journalism."

Edith kept her calm veneer in place. "I don't think I ever suggested that we would be embracing journalism for this experiment. This is about clicks. It's about exciting the public. It's about bringing in advertising dollars. I never said this was a journalistic endeavor."

"How is that a good thing?" Edie Butters demanded. She was sixty-two, only a few years from retirement, and she looked wrecked. It was enough to have me lowering my coffee because my stomach hurt too much.

"If you think this is how I wanted things to go, you're wrong," Edith said. "I believe in journalistic integrity. I thought I would be finishing my career in a specific way. That is not how things turned out. Complaining to me won't change anything. I have no control over how things have changed. I can only move forward."

Annabelle cleared her throat as she raised her hand. "I think it would be helpful if we had goals," she said. "I can't speak for anybody else, but the real difficulty for me is knowing what we're supposed to be doing.

"Like everybody else, I can carry out an assignment," she continued. "I'm good at it. I'm deadline oriented. But there are no set goalposts for what we're supposed to be doing. One day we're supposed to be doing cooking classes with our co-workers and the next we're supposed to be going on useless tours in the Quarter. It's unbelievable." She shot an accusatory look toward me.

"I can't give you goals to focus on," Edith replied. "I understand your frustration, but the end result isn't a straight line. This is an experiment, for all of us. The goal is buzz, word-of-mouth. It's advertising dollars to pay your salaries. It's finding something new that people value."

"Yes, but we have no idea how to do that," Annabelle shot back. "I've turned in five pieces the last two weeks. All of them have been professionally edited. They've all been hooky. I can barely get any views on them."

"Then try something different," Edith suggested. "The name of the game is experimentation. There is no set itinerary you have to follow. Look at what Shay and Grady are doing. They jump from activity to activity. It's not even what they do that's garnering views. It's the way they do it that's inspiring people."

I pressed my lips together, my cheeks burning under the strong praise. I wanted to be good at my job, but I didn't want my co-workers glaring at me as if I was the Antichrist, as if I was somehow to blame for how this had all played out.

"Yes, well, I think I speak for everybody here when I say that I'm suspicious regarding the numbers that Shay and Grady have been bringing in," Annabelle said. "There's no way that a stupid video about them screwing up gumbo had twenty-thousand hits. There's just no way."

"And yet that's what happened," Edith fired back. "Not

only did that video get twenty-thousand hits, it had three-thousand comments. People loved it."

"They're manufacturing those numbers somehow," Annabelle protested. "It's the only explanation."

"I don't see how they'd do that, but I'll play." Edith's expression was icy. Her dislike of Annabelle had been obvious before the world shifted. It was ten times worse these days. Edith was under a great deal of pressure, and Annabelle wasn't making her life any easier. "Even if they are somehow generating fake clicks, that still causes people to want to advertise. It's the clicks that lead to advertising, plain and simple."

"But ...." Annabelle's frustration was palpable.

Edith raised her hand. "I don't want to hear it. We are done with excuses, people. You're either going to get with the program, or you're going to get into the unemployment line. Those are your only options."

Annabelle threw up her hands. "This sucks."

"I don't disagree." Edith planted her hands on her hips and glanced around the room. "So, those of you doing well, keep doing what you're doing. Those of you having more difficulty with the transition, it's time to get it together. The final decisions aren't far off." She paused for a beat and then sighed. "I need to see a few people in my office now."

Everybody knew what that meant, and whispers rippled through the room.

"I'm sorry," she said, anxiety washing across her features. She rattled off seven names—including Brandon's—and gestured to her office. "Let's just get this over with."

My stomach felt as if it was full of curdled milk as I made my way to the front of the building. I dumped my half-finished latte into the trash and plunged outside to suck in fresh air. Even though the heat was building to something oppressive, anything was better than being inside the office.

"Shay, you can't take this to heart," Grady said as he

followed me. "I know you don't want to see anybody lose their job, but you can't control what's happening. All you can control is what we're doing. Focus on that and be proud. We're killing it."

"I am proud." I braced my hand on the side of the trash receptacle. "But I feel guilty for being proud. I don't know what's wrong with me."

"You're freaky. You can't help it." Grady removed my hand from the greasy receptacle. "Where are the wipes you carry everywhere you go?"

My mouth dropped open. "I don't carry wipes. That's something uptight people do."

Grady pinned me with a "Don't play with me" look.

"Fine." I dug into my pocket and came back with the travel package of wipes I always carried for emergencies just like this one. "I'm not uptight."

"Not my sweetheart," he agreed as he used one of the wipes on my hand. "You'll get scurvy or something if you're not careful."

"I don't think that's how scurvy works."

"Hey." Grady snapped his fingers in front of my face to get me to look at him. "You're doing what you need to do for yourself. You cannot be held accountable for what the others are—or rather are not—doing. This isn't on you."

"I can't help it. I want everybody to be okay."

"You're a good person, but you can't keep everybody safe. You need to let it go."

He was right. I felt it deep down in my bones. I hated worrying about how my co-workers were going to put food on their tables, or pay mortgages and bills, but there was nothing I could do to help them. "You probably think I'm a moron." I shot him a rueful smile. "I kind of think that sometimes myself."

"I don't," he countered quickly. "Far from it. In fact, I think you're one of the smartest people I know."

"That's sweet."

He raised a finger to still me. "I do think you're a lot of work. You're neurotic. You're a worrier. Thankfully, I happen to find it cute on you."

"I guess there are worse things."

He grinned. "You need to let loose and embrace the wonder that is you. You'll be much happier when you stop worrying about others."

"Any suggestions on how I do that?"

"Just one." He extended his hand.

This time I didn't look around to see if anybody was watching. I slipped my hand into his. "What's the plan for today?"

"It's a surprise."

"I hate surprises."

"You're going to like this one. Trust me."

Twenty-Two

"Come on." Grady gestured to the dressing room of a costume shop. He wasn't impatient but there was a "hurry up" edge to his attitude. "Get in there and put this on." He pushed a slinky black dress in my direction.

When he said he had an idea for an outing,ptsI was gung-ho...right up until the moment he led me into the shop. I'd seen it during my walks through the Quarter, but I'd never been inside. Costumes had never been my thing.

"Um...what are we doing now?" I held up the dress and tried to imagine wearing it. We had a problem. "I don't have enough cleavage to fill this thing. Whatever you're thinking we should do, I'm thinking it's a terrible idea."

His smile was soft. "You have more than enough cleavage to fill it. Don't sell yourself short."

"Who knows my cleavage better?" I demanded.

"I'm pretty sure I spent a lot of time with your cleavage last night." He didn't back down, which was frustrating. "I've also been eyeing your cleavage from afar for quite some time. The dress will look great on you."

I clutched the hanger tighter. "Grady." I seemed to be channeling my mother with my disappointed tone, and it wasn't a happy realization.

"Shay." He matched my tone with a mocking grin.

"Just tell me what the plan is." I used my most reasonable voice. "I'll do whatever you want. I just need to know the plan."

"It's a surprise."

"I hate surprises."

"No, you don't."

"I do."

"No, you really don't."

An impatient growl bubbled in my throat. "Grady, I know what I do and don't like. Surprises suck."

"I surprised you last night." His fingers were gentle as they brushed my hair from my face. "You surprised me too. Why can't you just unclench and have a little fun? That's all I'm asking. Just a little bit of fun after a hard morning. I think we both could use it."

I bristled at the statement. "I'm fun." I sounded petulant, but I couldn't stop myself. "In fact, I'm tons of fun. I'm a fun girl."

"You *are* a fun girl." He leaned in until I had to press myself against the wall to keep sight of his face. "Shay, I've had nothing but fun with you. Even the puking was fun."

"Oh, well, that's laying it on a bit thick."

His grin widened. "I have a plan for us. It's an easy assignment. It'll also allow us to cut loose. We both need it. The stress from what's happening with our jobs is dragging us both down. Can't you just trust me?"

That was what he was really after, I realized. He desperately needed me to trust him. That's what he wanted more than anything, and I was falling down on the job.

He wasn't what I expected him to be. All the rumors I'd

heard, all the flirty behavior, none of it was real. At his core, he was a loyal guy who tried to do the right thing. Did he always manage to do the right thing? No, but nobody was perfect.

"Fine." I pressed the dress to my chest. "If I'm not comfortable, I can't wear this. I'm not going to unclench if I'm uncomfortable."

He hesitated and then nodded. "Okay. That's fair. I don't want you to be uncomfortable. I do want you to have fun."

"What did I say? I'm a fun girl."

His grin was back. "This is going to be a great day. I promise. Just…give me a little wiggle room."

I looked at the dress again and sighed. "I don't have enough cleavage to fill out this dress. I'll look like an idiot. I promise to at least try to have some fun despite that."

"That's all I ask."

AN HOUR LATER, WE WERE OUTSIDE A theme bar on Dumaine Street. There was a small trolley with open windows out front. I kept fidgeting because I was certain there were a million men staring at my chest.

"I told you I couldn't fill out this dress," I hissed.

He'd selected costumes that had us decked out as Morticia and Gomez Addams. Neither of us needed a wig, which made things easier, but I felt as if I was on display…and I wasn't certain I liked it.

"Baby, you fill out that dress and then some." He gave me an appraising look as he slid his arm around my waist. It wasn't a proprietary move. I knew that instinctively. He simply wanted to touch me. I understood the feeling because I'd caught myself touching my fingers to his numerous times during the walk to the bar. "You look great."

"I don't know that I believe you." I craned my neck to get a look at my reflection in the window. "My hips look wide."

The sigh he let loose was long and drawn out. "Your hips are perfect."

"I look pale."

"You're making yourself pale because you're melting down over nothing."

I narrowed my eyes. "You know, if we're going to make this work, you're going to have to get used to the fact that I'm high-strung. I won't change myself to fit anybody's idealized vision of me."

That had his lips curving. "You're only high-strung fifty percent of the time." He snagged my hands and brought them up to his lips in a ridiculously romantic gesture that had my heart stuttering. "The other fifty percent of the time you're easygoing. As for changing you, that's not what I want. I like you the way you are."

"You do?" I couldn't contain my surprise. "Why?"

"Ugh." He shook his head. "I should think that would be obvious. I like who you are."

"Even though I'm high-strung?"

"Even though." He pressed a kiss to the tip of my nose. "Besides, you're only high-strung half the time. I just told you that, but apparently you only hear what you want to hear. The other fifty percent is when you forget to worry. Then you're the easiest person I know to get along with."

It seemed there should be an insult buried in there, but I couldn't find it. "Well, that's sweet," I said. "At least I think it is."

"I just want you to have fun." He was earnest. "This morning was tense. You're wound up about our job situation. I want you to relax, have fun, and not make yourself sick over something we can't control."

That wasn't the sort of thing I wanted to hear if I was going to relax. "Aren't you worried about our job situation?"

He shrugged. "I was when the announcement was first

made. Now, though...." He trailed off, contemplative. "Here's the thing," he said when he'd given it some thought. "Freaking out won't change the outcome. If we don't keep our jobs, then we'll find new jobs."

"You make it sound so easy," I muttered. "What if we can't find new jobs? What if I can't pay my rent? I went to school to be a journalist. It's all I know how to do."

"Those skills aren't exactly worthless," Grady noted. "You can use your writing abilities for other things."

"What?" I was genuinely curious.

"You could write press releases for the area bars. Heck, you could become a bar promoter. You have good ideas...and let's face it, if it's one thing that New Orleans has in abundance, it's bars. You could even do the same thing for the tour companies."

It was something I hadn't considered. When I glanced up, I found amusement in his eyes. "What?"

"You're adorable." He leaned in to kiss me again. "Absolutely adorable. I love the faces you make."

I went warm all over. "It's weird that you're attracted to me despite the things that have happened."

"What things?"

"I dressed up in an ugly bridesmaid dress and made a fool of myself in Jackson Square."

"You never stopped smiling on that runway." Grady handed over the tickets for the pub crawl as the woman collecting them appeared at our side. She gave him an appreciative once-over, but his gaze was solely for me. He waited until she'd provided us with our wristbands and moved down the line to speak again. "Shay, when your heart is open to new experiences and you allow yourself to laugh, you're the most beautiful person in the world. How can you not see that?"

The question caught me off guard and before I knew what was happening, my cheeks flooded with color. "I...um...."

"Adorable." He tapped the end of my nose as the line began moving onto the trolley. "Have fun with me today, Shay. Just...open your heart to me." He almost sounded as if he were begging. I had to give him something.

"I've already opened my heart to you." I couldn't meet his gaze when I said it. Instead, I slid my fingers into his and allowed him to lead me to two seats at the rear of the trolley. "I didn't want to." I opted for the truth. "I tried really hard not to let you in, but I couldn't stop myself. The things I was feeling...sometimes...." I couldn't finish.

"Tell me," he prodded. "Just...take a leap of faith."

I licked my lips, debating, and then nodded. "Do you believe in destiny?" I was nervous, but when I raised my eyes to his I found him grinning.

"I believe in fate," he confirmed. "Why? Do you think I'm your fate?"

I couldn't answer that, and not because I was embarrassed. It was something I needed to think about. "I think that I was always meant to meet you. We were always meant to do this. I don't know if we'll be able to keep it up over the long haul, but I'm not sorry that we're together now." It was as close as I could get to explaining. I hoped it would be enough for him, at least for now.

"Some things are meant to be," he whispered.

"Like Gomez and Morticia?"

He nodded. "Yup, and maybe you and me."

My heart did a little dance and I had to shift on my seat because I suddenly felt squirmy. "I don't know where this is going," I warned.

"It's too soon to know."

"I want to see where it ends, though," I admitted.

"Maybe it won't end. Have you considered that?"

I didn't want to consider it. If I got too attached to him and he disappeared from my life, well, I just couldn't think about it. "Let's have fun," I said to redirect the conversation. "What would Gomez and Morticia do?"

The look that crept into his eyes was sly. "Well, I'm glad you asked. There's a reason I picked these costumes. Gomez and Morticia weren't afraid to embrace the public displays of affection. You're still nervous about us, so I thought embracing our roles would be good. We're in costume, so it allows us a little wiggle room."

Understanding dawned. "You just want me to hold your hand in public."

"Definitely."

"And maybe kiss you."

"There's going to be kissing, baby. Two beers and you won't be able to stop yourself."

I shook my head but there was no hiding my grin. "Your ego is something to behold."

"Stick with me, Shay." He gripped my hand tightly. "There are a lot of things I want to show you."

WE GOT DRUNK. IT WASN'T MY INTENTION—I told myself to stop after three beers—but we were on unsteady feet when the pub crawl ended hours later. For an additional fee, we could've stayed with the group. Grady was willing to pay it, but I knew better than agreeing to continue.

"Just one more beer," he pleaded as he tugged my hand and pointed to a cutesy bar on our left. "It will be fun."

"We've had endless fun," I countered. "I can't remember the last time my stomach hurt this much from laughing. We don't need any more beer. Beer is not necessary for fun."

"Oh, no?" His expression changed in an instant to sexy. He stalked toward me, as if trying to pin me down as prey, but he was drunk enough that he accidentally fell into me. That had us both falling into fits of convulsive laughter. "Maybe you're right," he said when he'd recovered, his fingers gentle against my cheek. "Maybe we don't need beer."

"Oh, I'm totally right." I bobbed my head. "What we need is food."

"I'm not hungry."

"You are, but you don't realize it."

"I don't need anything but you," he said as he tugged me tight against him. Instead of a kiss, he gave me a heartfelt hug. "Let's just do this." He rested his cheek on my forehead.

It was a sweet gesture, but drunken people passing by kept jostling us, so it wasn't exactly a comfortable place to plant roots.

"This is nice." I hugged him back.

"Really nice," he agreed, letting out a contented sigh. "You have no idea how long I've waited for this. I was getting to a point where I thought it might not happen. You're so stubborn."

I lifted my eyebrows in amusement as I tilted my head so my chin was settled against his chest. "You could've just told me what you had in mind from the start. You didn't have to go the seduction route."

Grady shook his head. It was warm enough that we were both sweaty after the copious amounts of beer. Neither of us seemed to mind. "You need to come to terms with things slowly. I tend to rush things. We needed balance, so I had to wait for you to become ready."

"Is that what you did?"

He slid his eyes to mine and nodded. "I knew you wouldn't give me a chance if you didn't get to know me." He brushed his fingers over my cheek. "I needed you to give me a chance."

"Because you'd been pining for me for a year?" I meant it

as a joke but his solemn nod had me frowning. "You've been pining for me?"

"Pining might not be the right word," he conceded. "I felt this...spark...whenever I was around you. It was like my heart recognized you. But your heart didn't recognize me. It was painful."

I thought back to our interactions. "I don't know that my heart didn't recognize you," I said. "I think my heart just needed a bit of time to catch up."

"You protect your heart," Grady countered. "I get it, but I'll never hurt you. Not on purpose. I don't have it in me."

I believed him. "That's really sweet."

"Yes, I'm a sweet guy. I'm also awesome in bed." He shot me a wink. "Let's go back to your place so I can show you."

I had something similar in mind. "Let's pick up food on the way. If all goes as planned, I can stuff you full of gumbo and you'll be halfway to sober by the time we're done eating. Then we can talk about the other stuff."

Rather than agree, Grady puffed out his chest. "I'm a man of action." He said it in such a serious manner I couldn't stop myself from laughing.

"Well, man of action, let's get food. My place is only three blocks from here. Once I'm reasonably assured I wouldn't be taking advantage of you, we'll make plans for the rest of the evening."

He nodded, but I wasn't certain he even understood. I grabbed his hand all the same and started down the street. Then he spoke again. "Those plans include sex, right? I want to romance the crap out of you."

On the surface of it, the statement was funny, but his voice contained a hint of earnest yearning that had me going warm all over. "I want you to romance the crap out of me." Surprisingly, I meant it. "Food first. I don't think we need another showing of vomit pyrotechnics."

"Good point." He sagely bobbed his head. "You're the smartest person I know. Have I mentioned that?"

"No, but it's always nice to hear."

"You're awesome. I'm so glad you finally gave me a chance."

I was right there with him.

Twenty-Three

Two weeks of bliss was enough to have me sinking into a relationship I didn't know I wanted. Grady and I continued with our daily outings—some more successful than others—but our viewership continued to grow, to the point we were now getting recognized on the street.

We spent our days exploring New Orleans with fresh eyes and our nights exploring each other. We didn't sleep apart. There was no easing into the relationship. Once we were together, we were together, and it was hard for me to remember when we were ever apart.

"So, I was thinking maybe we should take the day off." Grady's eyes were alert when he turned to face me. I'd yet to visit his apartment. He'd simply taken over half of mine, including the closet. It was almost as if we were living together, even though that discussion had never taken place.

"You want to take the day off?" I plucked his hand from on top of the blanket and idly traced the lines in his palm. "I don't know. We've been doing five pieces a week since we joined forces. Don't you think our fans will be disappointed if we don't feed the beast?"

He rolled on top of me, his smile impish. "I have every intention of feeding the beast." He rolled his hips suggestively. "Come on. It will be fun. We haven't played hooky since this whole thing started."

He'd trapped me on a basic level. I was a good girl at my core, feeling I should work the standard five days a week. On the other hand, he was ridiculously handsome and there was little I loved more than spending time with him. "You want to spend the whole day in bed?"

"Absolutely." He bobbed his head without hesitation. "Or maybe we could spend the morning in bed and then head out for lunch. We need to brainstorm some new outings. We're getting near the end of our list."

"I don't know." I adopted a breezy tone. "That seems like something slackers would do."

"Oh, baby, I have no intention of slacking." He nuzzled my cheek. "Come on. We don't even have to go out. We can have food delivered."

I briefly pressed my eyes shut, enjoying the warmth of his body against mine. Before I realized what I was doing, I nodded. "Okay, but just one day. We can't start slacking. I know we're at the top of the heap, but it's not as if Annabelle will let us coast into happily ever after."

Grady pulled back to study my face. He was so intense, discomfort rolled over me.

"What? Did I say something wrong?"

He shook his head. "You rarely say anything wrong."

"Two days ago, you insinuated I couldn't control the words that come out of my mouth. You said I suffered from chronic verbal diarrhea."

"I didn't say it was a bad thing." His grin was back. "I like that you always say what you mean. When you think too hard, it gives me stomach worms."

My eyebrows drew together. "Stomach worms? That is not the picture you want to put in my head if you want a morning in bed."

"Fair enough. I get itchy when you think too hard. I know when you blurt things out that it's how you really feel."

"I always say what I think."

"Almost always," he agreed. "There are times you try to be strategic. Those are the times I get itchy."

"You're not known for holding back how you feel," I pointed out.

"No." He slipped his arm around my waist and reversed our positions, so I was on top of him. His hands moved to my bare back to rub at my sore muscles. We'd had an engaging night—I wasn't complaining—but it had also been strenuous. "I like that I can tell you what I'm thinking these days and not worry you'll balk and run."

I snorted. "Like you ever worried about that."

"Oh, but I did." He was solemn. "There's a reason I took my time with you at the start. You can't be rushed into things. You need to think long and hard before you engage."

"I think you're saying I'm boring."

"I'm saying that you need to work things out in your head before you put your heart on the line. I admire that about you, even though I do wish you would've opened yourself to me the day we met. I think about all the time we wasted not being together and it makes me sad."

I lifted my head to stare down at his guileless face. His hair was a mess—much like me, he was plagued by rampant bedhead, although it only added to his sexiness—but his smile was ever present. "Do you want to know the truth?" I asked on a hesitant breath.

He nodded. "Always."

"I think things happen when they're supposed to." I took a moment to organize my thoughts. "I wasn't ready for this when we first met. I was too focused on the job. That's why I came here. I needed to be successful."

"Why?"

"Because...I had to be. I can't ever go back home."

"Why?"

"Because...." He was starting to frustrate me. "Because I don't belong there. I never did. You know how some parents always say, 'This will always be your home?'"

He nodded.

"My parents never said that. Even when they were together, they made jokes. 'Fifteen years and she'll be out of here.' 'Ten years and we won't have to deal.' I always knew there was an expiration date on their love."

His face twisted. "Oh, baby." He scooped his hand over my hair. "I'm so sorry. You never talk about them. Are they still together?"

I shook my head. "I haven't seen my father in years. He just got fed up one day. He calls every few months. Most of the conversation is about him, but he drops his version of wisdom on me, what I should be doing, and then he disappears again. My mother did her best. She really did. She was just...limited. Growing up I assumed I was limited too."

"Shay, you're the exact opposite of limited." He held me close. "You give so much of yourself without even realizing it. I'm sorry they never made you feel safe, but that's the answer to the riddle."

Now I was confused. "What riddle?"

"You can't open your heart until you feel safe. I get it, and it's okay."

I wanted to argue that he was wrong because it made me sound standoffish, even a little full of myself. But he was right. I had issues. "I don't ever want to be my mother." My voice was low and I didn't know if he could hear me. "I want to be better than that."

"You are. You're the best person I know."

"You've spent the last few weeks telling me over and over again the exact opposite. I kept you at arm's length. I was ready to believe the worst about you because it meant I didn't have to engage with you."

"You needed time. Don't expect me to give you grief about that. I knew when I met you that there would be no rush to happily ever after. That's what you said just now that threw me. You mentioned we could get a happily ever after, and all I could think was, 'Finally. Finally, she gets it.' That's what was going through my head. Nothing else."

Shame coursed through me. "I guess I really have held you at arm's length. The thing is, I didn't realize I was."

"I know. Don't blame yourself." Sincerity shone brightly from his eyes. "It's okay. We can figure this out together. We don't have to have all the answers now. I just want you to remain open to this, to us being together.

"When you need to talk about something, I want you to talk about it with me," he continued. "When you're afraid, I want you to tell me so I can at least try to make it better. When you need to feel safe, I want to make you feel safe."

I swallowed a huge lump that had appeared without me noticing. "I might be more messed up than I realized."

"We're all messed up. We all have issues. Believe it or not, I'm not perfect."

I laughed, swiping at an errant tear as I sucked in a breath to calm myself. "Oh, yeah? What's your biggest fault?"

"I jump in with both feet without thinking. Without sounding trite, I'm a romantic. Most men won't admit that, but I'm happy to. It's gotten me into trouble a time or two."

"Like with Annabelle?"

He scowled. "I knew she was a poor fit before we went

out, but that didn't stop me. She would be a shining example of the poor decisions I've made."

"Are you worried I'm a poor decision?" I held my breath waiting for his answer.

"Not even a little." He fervently shook his head. "You're the best decision I've ever made. I just don't want to make the wrong move and scare you off."

"You won't." I meant it. "I'm not scared in the least."

"Good." He held me tight as I rested my head on his chest. His heartbeat was a calming rhythm in my ear. "So, where did we land on spending the morning in bed?"

I smiled as I rested my fingertips on his stomach. "You've talked me into it. In fact... ." The bedroom door flew open to allow a third person to wander into my bedroom.

My first inclination was that we were being robbed, but the flurry of messy hair that accompanied our visitor had me jolting...and for all the wrong reasons.

"Cally!" My voice was accusatory. "Just because you have a key to my place, that doesn't mean you can use it whenever you want."

My best friend pulled up short and took in the scene. Grady and I were naked, wrapped together in bed, and there was no way to hide what was going on. "You guys were right in the middle of doing it!"

"What does that matter?" I demanded as Grady's chest shook with silent laughter. He'd interacted with Cally multiple times the last two weeks, and they seemed to get along well. If he was bothered by her invasion, he didn't show it.

"I didn't hear any noises when I was creeping through the house," she replied. "I listened, just to be on the safe side. If you guys were groaning and moaning, I had every intention of being polite and waiting it out in the living room."

I thought my eyes might bug out of my head. "That's being polite?"

"Yup." She plopped down on the bed next to Grady without invitation. Thankfully she didn't try to pull the covers over herself. "I'm nothing if not polite."

"What are you doing here? If this is about the Square statues again, we can talk about it later. I don't care if you've found a new love of your life." I realized what I'd said after the fact and frowned. "Wait. That came out wrong. I do care. I just don't want to talk about it right now."

She patted my hand, which was still on Grady's chest. "Don't worry. I'm not offended. Oh, these are nice." She moved her fingers to Grady's pecs, causing me to cringe. "How often do you work out?" The question sounded clinical. "You're muscular but not so much that you look hard. Your body is very nice. I'm guessing you work out three times a week."

If Grady was bothered by her invasive question—or fingers—he didn't show it. "That's about right," he confirmed.

"Very nice." She beamed at him. "Why are you guys still in bed? You're usually up by now."

"We're playing hooky," Grady replied calmly, his fingers lightly running over my back. "We're taking the day off."

"Oh, that sucks."

I frowned. "Why does it suck? You've been trying to talk me into taking a day off for weeks."

"There's no way you can take the day off now." Cally's expression changed. "Hasn't anyone from *The Bugle* called?"

I was instantly on guard. Cally had a reason for being here. Sure, she was getting to it in her own sweet time—as was her way—but she wasn't here simply because she was bored. Something was wrong, and I should've picked up on it earlier. "What is it?"

Cally hesitated, running her tongue over her lips, and then sighed. "I went on the website to watch the most recent videos. I freaking loved your trip to Grand Isle. Your coverage on the work they're doing there, how they're recovering after Hurricane Ida, was both entertaining and poignant."

"Thank you," I replied stiffly. "I think."

"When I was on the site, something else caught my eye." Cally wet her lips again. It really wasn't like her to beat around the bush like this.

"Just tell us what's going on." I shifted so I was next to Grady rather than on top of him, the sheets clutched to my chest. Cally had seen me naked more times than I could count but it wasn't as if I was going to put myself on display given the circumstances.

"Shh," Grady said. "I'm sure it's okay."

"I'm not sure it is." Cally shot me an apologetic look and then pulled out her phone. "You should see it." She touched her screen a few times and then handed it over. "The video is queued."

I was confused, but I accepted her phone, letting out a breath when Grady's warm chest pressed against my back so he could watch the video with me. I touched the triangle button and the video started almost immediately.

"New Orleans is a city of love," a familiar voice intoned. "It's a city of fun, but love is at the heart of the entire city. Every corner you turn, there's love on display...which is exactly what Shay Archer and Grady Dalton have been selling you on. The idea of love. The idea that you've been watching them fall in love. The thing is, they've been hiding the fact that they're already together."

I sucked in a breath, horrified. Why was Annabelle putting our private business in her video?

"They've been playing a game with all of you," Annabelle continued in a fake perky tone. "They wanted you to believe that you were falling in love with them when they were falling in love with each other, but it's all been an act. They've been manipulating you."

I turned to look at Grady and found a muscle working in his jaw. He looked furious.

"I'm a truth-teller in a city of love," Annabelle said. "You don't deserve to be manipulated. If you want love, follow me. I'm going to take you on a trip so we can all fall in love together. No lies. No bull. No fake emotions. Just Annabelle...uncut and ready to rock this city."

That was it. I didn't know what to make of it. "I don't understand."

"She's jealous," Grady replied. "She can't find a viewership of her own so she's trying to alienate ours and steal them."

"That won't work, will it?" I was suddenly nervous. "She won't be able to derail our efforts?"

"Of course not," Grady replied.

"I don't know." Cally was more subdued. "She has hundreds of people commenting on the video. Some feel betrayed. She pushed some buttons. I think she might've managed to stir up trouble for you guys, which was obviously her intention. I wanted to make you aware."

"Thank you," I murmured. I didn't know what to do. I was suddenly adrift...and seemingly frozen in fear.

"It'll be fine," Grady reassured me, perhaps sensing that I was about to go off the rails. "Don't get worked up yet. I—" He was cut off by the sound of his phone chirping. "Son of a —" He viciously swore as he retrieved it, glaring at the screen as he studied the incoming text. "It's Edith. She wants to see me."

My phone chirped as if on cue. "I'm guessing that's Edith too." The fear I'd managed to tamp down the last two weeks was back with a vengeance. "What do you think she wants?"

Grady was grim. "I don't know, but she demands to see us in an hour."

Twenty-Four

Grady insisted on stopping for coffee before the meeting with Edith. The last thing I needed was caffeine—I was a jittery mess—but he was adamant. By the time we reached the office, I was practically bouncing off the walls.

"They're going to fire us."

"You don't know that," Grady said. "She might just want us to come out publicly as a couple."

"How is that better?" I asked.

"Because then we don't have to hide. We can be ourselves on the videos and stop worrying that other people may out us for something that's none of their business. We can share what we want and start going out in public together when we're not on an assignment."

He made it sound so easy. "How can you be so calm?" I was honestly curious. "I'm a basket case."

"You're just high-strung. It's okay."

"How many times do I have to tell you I'm not high-strung?" Sure, I'd used the term to describe myself, but it was different when he said it.

"Just until I believe it." He pressed a kiss to my temple. "Try not to freak out. Whatever happens, we're going to be okay."

"What if we're not?" All I could think about was losing my job. "What if this is the end, Grady?"

His expression was impossible to read. "There's no 'end' happening here. Hold it together. Just...let me do the talking."

That made me bristle. "If I'm high-strung, then you're a control freak."

"I don't agree, but it's going to be okay." He reached over and twined his fingers with mine. "Just take a deep breath, baby. I promise, this is all going to work out."

I wished I had his faith. Something very bad was about to happen. I could feel it.

THE NEWSROOM WAS EMPTY AND QUIET AS WE made our way through it and headed straight to Edith's office. I heard voices inside and slowed my pace, desperately trying to make them out. I recognized Edith's measured tone right away —she was hard to mistake for anybody else—but the other voices were more muffled.

Grady squeezed my hand tightly when I tried to separate from him and walked through the open doorway first. He didn't bother knocking. "Good morning," he drawled in his Grady way. "It's a lovely day." He drew me in beside him and refused to let go of my hand.

My heart dropped. With Edith was Annabelle, seated across from the editor. But it was the person next to Edith who made my insides shrivel.

Lacey Andrews, *The Bugle's* Human Resources manager, sat behind the desk, next to Edith. She had three folders in front of her, and the look on her face was grave. "Have a seat," she said stiffly, refusing to make eye contact with me. Her gaze was for Grady.

"Sure." Grady was calm as he led me to the chairs. He had to release me long enough for us to sit, but he grabbed my hand again before I could fold it into my lap. Whether he was trying to calm me or himself, I couldn't say. "What can we do for you?"

"I take it you saw Annabelle's piece this morning," Edith started. She was never the most welcoming person—sometimes I was convinced that she acted as if she was constantly constipated—but it was worse today.

"We saw it." Grady leaned back in his chair, long legs stretched out in front of him. He looked calm, but I felt the anticipation coiling inside of him. "I can't say we liked it."

"Of course you don't like it," Annabelle sneered. "It means that your little charade is ending."

Grady's eyes narrowed. "Why is she here?" He directed the question to Edith. "If you want to talk to us, why is Annabelle part of this?"

"Because she brought the problem to our attention," Edith replied. "I thought you would want to face your accuser."

"Really?" Grady made an incredulous face. "Our accuser? What is this about?"

"It's about company policy," Lacey replied. "You're aware there's a 'no fraternization' rule, correct?"

"Are you kidding me?" Grady looked as if he was the one who might tumble over the rage cliff any moment. "Half the people who used to work in this building hooked up with each other."

"That doesn't change the fact that the rule exists." Lacey was firm. "I believe you were made aware of the rule more than a year ago. I made you aware of the rule...after you broke it multiple times."

Grady rolled his neck until it cracked.

Did she say "multiple times?" I thought.

"Don't worry about it," Grady said. "This is just Annabelle being Annabelle."

"Oh, no." Annabelle made a tsking sound and feigned seriousness. "I want this company to stay in business. Any threat is a serious threat...and you are a threat."

"How do you even know we're together?" Grady demanded. This time he couldn't bank his fury. "Seriously, how are you aware of what's going on with us? Did you follow us?"

"I asked the same question," Edith assured him. "I was...concerned...about how this was all playing out. It turns out that Annabelle saw you on a pub crawl together. You were anything but professional."

"There were costumes," Annabelle said, wrinkling her nose. "Very inappropriate costumes."

"We were Gomez and Morticia Addams," Grady shouted. "How was that inappropriate?"

"There was a lot of...this." Annabelle cupped her hands in front of her breasts and leveled her gaze on me. "When working on a story, there should never be any of *this*." She waggled her fingers again.

"Oh, give it a rest," Grady growled. "You don't care how she was dressed. You're just jealous."

"And why would I be jealous?" Annabelle was the picture of innocence. "What is it you're suggesting?"

"I think we're getting off track," Edith interjected.

"No, we're right on track," Lacey countered. "Grady has been warned about fraternizing with co-workers twice. The first time he could be excused for not knowing the rules. The second time he was written up. This is serious."

My stomach gurgled and I slowly pulled my hand from Grady's, doing my best to ignore the worried look he shot me.

"I think we need to start at the beginning," I prodded. "I'm feeling a bit out of my depth."

"Surprise, surprise," Annabelle snarked.

Edith shot her a warning look before smiling at me. For some reason, the smile made me feel worse. "When you joined the staff, you checked a box on your paperwork that you understood workplace romances were forbidden."

Had I? I couldn't remember everything that had been on the paperwork. Inherently I knew that workplace romances weren't allowed, but I genuinely didn't remember the box. "Okay, but...we're not hurting anybody."

"Definitely not," Grady agreed. "We're minding our own business, something everyone should do." He shot Annabelle a pointed glare.

"Don't blame me because you broke the rules," Annabelle shot back. "You pretended not to know when we got called into Human Resources too. Then I found out you were familiar with the rule. That didn't stop you from dumping me then and there."

"I don't understand," I said as I pressed the heel of my hand to my forehead.

"Annabelle is jealous and is trying to break us up," Grady barked. "That's all you need to understand."

"That's not the point," Edith countered.

"And I'm not jealous," Annabelle hissed. "I don't give two figs about you. I just don't want this fragile business plan we're building as we try to save *The Bugle* to crumble. I'm worried about our co-workers. I don't care about you."

Her tone told me otherwise, and yet there was more going on here. "Just lay it out for me," I demanded.

"You and Grady shouldn't be dating," Edith replied. "It creates a problem. I had my suspicions when I saw the videos —there was always a flirty edge to them—but the viewers seemed to love them, so I let it go. Once Annabelle uploaded her video, I no longer had that option."

I felt sick to my stomach. I was about to lose everything, and yet I persisted. "I don't understand why it's important."

"Annabelle's video has twenty-five-thousand views," Edith explained. "You two have become pseudo-celebrities quickly. People love you because you're down-to-earth, and they trust you. Unfortunately, given what Annabelle has done, that will likely no longer be the case."

"Likely?" Grady challenged.

Edith nodded. "We've had two advertisers pull out. They're concerned that a romance gone sour could hurt them."

"This is a bunch of crap," Grady sneered. "Our relationship is nobody's business."

"Except you put yourselves out there," Edith argued. "You made yourselves the focus of your own stories. For better or worse, you were the hook...and now this is going to blow up in our faces. We have to add sponsors, not shed them."

"What sponsors dumped us?" Grady asked.

"It doesn't matter." Edith looked tired. "If you guys had come to us when this all started and told us you were going to build it as a love story, we might've framed things differently."

I sputtered. "What?"

"What we do in our private lives is not for public consumption," Grady snapped. "Why would we tell you?"

"Because now we're in a pickle." Edith's fury was palpable. "Do you know how many emails I've gotten today? This story is taking on a life of its own. The freaking radio jockeys have picked it up and are coming up with ridiculous theories about your relationship.

"Some of them are framing it as the two of you leading people on, making them fall in love with you, and faking everything else," she continued. "Others are suggesting there's some weird sex stuff going on, and the more conservative sponsors won't touch you with a ten-foot pole. This is serious, Grady."

"When you add to that the fact that you've been warned twice, you can't use ignorance as a defense," Lacey added. "It was bad enough when you trampled all over my feelings, Grady. Then you went and did it to Annabelle. Now you're here with Shay. It's a pattern."

My mouth dropped open. "Wait...you were with Lacey?"

Grady shook his head. "We went on two dates. It wasn't a big deal."

"Maybe not to you." The way Lacey's eyes fired told me it was a big deal. Likely far bigger than it was to Grady. In the shadow of her annoyance, which could also be construed as heartbreak, my reservations regarding Grady's motivations when we first started working together returned with a vengeance. "Shay, I understand this isn't your fault." She squared her shoulders as she looked at me. "That makes this all the more heartbreaking. There's nothing I can do to remedy the situation, however."

Now I was back to confused. "I don't understand."

"I don't either," Grady growled. "Just tell us what's going on here and we'll deal with it."

"You're a victim of society, Shay," Edith supplied. "The majority of the viewers watching you and Grady online are female. They paint you as the villain, likely because they think he's hot. The majority of our advertisers say they'll stay with us, but only on one set of videos. Several of them said they would only advertise on Grady's videos specifically, so ...." She trailed off, her face contorting.

"So I'm being let go," I surmised. I was surprisingly numb as reality set in.

"Yes." Edith nodded once. "I'm so sorry."

"Wait a second!" Grady jumped to his feet, his eyes wild. "What is happening here?"

"Well, against my better judgment, you're being given yet another chance," Lacey replied, a momentary flash of disgust in her eyes. "It wasn't my first choice—I thought you should both be let go—but apparently advertising dollars are more important than ethics."

"You'll keep doing your videos, Grady," Edith informed him. "You have a built-in readership. I'm guessing the majority of the women will forgive you and blame Shay for what happened. That's usually the way these things go."

I stared at my hands in my lap, briefly wondering what I should do with them. They didn't feel as if they were attached to my body.

"So you're firing Shay?" Grady vehemently shook his head. "No. She started the videos. We began dating later. If anybody goes it should be me."

"Oh, look at him falling on his sword," Annabelle trilled. "Stop pretending, Grady. You've made a name for yourself as an office lothario. You use women for your own gain. You've been doing it since you got here, which is why you started with the Human Resources manager before moving on to me. You refuse to let yourself feel anything real. This time you used Shay to keep your job, and it worked. Congratulations."

My stomach tilted and I thought I might be sick. The only thing saving me was the fact I'd skipped breakfast and had only taken two sips of coffee.

"There will be a small severance, Shay," Edith offered. "It won't be much, but enough to get you through a month or two. Given the skills you've shown online, I'm sure you'll be able to find a job."

"You're sure," I echoed in a low voice. "Well, if you're sure …." I was already doing the math in my head. I would have to give my notice on the house as soon as I got home and hope that Cally's father would let me out of my lease early. If not, my credit would be shot, along with everything else.

"I'm assuming you have some paperwork for me to sign," I said when I'd sufficiently recovered the ability to talk without crying.

Lacey handed over a stack of papers, pity etched across her face. "I truly am sorry. This isn't your fault, but my hands are tied."

"Right." I studied the paperwork through glassy eyes, doing my best to ignore Grady as he returned to the chair next to me.

"Don't sign that, Shay." He jerked the papers out of my hands. "I'm sorry," he said when I looked at him. "I didn't mean to upset you."

"I need to go." My voice sounded tinny and hollow, even to my own ears. "I have...things to do."

"We're not done here," Grady insisted. "They're not seeing the bigger picture."

"We are done," Edith said. "The higher-ups are trying to sell this business. They can't do it with controversy swirling. You're smart enough to realize that, Grady. You've been deemed more valuable to the company, though I beg to differ. But I don't get a say. That means it's done."

"It's not done." Grady was imploring as he leaned closer to me, making sure to keep the paperwork from my grasp. "Shay, just give me a bit of time. I can fix this." He looked so earnest. It was hard to believe he was the monster they painted him as, and yet he'd clearly been holding out on me.

"Can you send the paperwork to my place?" I asked Lacey. "I need to get out of here."

Her gaze was pitying. "I can have them messengered over this afternoon. I really am sorry about this."

When I pushed myself to a standing position, I was surprised my legs held my weight. "I need to leave now."

"You're not going without me." Grady stood to follow.

"We're not finished," Lacey said. "We have some new rules for you, Grady."

"They can wait." Grady insisted. "I'm going with Shay. She...needs me."

Did I? Quite frankly, right now all I needed was my bed and oblivion. "I'm fine." I lifted my chin and met his eyes. "You should stay and deal with this."

"I'm going with you."

"You're not."

"We need to talk about this," Grady demanded. "What they're saying, it's not right. We need to come up with a different plan."

"There is no 'we.'" Saying it caused my heart to constrict. "There's no anything now. There's you and your job, and me and my...problems. Focus on your job." I turned my back to him and woodenly moved toward the door.

"Shay, don't say that. There is a we. There's always been a we. You just weren't ready for it."

And I wasn't ready for this. "Good luck with your videos, Grady." I glanced back at the women, frowning at Annabelle's smugness. "Good luck with *The Bugle*. I hope everything works out."

Edith looked pained. "Shay, if you need a recommendation, I'll provide you with a glowing one."

"Thank you. I'm not sure what I'm going to do just yet. I need a bit of time."

"Of course." Edith bobbed her head. "Take a few days. We'll talk."

"Yeah, we'll talk." I refused to look at Grady before exiting the room. I heard him swearing—whether at himself or them I couldn't say—but I refused to make eye contact. If I did, I would fall apart. At least this way I had a shred of dignity to hold onto as I walked out the door for the last time.

Twenty-Five

I went to bed when I got home. I didn't know what else to do. My sheets smelled of Grady, so I thought about stripping the bed and washing them, but I couldn't. I wanted to remember the happiness from hours before even if it was already lost to me. Instead, I closed my eyes and let sleep claim me.

I have no idea how long I was under. My dreams weren't of the restful variety. No, my mind decided to cast Edith, Lacey, and Annabelle as monsters. They chased me through the Quarter, other monsters joining the fray. When I found Grady, I begged him to help me. Instead, he took off with a blonde, laughing all the way.

I woke to the sound of munching, and when I looked to my left, I found Cally in bed with me. She was focused on her phone, an open bag of dill pickle chips between us.

"What are you doing here?" It wasn't the most gracious of greetings, but I didn't care. I turned my back to her and covered my face with the blanket. The last thing I needed was a Cally pep talk.

"I'm checking on you," she replied. "Good thing, too. You've slept the entire day away."

I remained under the covers. "What time is it?"

"It's almost seven."

I bolted upright. "At night?"

Amusement flickered across Cally's features. "Yup."

"But...how?"

"I tried calling, several times, but you didn't pick up. That's when I decided to come over and rouse you."

I flopped back on the pillows. "I got fired today."

"I heard."

Suddenly, I was suspicious. "How? Please tell me that Annabelle didn't post a video about it."

"She didn't, at least not that I've seen."

"Ugh. Did they already issue a news release?" That would be just like them. "I guess I shouldn't be surprised. They need to shore up those advertisers."

"Grady called me."

My heart skipped. "Why?"

"Why do you think?" She tipped the potato chip bag in my direction, but I shook my head. If I ate, I would throw up.

"He probably wanted to make sure I wasn't going to hurt myself," I replied. "He wouldn't want that on his conscience. He's *The Bugle's* golden boy, essentially untouchable. He ended up getting everything he wanted out of our partnership. My death would taint that."

"Wow." Cally shook her head. "That was dark."

"If you wanted sunshine and roses, you should've found someone else to bother." I knew I sounded petulant, but I couldn't help myself. "Why are you here? I don't have energy to deal with your stuff on top of mine right now. I'm sorry."

She looked offended. "I'm here for you. That's what best friends are for. I'm a little hurt that you didn't call me the second you found out."

"I couldn't. I just...I needed some time."

"To hide?"

"To...get my head around things."

"Oh, yeah? What have you come up with?"

"Grady lied." That bothered me most. "I knew he was a ladies' man when we first started working together, but somehow I let myself forget along the way. How could I be that stupid?"

"I'm not sure I understand what happened," Cally said.

"I'm sure Grady told you."

"Actually, he was busy yelling at someone in the background. He sounded positively furious. I think he was dealing with something."

"Well, at least he took time out of his busy day to make sure I wasn't dead in a gutter somewhere. It's nice that he called you instead of me. He probably figured that would be easier."

Cally made a face. "That doesn't sound like him."

"You don't even know him."

"I've gotten to know him a bit since you guys started working together," she countered. "We're not best friends or anything, but he seems like a good guy."

"He's a good guy who slept with the Human Resources manager," I noted. "He was warned about office relationships then. That didn't stop him from dating Annabelle...and at least one of the ad reps. He was warned again after Annabelle. He keeps getting free passes but everybody else he's dated in the office is essentially treated as roadkill."

"That's a cheery thought." Cally patted my knee. "Tell me what happened. We'll go from there."

I rubbed my eyes, willing the depression that was dragging me down to leave or at least take a break. I hadn't even been with Grady that long. I shouldn't be reacting this way. "Annabelle claims she saw us on the pub crawl and recognized that we were together. She said that she didn't want *The Bugle* to fold."

"I have trouble understanding how your relationship with Grady would sound the death knell of *The Bugle*."

"It's the advertisers. They want something wholesome. If Grady and I were to break up, which was apparently bound to happen eventually, the viewers might turn on the advertisers."

"I doubt very much that would've happened."

"Well, the newspaper owners weren't willing to risk it. They're trying to sell. They can't have drama attached to the sale."

"So you and Grady were fired." Cally shook her head. "That's unbelievable."

"Grady wasn't fired."

"What?" Cally jerked up her head. "You were fired, but he wasn't?"

"Our viewership is largely female. They all had crushes on Grady, and in typical fashion, the comments on Annabelle's piece blamed me for what happened. That's just how it works."

"That's bullshit."

"I don't disagree."

"I can't believe Grady didn't say anything." Cally looked disappointed. "I thought he was different for some reason."

"He tried. I don't know how much effort he put into things, but he tried. He told them to fire him instead, but I think he already knew that wasn't going to fly. He was still there when I left. He even tore the papers Human Resources needed me to sign from my hand and demanded I not sign them. He put on quite the show."

Cally's forehead creased. "I think I'm still behind on this. Tell me everything from the beginning."

I did just that. When I finished, she looked more confused. "That doesn't make sense. I don't understand why they just couldn't wait a few days. It's entirely possible the hubbub would've died down."

"You'd have to ask them."

"Sure. Tell me who to ask." Cally's expression was serious. "No, really, I'll place a call. You know who my father is. He's a big advertiser. He might be able to help."

I shook my head. "I don't want that. He's done enough for me."

Cally was incredulous. "What has he done for you?"

"He gave me this house for half the rent. He did that for you, and I'm grateful."

"So what? He's rich. It's not as if he's going without for you."

"You realize I have to ask him to break my lease? I can't afford this place now that I don't have a job."

"No, I don't realize that." Cally folded her arms across her chest. "I'll talk to him. He'll be okay if you need a month or two to find a job."

"That's not fair to him."

"I'll handle it."

It was a nice offer, far more than I expected, but I couldn't accept it. "I'm an adult, Cally. I'm supposed to pay my own bills. I can't just take advantage of your father because we're friends."

"You're not taking advantage of him."

I shot her a dubious look.

"You're not," she insisted. "I'm taking advantage of him, and it's going to be fine. He likes you. He says you're the most stable friend I've ever had and he hopes you'll rub off on me. Trust me, you staying here benefits us all."

"I doubt he'll think I'm all that stable when he hears I've lost my only source of income because I fell for a charming smile and a perfect set of dimples."

"Grady's dimples are divine," Cally agreed. "As for my

father, he'll be fine. In fact, I think he can help your work situation. I'll call him. He'll want to help."

"It's over. I'm done there and you know it."

"That doesn't mean you're done here." Cally was adamant. "Just...give me a little time. I'm sure I can find you a job."

"It's my job to find me a job."

"But you'll be bad at it. I have a head for these things." She tapped her temple. "Where is your phone?"

"I...don't...know. I didn't pay attention when I came home. I just climbed into bed and...rested."

"You mean you hid." Cally shot me a "Don't bother arguing" look as she got up from the bed. Her eyes were intense as she searched the floor. A few seconds later, she got comfortable again. This time she had my purse. "I bet it's in here." She dug around inside without asking for permission and came back with my phone. "Wow. Looks like you were popular this afternoon."

"What?" I moved closer to her, and then because it was there, I rested my head on her shoulder as I studied my phone screen. "That's a lot of missed calls," I said finally.

"It is," she agreed. "I believe there are forty here from Grady alone."

"I doubt he called."

Cally arched a challenging eyebrow. "That's his number, right?"

She was right. Not only had Grady called once I left the office, he'd done so incessantly. "He probably wanted to apologize for using me."

"Or he wanted you to get your head out of your ass and stop blaming him," Cally muttered.

"Excuse me?" This wasn't the time to be annoyed with my best friend, but she was the only one here. "Human Resources warned him repeatedly, but he still chased after me. Annabelle said he wanted to use what I had going for his own gain. In fact, she told me that after the first piece we did together. Maybe I should've listened."

"To Annabelle?" Cally's expression told me exactly what she thought about that suggestion. "Great idea. You should've listened to the woman who has gone out of her way to torture you since you joined the staff."

"I don't know that I would say 'torture,'" I grumbled.

"I would. She's been after you from the start. She cut you out of lunches, talked about you behind your back, and was disagreeable at every turn. Want to know why?"

"I thought it was just her personality."

Cally barked out a laugh. "It probably *was* her personality, but there was another reason."

"What?"

"Grady."

I blinked several times. "What about him?"

"Oh, you're so stupid." She tapped the tip of my nose. "It's a good thing you're pretty, because sometimes your IQ sinks through the storm drains or something. Pay attention." Her touch turned mean when she thwacked my forehead. "She's in love with Grady. You realize that, right?"

I was officially dumbfounded. "She hates Grady. She warned me away from him several times."

"She didn't warn you away from him out of the goodness of her heart. Buy a clue. She wanted you away from him because she was determined to reclaim him. Sure, part of it was because she's a disagreeable bitch, but the other part was because she saw what you've never been able to see."

"What's that?" My voice was barely a whisper.

"Grady is in love with you."

"No." I shook my head. "He used me to get ahead at work."

"That's just your insecurity talking. I knew the second I

saw you together that he had legitimate feelings for you. It's written all over his face whenever he looks at you."

"He dated several women at work and ignored me."

"Because you were the one that mattered," Cally fired back. "You're so blind to what he's feeling I'm surprised you can see anything. Good grief. You told me yourself he talked to you every day. He didn't always say something smart, but that's because you made him nervous.

"What he wanted more than anything was for you to like him," she continued. "He dated those other women to distract himself. He might've even dated them in an effort to make you jealous. When he realized that wouldn't work, he became more direct.

"I'm not saying he's smart—because Lord knows that boy needs a good kick in the pants to find his brain—but he's been in love with you for quite some time. You just can't see it because you're you."

I stared at her for a long time. Could that be true? My heart wanted it to be true, but my head wouldn't even consider the possibility. "No. He got what he wanted. His job is safe. Now I'm gone and he can move on to his next victim."

"Oh, you are the worst." My reflexes were dulled from heavy sleep—at least that's what I told myself—so I didn't move fast enough to avoid Cally's finger flick to the forehead. "Get up."

"To do what?" I demanded. "I'm jobless and soon I'll be homeless."

"Oh, you're so dramatic." Her eye roll was pronounced. "I said get up. You need to brush your hair and fix your makeup. We're going out."

"Did you hear me? I lost my job. I have no money to go out."

"I'll pay."

It was always so easy for her. She had a job she loved and a father who loved to spoil her. I had neither, which made me want to wallow. Why couldn't she see that? "I'm going to stay here."

"No, you're not." She vehemently shook her head. "I'm going to snap you out of it. I can't do it here when you're sleeping in your sex sheets and feeling sorry for yourself. We need a change of environment. We're going to Moxie's and you don't get a say in the matter."

"But...what happened to me feeling sorry for myself?"

"You've done enough of that. Now we have to come up with a plan to fix your life."

"What if there is no way to fix it?" That was my biggest worry. I was going to turn into the loser my mother always knew I would be.

"I don't accept the question," Cally replied. "You're smart and fun. You're driven...your day in bed notwithstanding. There's a solution out there. We just need to find it."

I wished I had half of her energy and faith. "I want to feel sorry for myself. I think I've earned it."

"Well, I won't allow that. We're heading out. I won't take no for an answer."

And just like that, I had no control over my own life. Again. This day just kept getting worse.

Twenty-Six

I refused to get dressed up for the bar, opting for denim capris and an oversized T-shirt. I wouldn't have bothered running a brush through my hair if Cally hadn't insisted. She also attacked me with a washcloth to the face and suggested I put some makeup on. I politely declined.

"You look as if you just came from a funeral," she complained as we entered Moxie's Cantina. "You could've put in the bare minimum of effort."

"I believe I did." I glanced around. The bar was busy but not packed. I pointed to a table in the rear corner. "Let's sit there."

Cally made a face. "It's right by the bathroom."

"So?"

"You know I hate sitting next to the bathroom."

"Well, I don't want to sit anywhere else. If we're in the middle of the bar, we'll be visible from the street should anybody look through the window."

Cally didn't bother to hide her impatience. "So?"

"I don't want to see anybody."

"You mean you don't want Grady to walk by, see us, and make things better."

"He can't make things better."

"So you've said – repeatedly."

I held out my hands. "It's either that table or I go home."

"You're not going home."

"You can't stop me from going home."

Cally didn't look convinced. "Did I ever tell you I was on the wrestling team in high school? The boys' wrestling team. I even won awards."

I narrowed my eyes. I truly believed Cally could do anything she put her mind to, but wrestling seemed a stretch. "You weren't on the wrestling team," I said.

"I was. I wrestled with boys all the time in high school."

"That's not the same as being on the wrestling team. Come on. I know darned well you would never wear one of those outfits. You think spandex is for Quentin Tarantino-themed parties and nothing else."

Cally held my gaze for a long time—perhaps too long—and then let loose a sigh. "Fine. I wasn't on the team. They would've totally wanted me, though."

"Of course, they would." I moved to the table hidden in the alcove by the bathrooms. "Who wouldn't want you?"

"I was an excellent wrestler. All the boys told me I was their favorite."

"I don't want to hear about you and the boys." I was adamant, to the point I was back to being anti-relationship. "Let's order drinks."

"That's the plan." Cally raised her hand and motioned for Moxie.

The bartender was all smiles when she arrived. "Ladies. What are you doing over here?"

"We just want a little quiet," I replied.

Cally made a face and rolled her eyes. "Shay is in hiding, so apparently I'm forced to hide too. Do you have those yummy smoking drinks on the menu tonight? I would love the Witch's Brew."

Moxie bobbed her head. "We do." Her eyes were probing when they landed on me. "You okay?" She slapped her hand to my forehead before I could respond. "You're not sick, are you?"

"I'm fine," I assured her as I gently nudged her hand away. "Just been a long day. I'll have a Witch's Brew too."

Moxie didn't look convinced. "A long day?"

"She got fired," Cally volunteered.

"Cally!" I wanted to kill her.

Cally barreled forward as if I hadn't said a word. "The office troll reported her and Grady for being in a relationship."

"I don't understand." Moxie looked baffled. "Why is that a bad thing? Also...why is this the first I'm hearing about this? I knew you two were going to get together. I have a bet with Gus. He totally owes me an hour-long massage."

"You had a bet with Gus?" I didn't know if I was mortified or impressed at her observational skills. "Why would you assume Grady and I were going to get together?"

"I saw you interact – under this very roof, if you remember correctly." Moxie was blasé. "You two had chemistry coming out of your butts."

"That's much better than the stuff that normally comes out of your butt," Cally offered helpfully.

I glared at her.

Moxie let loose a nervous snicker. "Let's not fight, huh? Adding an argument to the mix won't help. I don't understand why you got fired."

"Office relationships are frowned upon," Cally explained. She was apparently not interested in letting me tell my own story. "Grady supposedly is the reason for the rule. He might've broken a few hearts, including the one that belongs to the Human Resources director."

"Uh-oh." Moxie looked distressed. "How is Grady taking being fired?"

"Grady wasn't fired," I replied, hoping I sounded breezy rather than bitter.

"But...why were you fired if he wasn't?"

"It was explained to me that the female fans like him more. They couldn't risk getting rid of him because of the advertisers."

"Oh, what a load of crap." Moxie's fury was on full display. "We're advertisers. We'll talk to them."

I shook my head. "I appreciate the offer, but I can't go back there. Not now."

"This is all because of Annabelle," Cally groused. "She's always been jealous of Shay. She's been working against her from the start. It's not just professional jealousy. She's hot for Grady, and this is her way of eliminating the competition."

"I still can't believe this happened." Moxie rested a sympathetic hand on my shoulder. "I'm so sorry. How did Grady react?"

I bristled at the question. "He kept his job. He was fine with it."

"Oh, now let's not go making up stories," Cally admonished. "You said he was upset."

"He still kept his job."

"Oh, geez." Cally wrinkled her nose. "Can you make her Witch's Brew a double? She's being a real pill and I need her to loosen up a bit. Her head isn't in a good place."

Moxie hesitated. "Do you think alcohol is going to solve that problem?" she asked.

"Oh, it'll make things worse," Cally confirmed. "But she needs to wallow. She needs to get it all out of her system.

Tomorrow is earmarked for a hangover and some serious pouting. After that, we'll start fixing things."

"Ah." Moxie bobbed her head in understanding. "Let me ask around about jobs. Shay turned out to be a whiz at promotion. There might be something I can come up with."

"Awesome." Cally looked thrilled. "I'm going to put my father on it too. He knows everybody."

"Does he know the repo man?" I asked. "I'm sure that the repo man will be coming for me."

"See, her head is a mess." Cally shook her head. "Honey, I hate to break it to you, but you have nothing worth repossessing. My father isn't going to kick you out of your place. I won't allow it. Besides, he's not as bad as most people think. He likes you. He'll want to help."

"We'll all help," Moxie reassured me. "You're far too talented to lose. We just need to find a job that's the right fit for you."

She made it sound so easy. "I think I just want to drink."

"Of course, you do." Sympathy practically rolled off her in waves as she patted my arm. "Getting drunk tonight is a good idea. Once you purge all this anger and sadness, we can start making things better. It will work out, you'll see."

"Sure. It will all magically get better."

"Magic is all how you look at it." Moxie insisted. "I didn't believe in magic when I got here but look at me now. I have a man I love more than anything, and he's great."

Gus, cutting behind Moxie, gave her a playful swat on the rear. "Thank you, baby. I feel the same way about you."

Moxie beamed at him as he headed toward the bar. "I have a job I love. I have roots, and I didn't think I would ever have roots again. I got everything I could've wanted…and that's going to happen for you too. Just wait and see."

Unbidden, an image of Grady's smiling face appeared in my mind's eye, causing a lump to form in my throat. I brutally swallowed it. He'd used me, just like he'd used the others in the office. He was all about getting ahead. He didn't care about those he left behind in his wake on his way to world domination.

"It's going to be okay," Moxie replied in a soft voice. "Don't let this get you down."

It was difficult to be anything other than down. Before I could point that out, Cally went ramrod straight in her chair. She stared at the door.

"What are you doing?" When I swiveled, my heart lodged in my throat. Grady was cutting a swath through the tables, scanning the faces. I tried to shrink in my chair in the hope he wouldn't see me, but as if he sensed me, his eyes sought—and found—mine.

"I've been calling you all day," he snapped, his tone accusatory. "Why haven't you been picking up?"

Was he kidding? "I don't think I have anything to say," I replied in a soft voice barely audible over the noise of the bar.

"There's plenty to say." Grady planted his hands on his hips and glanced between Moxie and Cally. "I don't suppose I could have a few minutes alone with Shay?"

"Of course," Moxie responded.

"Not in a million years," Cally fired back. She reminded me of a dragon, she was so annoyed. The only thing missing was fire coming out of her nostrils. "You have a lot of explaining to do."

"I know." Grady held up his hands in supplication. "I need to do my explaining to Shay."

"She's not in the best headspace." Cally was having none of it. "You need to explain to me by proxy and then I'll see if I want to help you explain to her."

Grady worked his jaw, annoyed. Then he moved his eyes to me, and there was despair there. "Okay." He lowered himself into the chair on my left. "We'll do it your way."

"That is the way I like to do things," Cally replied. "To start with, I'm hoping you have an excuse for being a man whore."

Grady's forehead wrinkled. "I'm not a man whore."

"Oh, really?" Cally asked. "So that wasn't you that romanced the Human Resources woman and Shay's archnemesis and caused her to lose her job? Seriously, you must be magic in bed to have all these women chasing you. I guess that means you're not hung like a crayon. I can't tell you what a relief that is, because there are so many hot guys out there walking around with spaghetti noodles in their pants."

I was mortified. Grady, however, merely looked intrigued.

"I don't really want to talk about my performance in bed," he said. "I can safely say I don't suffer from the spaghetti syndrome. I can't tell you how much I want to hear more about that, but it will have to wait.

"As for Lacey, I didn't sleep with her," he continued, fixing his imploring gaze on me. "She asked me out for coffee. I agreed because...well...I'm a moron."

"A complete and total moron," Cally agreed.

Grady ignored her. He refused to tear his gaze from my face, which was making me distinctly uncomfortable. "I didn't like her. I never liked her."

"That doesn't make it better," I said. "I didn't even know you dated her. How many women in the office did you date?"

He hesitated and then growled. "Too many. But I didn't want any of them. I was attracted to you right from the start, but you wouldn't give me the time of day."

"Grady, that doesn't make it better," I said. "Hearing I'm the last in a long line of women you dated to get ahead doesn't make me feel special."

"I didn't date you to get ahead." Frustration clouded Grady's handsome features. "I've always liked you for you. That's why I was constantly bugging you. I figured any attention, even negative attention, was better than you not knowing I was alive."

"I knew you were alive." I remained focused on the table. "I always knew." He looked pained when I finally managed to look in his direction again. "Do you know what I saw when I looked at you?"

"A man whore," Cally offered in an aside meant for Grady's ears only.

"Thank you, Cally." Grady sent her a grim smile before turning back to me.

"I saw a guy who needed attention," I said. "I didn't see anything of substance because you wouldn't let me see that side of you."

"I didn't understand what I was doing," he explained. "I just...wanted you to notice me. I didn't realize that you had noticed me. I know that I went about it the wrong way. I just thought if you believed other people found me desirable you might decide I was too."

"You could've just asked me out," I noted. "You didn't have to play games."

"He's a man," Cally said sagely. "They're trained to play games. Television and movies are the teachers and they're powerless to do the sensible thing because it's the opposite of what they've been shown."

"I don't want to agree with Cally," Grady said. "You have no idea how much I don't want to agree with her, but she's not wrong. I thought you would eventually look at me and realize what you'd been missing. After seeing you in that ugly bridesmaid fashion show, I knew I'd been reading you wrong.

"You're not like the other women I've dated," he continued. "I recognized that from the start and yet I treated you like the other women. That's on me. I never cared about any of them." He raised a hand to silence me when I opened my mouth. "Let me finish," he pleaded. "Just...let me get this out."

I nodded. I owed him that.

"I know that telling you I didn't care about the other women I dated doesn't instill faith in me," he said. He looked to be choosing his words carefully, something I'd rarely seen him do. "I know that dating them to get your attention was worse than wrong. It was disrespectful to them and to you. It goes back to that idiot thing.

"I only ever wanted you and I thought acting out to get your attention would work," he continued. "The thing is, I didn't realize I was acting out at the time. Hindsight makes that obvious. When it was going down, I convinced myself it was okay to distract myself because I couldn't have what I really wanted.

"The past few weeks with you have been the best of my life. I've learned so much, and more than that, I've realized I want to be a better man. Not just for you, but for me too. I realize that I've let myself down as much as you.

"Here's the thing, though," he said, grabbing my hand and holding it between both of his. "I need you to give me a chance to make this up to you. I know I can."

It was only when he said it that I realized I wanted it to be true. "I don't...." What was I supposed to say? I was still angry. Worse than that, I was hurt. My mind was too clouded to make that decision now.

"Did you quit?" Cally asked.

"What?" Grady was confused.

"Did you quit your job?" Cally's voice was level, but there was a challenge in her eyes. "You kept your job, but Shay lost hers...and in embarrassing fashion. I'm assuming you quit in protest."

Grady's cheeks flooded with color. "I didn't, but I will. I

didn't really think about it. I was too surprised by what was happening."

"You were too surprised." Cally rolled her eyes. "Wow. I can't believe you just said that with a straight face."

"I have a plan," Grady insisted. "I can't quit until I enact my plan."

"Oh, you have a plan." Cally got to her feet. "Let's go."

For what felt like the fiftieth time that day, I was surprised. "What?"

"Let's go." Cally was firm as she extended her hand for me to take. "We're not listening to this."

"Where are you going?" Grady demanded when I allowed Cally to pull me to my feet.

"You're not saying what needs to be said," Cally replied. "You're not making things better. You're trying, I'll give you that, but you've sacrificed nothing in this, and Shay has lost everything. Don't you see that?"

"I said I was trying to fix it," Grady growled.

"Whatever." Cally's tone was dismissive now. "Come back when you've fixed things. Until then, you're banished."

Flabbergasted disbelief washed over Grady's face. "Banished? You can't banish me."

"I just did." Cally was matter-of-fact. "I spent the better part of the last three hours telling Shay you were a good guy and that she was misreading what happened. I was wrong."

"I'm not a bad guy."

"No, but you're not ready for her yet. She deserves the world. You can't give it to her. We're at an impasse until you pull your head out of your ass. And I don't want to see you until you've figured things out."

"But...I'm going to fix things." Grady was desperate when he reached for me, but Cally used her hip to nudge him away. "Don't take her from me."

That was enough to break me out of my reverie. "She's not

taking me. You lost me. I just...can't right now. It's like you don't even understand what happened."

"I do understand." Grady's voice cracked. "I have something in the works. I swear to you that it's going to work out. I just need you to have faith in me."

"I'm all out of faith." I felt numb. "I started the day so happy. I thought things were going to work out. Now it's all gone."

"I'm not gone." Grady was vehement. "I'll never be gone."

"And yet you're not really here. Cally is right. You don't get it. The sad thing is, I'm not sure you ever will." With that, I swept toward the door. I was over this day and wanted to go back to hiding, at least for what remained of the worst day of my life.

"This isn't over, Shay," he called to my back. "I really am going to fix this."

"I hope you do." I meant it. "For both our sakes."

I swept out the door without looking back.

Twenty-Seven

The sky opened up during the walk home. That wasn't unusual for New Orleans. The heat built during the day, drawing moisture from the Gulf, and storms frequently broke in the afternoon. But this rain didn't stop for a solid week. It was as if the heavens were mourning right along with me.

When the skies finally cleared, I was in a better place. My house was clean and organized—Cally helped me with that—and I had a job interview. A consortium of local bars had formed a business oversight committee, and I was being considered to run the public relations department. It wasn't something I'd ever considered. Heck, I wasn't certain if I was qualified. Moxie was a member of the group, though, and she placed my name in contention. The money was good. The hours would be set. I was ready to sell myself.

I dressed in my best suit and headed out thirty minutes early. After a week of rain, it was nice to see the sun. It was already steamy when I left the house, but I didn't mind. This was New Orleans, after all. Heat was part of the package, and

I'd come to the conclusion that I loved the overall package. I didn't want to leave the city.

I swung my little briefcase satchel as I walked. It was a gift from Cally, who was determined to make sure I didn't leave town. If I hadn't already known she was the best friend I would ever have, it was impossible to ignore now. She'd been with me through every step of my transition. She scoured job boards, fielded calls, and helped me shop for an interview suit. She'd been invaluable...and was prepared to celebrate—or commiserate if things went poorly—after my interview.

As for Grady, I hadn't seen him. He'd texted incessantly for three days and then stopped communicating. I heard through the grapevine he was still working for *The Bugle*, but I refused to go to the website and check out his pieces. It would hurt too much. Besides, that life was gone. I was emotionally removed from it, if not him. It was better to make a clean break.

The interview was held in an office on Royal Street. I was early so I distracted myself by looking in the kitschy shop windows. One of them, a jewelry store, sold a series of bracelets I adored. They were made of stamped metal, colorful stones in the shape of hearts dangling all around, and I made a mental promise to buy myself one if I got the job. I wanted something to remember the day I took my destiny into my own hands.

After fifteen minutes of window shopping, I let myself into the building and smiled at the perky secretary behind the desk. I gave her my name and then sat in the waiting area as she directed. My nerves were shot, but I forced myself to sit upright. I wanted to paint a professional picture, and that meant acting as if I wasn't afraid to be in a room with a bunch of powerful bar owners. I figured if I could convince them it was true, eventually I would convince myself.

"Ms. Archer?" a male voice asked from the hallway beyond the lobby, jolting me back to reality.

I hopped to my feet and turned. I had a smile at the ready for the well-dressed man who regarded me with friendly interest. "Hello." I shook his hand firmly. "I'm Shay Archer."

"Gerald Bishop. I own Two Beers and a Beignet."

"Oh, I love that place." I beamed. "You have those skull Pilsner glasses, right? Your place is really cool."

"That's me." He led me down the hallway. "I want to say, before we get started, that I loved the pieces you were doing for *The Bugle*."

My insides went rigid. It was a compliment, but I couldn't help feeling that something else would come of the statement. It turned out I was right.

"Moxie Stone told me what happened to you there and I have to say I'm disappointed."

I was glad I'd foregone breakfast.

"I expected more from Edith Felders," he continued. He was either oblivious to the change in my demeanor or putting on a good face to pretend he hadn't noticed. "What happened to you was unfair. I want you to know that we don't play games like that here."

"I've learned my lesson about dating at work," I offered when I found my voice. "That won't happen again."

He chuckled. "I didn't mean that. We don't care who you date as long as it doesn't affect your work. I'm talking about the way they made you compete to keep your job and then pulled the rug out from under you. That will never happen here."

"Oh." I was taken aback by his forthcoming nature. "Well, that's good."

"I just don't understand how the management at *The Bugle* thought that was appropriate," he said. "Everybody has heard about it."

My stomach sank again. "Everybody?" That didn't bode well for my job-hunting prospects.

"Yes, and we're all disgusted you were so unceremoniously dumped," he continued. "We just hope the paper's new owner fixes things. We hear he has grand plans to restore the newspaper to its former glory."

I almost tripped on the rug. "I didn't realize *The Bugle* had been sold."

Gerald nodded. "Two days ago. The formal paperwork is being signed today. Apparently, the new owner doesn't want to drag things out. He was in the midst of negotiating when the story about you came out. He rammed things through after that."

I had no idea what to make of that. "Well, I hope the people still there make out okay. It was a rough transition."

"I'm sure they'll be fine. I heard the new owner is bringing much of the staff back, even adding to it."

That would've been the best news in the world a week ago. Now I merely offered up a flat smile. *The Bugle* was no longer my concern. "I wish them well."

Gerald's eyes crinkled at the corners. "Don't worry about the interview. We want you to be yourself. This is New Orleans."

"I think I know what you're saying." I grinned. "You want the Shay from the videos."

"We love Shay from the videos. We just want you to be you."

"I'll do my best."

He held open the door to a conference room. "I think everything will work out fine."

THE INTERVIEW LASTED TWO HOURS. Thankfully, I was only a nervous wreck for the first fifteen minutes. After that, I managed to settle. By the time I left, I felt as if I knew the four people sitting in on the interview...and I liked them all. They said they had three candidates left and would get back to me the following week. I thanked them and left. I thought I would head straight back to my house and change.

The world had other plans for me.

"How did it go?" Cally practically had me jumping out of my skin as she detached from the outside of the building and planted herself in my path.

"Don't do that," I complained when I caught my breath. "Make a noise next time."

Amusement flitted through Cally's eyes. "I'll get a bell for next time."

"Good idea."

"So, how did it go?" She rubbed her hands together, as if anticipating a juicy porterhouse to appear out of thin air.

"It went well." I beamed at her, the earlier anxiety now gone. "I was in there two hours. I think that's a good sign."

"I should say so. Tell me about it."

I did just that as we meandered down Royal Street. Cally made the decisions on our route. She listened with rapt attention, and before I realized what was happening, she nudged me into one of the nicer restaurants that bordered Jackson Square.

"What are we doing?" I asked.

"We're having a celebratory lunch. Don't worry. It's on me."

I was exasperated. "There's nothing to celebrate yet. I won't know until next week."

"Yeah, I've decided to celebrate now." Cally's smile was impish. "I know you're going to get what you want. Can't you just let the hope in a little and celebrate with me?"

I couldn't deny that face. "Sure. I mean...you are buying."

"Awesome." She led me into Tableau and requested a

balcony table. The restaurant was about half a block from the park but still offered a lovely view. We settled at the table and accepted our menus from the waitress. I waited until she'd left with our drink orders to speak.

"So the head guy interviewing me was Gerald Bishop," I started.

"My father knows him. He owns that beer and beignets place." Cally said. "He's supposed to be a good guy. I'll have my father call and pressure him."

My mouth dropped open. "Or you could not do that."

"Why wouldn't I?"

"Because I would like to see if I can get the job on my own."

"Ugh. You're such a stickler when it comes to cronyism." She pressed her finger into my cheek and grinned. "I'll consider it. I can't make promises until I've given it some thought. At the very least, my father can place a call to see who you're up against. That alone might be enough to tip the scales in your favor."

Obviously, she didn't understand when I said I wanted to get the job on my own. I decided to let it go. "I've only eaten here once, but I can't remember what I had. What's good?"

"Everything."

"What's especially good?"

Cally pursed her lips as she studied the menu. "I'm getting the pan-roasted duck."

"As in quack-quack?"

"As in yum-yum."

"I've never eaten duck. I don't believe I want to start on a day when my stomach is tied in knots. I think I'll have the mushroom risotto."

"That's good too."

The server returned with our drinks and took our orders. I had to wait to unload my gossip until she was gone.

"So, as I was saying, Gerald told me something interesting," I said. "He said someone swooped in and bought *The Bugle*. Apparently, they're going to be bringing staff back."

Cally's eyebrows drew together. "You're not thinking of going back?"

I shook my head. "No. That door is closed."

"Are they bringing back the print product?"

I shrugged. "I don't know. I hope so for the workers, but I didn't ask."

Cally studied my face. "Would you consider going back if Edith and that nasty Human Resources lady weren't there any longer?"

"No." I meant it. "I can't go back. Grady's there."

"And Annabelle."

"I could ignore her easily enough. I let her get to me for far too long. It was a waste of time. But I don't want to see Grady."

Sympathy replaced suspicion on Cally's face. "Has he tried to get in contact with you since that first day and the meeting at Moxie's?"

I had to hand it to Cally. She always got to the heart of matters. "I think it's best we go our separate ways and forget about one another."

"Do you think that's possible?"

"You're the one who says anything is possible."

"And I believe that. I want to know what you believe."

"I believe Grady is a good man who made some bad choices." I'd given this a lot of thought. "He was immature and did the wrong thing several times. I knew that going in. I should've followed my head."

"But you followed your heart," she added. "You never follow your heart, but you did with Grady. I always follow my heart and it almost always ends poorly. You always want to make the smart decisions, and you did it again this time."

"Yeah, well...." I held out my hands and offered up a rueful smile. "That's me. I'm a thinker. Perhaps if I hadn't lost my head things wouldn't have worked out this way."

"You mean getting a fabulous new job."

I snickered. "I mean that I wouldn't still miss him." I had no idea where that declaration had come from. I'd been careful not to talk about Grady with her because I didn't want to acknowledge the heartbreak. Now, here I was volunteering it to her. What was wrong with me?

"It's okay to love him, Shay," she said in a low voice. "You don't have to erase him from your life."

"What other option do I have?"

"You could forgive him."

"I'm not sure that there's anything to forgive. Yeah, he made some dumb choices."

"Super dumb."

"He never approached it from malice. He didn't want to hurt me. He didn't want to hurt them. I believe that with my whole heart."

"Then maybe you should give him another chance." Earnest hope stared back at me when I met her eyes. "I know I told him he couldn't come back until he fixed things, but I didn't realize that I was punishing you as well as him. If it hurts too much to be away from him, give him a second chance."

"Won't it hurt more to give him another chance and lose him a second time?"

"What makes you think you'll lose him again?"

"Because...it seems inevitable. He's still there, still chugging along. He's seemingly forgotten about me. Maybe it's best to let him go."

"He hasn't forgotten about you," Cally scoffed. "He's in love with you."

My heart skipped. "I...don't think so."

"You may not want to believe it, but it's true. He's totally in love with you. I think he's been in love with you for a long time, and that's why he made all those stupid decisions. He didn't know what to do with those feelings."

"That's all well and good, but...I just can't think about that. I need to focus on my future. I don't want to be homeless."

Anger flashed in Cally's eyes. "I told you my father won't evict you. I won't let that happen. Heck, he's already agreed to give you as much time as you need to find a job. Let that go."

I couldn't. If I went too long without a job, I would have to leave the house. I couldn't take advantage of the kindness of others. "We'll see how it goes." I forced a smile for her benefit. "I can make it two months. Hopefully it won't take that long to find a job."

"It won't." Cally's smile returned. "You'll have job offers coming out of your ears before you know it."

"Oh, well, that sounds fun." I flicked my eyes to the Square. It always bustled with activity, but today it looked especially busy. "Looks like they're setting up another runway," I said. "I wonder if they're having another fashion show."

"We'll check it out when we're done here." Cally glanced in that direction. "It might be fun."

"Sure."

"Just one thing before I let you successfully change the subject," she added, ignoring my exaggerated sigh. "True love doesn't come along very often." She was deadly serious and refused to let me avert my gaze. "It's a gift, miraculous even, but it's never perfect.

"I don't think Grady ever pretended to be perfect," she continued. "He's a work in progress. The thing is, he wants to do the work."

"How do you know that? Last I checked, you were insisting that we keep him at arm's length."

"Maybe I changed my mind."

"Maybe I haven't. I don't want to be hurt again. I'm starting a new adventure. It might be best to let the past go—except for you, of course—and look to the future."

"That's what I want for you. I think Grady is your future."

"It hurts too much to think of the past. I have to let him go. Besides, he's already let me go. I bet he's already romancing someone else in the office."

"I think you're wrong, but I'll let this one play out." Cally leaned back in her chair. "Let's enjoy our lunch, celebrate your awesome interview, and then see what's going on in the Square."

I beamed at her. "Sounds like the perfect NOLA day."

"Yeah, it's going to be an interesting day...no matter what."

Twenty-Eight

The noise from Jackson Square was deafening as we made our way down a side street. A crowd had begun to build, and we had to zigzag through it to see what was happening. I wasn't surprised to find another runway had indeed been set up. The fact that Bebe was running it again did throw me for a loop.

"That's Bebe Beignet." I pointed for Cally's benefit.

"That's who got you to dress up in that ugly bridesmaid dress last time, right?" Cally looked impressed. "I'm loving that beaded gown he's rocking." She stilled. "Wait...he or she? I don't want to screw it up."

"He. I asked." I understood her dilemma. "Let's see what he's doing." I tugged on Cally's arm. She was eager to follow.

Bebe looked up just as we reached him. "Hey, girlfriend." His grin was wide and it popped because of his sparkly red lipstick. "I was hoping to see you again. We have an outfit ready for you." He disappeared inside the tent before I could tell him that wouldn't be necessary. He reemerged holding what looked to be a costume from a *Gone With the Wind* theater production. "Get dressed." He shoved the frock into my hands.

"Oh, no." I shook my head. "We're just here to watch."

"No." Bebe was having none of it. "You're on in ten minutes."

"I'm not working at *The Bugle* any longer." It wasn't as hard to admit as it had been a week earlier. I was becoming accustomed to my new reality. "I don't need any footage for my blog."

Bebe shrugged. "So?" he challenged. "What does that matter? This is for charity."

"I know."

"It's a good charity."

"It is." I felt guilty. "I got fired. I'm just not in a great headspace right now."

"She's getting better," Cally offered. "She's no longer spending long stretches of time in bed dreaming about the one that got away." She was curious as she eyed the dress. "Can I play?"

Bebe beamed at her. "Absolutely. We have an extra lilac dress with your name written all over it. With that chest, whew! You'll rock the house."

Cally's smile was warm and lovely. "Awesome."

"You need to get your friend to dress up too." Bebe was adamant.

"No problem." Cally took the dress from him. "Give us ten minutes."

"I'm not doing it," I insisted as Cally dragged me into the tent. "You can't make me."

"It will be fun." Cally grinned when she saw the other dress hanging from a hook. It looked as if a lilac bush had thrown up eighty times and this was the only thing salvageable from the mess. "Perfect."

"Are you kidding me?" I was at my limit. "I'm not doing it.

I only did it the first time for work. There's no reason to do it now."

"What about because it's fun?" Cally challenged. "You told me that the ugly bridesmaid dress fashion show was one of the most fun pieces you'd ever done. Why not repeat that experience, only this time because you want to, not because you have to?"

I hated that she had a point. Absolutely freaking hated it! "Fine." I took the dress from her and stared down at it. The bodice looked a bit low for my comfort zone. "Why can't they have a pretty dress fashion show? I would get up for that."

"Because that's not fun. Now...get dressed."

It took me the full ten minutes to tug on the huge dress and get it situated. Bebe entered the tent long enough to fuss with my hair. Then he gave me a terrific shove toward the runway as I was still trying to slip into the shoes.

"I'm not ready," I complained. "You go first, Cally."

"I can't."

"Why?" She was acting weird. She'd been slightly off all morning.

"Because your partner is already walking out. You need to hurry to meet him," Cally replied.

"My partner?" I was beyond confused.

Cally didn't take the time to explain. Instead, she shoved me through the opening—with a little help from Bebe—and before I realized it, I was in front of the crowd.

"Work it, girl!" Bebe prodded with a great amount of exasperation when I didn't move. The sheer number of eyes focused on me had me freezing in place. "You look like a big pile of pink Pepto Bismol. Freaking go."

I started walking. Out of desperation, I put a bit of sway in my hips. The circumference of the dress was so wide I had to keep looking down to make sure I didn't trip. I was almost to the midway point when I realized someone was already standing there...and it was a man.

The oxygen rushed out of my lungs when I saw Grady. His long hair was pulled back in a ponytail, and he wore a suit of crushed velvet. His white socks went to mid-calf, and the shirt under his blazer was white and ruffled.

"What the ...?"

He graced me with a huge smile and then lifted his hand. He was holding a microphone. "Welcome to the first—and maybe never to be repeated—charity bash for The Rainbow Confederacy of New Orleans," Grady said into the microphone.

The audience roared their approval.

"I'm Grady Dalton, and I'll be your emcee this afternoon. You might be asking yourself what I'm doing here—I've been asking myself that since I woke up this morning—but I feel this is the place it truly started."

"Where what started?" I asked dumbly. There was no way Grady could hear me over the crowd.

"As everybody here probably knows, I'm with *The Bourbon Street Bugle*. I used to be a news reporter. You know, crime and political stuff. That was my great love. Recently, however, after a change in style, I started doing fun pieces with my co-worker Shay Archer." He gestured to me. "It was something we stumbled upon together, and we were having a great time...until about a week ago."

Was he really putting all of this out there for everybody to hear? Why would he even consider doing this? When I glanced into the crowd, I got my answer. Grant was there, in the center of everything, filming Grady with his phone.

"I like having a good time," Grady continued as he gestured toward his outfit. "I even like embarrassing myself, which should be obvious. Shay was a little more reticent when it came to things like this, and yet she embraced it fully. She embraced me fully, which is what I always wanted."

He took a breath before speaking again. "I'm going to tell you a little secret." He winked at the crowd. "I started at *The Bugle* the day Shay started. We interviewed on the same day. I fell in love with her that day."

I thought my heart was going to beat out of my chest. "What are you doing?" I demanded.

He slid his eyes to me but didn't respond. "I didn't believe in love at first sight until that day. Even after, I thought I was imagining the way I felt around her. I wasn't. Unfortunately for me, she didn't feel the same way, so I had to win her over."

I was panicked when I glanced over my shoulder and found Bebe and Cally standing together in front of the tent. They didn't look surprised at all by what was happening. "You did this," I snapped. "You knew."

"Shut up and listen to him, Shay," Cally ordered. "You might just get everything you ever wanted."

I was mortified. I didn't want any more relationship drama playing out in front of people. This was not the way it was supposed to work.

"Now, this won't come as a surprise to anybody who has ever met a man who is clueless," Grady continued. "I messed up winning her over. I thought that irritating her was the way to go. That's right, I pretended I was in fifth grade and we were on a playground. I'm betting you can guess how that went."

The crowd laughed appreciatively. Some even clapped.

"When that didn't work, I decided to make her jealous by dating women in the office. I wasn't looking for a relationship. I'd already decided that she was the one for me even though she had no idea. But I thought if she saw I was with other people she would know I was desirable. Who knows how that went?"

A guy in the audience shot his hand in the air. "Not well!"

"Worse than that," Grady countered. "It was a complete and total disaster. Not only did I date women I had no interest in, but the one woman I was interested in didn't notice. I was deciding how to regroup when circumstances changed and Shay and I stumbled onto the same assignment one day. That assignment was right here in Jackson Square, and it was very similar to what's taking place today.

"She wasn't sure about me when we first partnered, but I was determined to win her over," he continued. "What's funny is that I decided it was best to be myself and to stop forcing things. I figured she would come around to my charms eventually. I mean...who wouldn't want this?" He gestured toward his outfit and wiggled his hips in a suggestive manner.

The crowd erupted into applause.

"It worked." His grin was wide but there was sadness in his eyes when they locked with mine. "She got to know the real me and even liked me. Then I screwed it up again."

"Aw, honey, I would totally give you another chance," a woman yelled from the crowd. "Everybody makes mistakes."

"I've made a lot of them." Grady licked his lips and gripped the microphone tighter. "I regret all of the mistakes I've made. I was an idiot. I caused the person I most care about to lose her job in the process, and I will forever regret taking something so important from her. I don't regret letting her see the real me, though, and now I'm going to give her another look."

Slowly, he turned to face me. "You got embarrassed in front of the entire city, and it's my fault. I should've put my foot down that day in the office, but I didn't. I froze, like an idiot—I'm such an idiot sometimes—and you paid the price. You'll never know how sorry I am."

My heart heaved at his earnestness, but I couldn't find the words to respond.

"I went into this with the best intentions, Shay," he said. "I wanted to give you the world. Instead, I yanked the rug out from under you. I'm a walking disaster, but I want what's best for you – for us. I need you to give me another chance."

I lowered my gaze and stared at my feet. When I lifted my eyes again, I spoke to Cally. "You knew this was going to happen, that he was going to do this." My voice wasn't accusatory as much as resigned.

She'd moved close enough that she could hear me. "I knew. Grady and I had lunch yesterday — and a very long talk."

"You were the one who said he had to grow up," I protested. "You said he wasn't ready."

"I know what I said, and I meant it at the time. The thing is, nobody is ready until they're in the thick of things. I don't think you're any more ready than he is. That's the point. You need to get ready together."

I wanted to argue with her. Instead, I turned back to Grady. "What is it you think you want?"

"Just you," he replied. "I've always wanted you. I need you to give me another chance. I know it won't be easy, but I'll do better. I'll be better. Heck, I'll be the man you deserve. I know how to do it. I just...forgot. I didn't think about what was happening to you that day. I just thought about what I knew was going to happen this week."

It was an odd thing to say. "I don't understand."

"Did I ever tell you what my father does for a living?"

I shook my head.

"He's an investor. He puts together teams to save businesses on the brink of bankruptcy and then he builds them back up. He just closed on a deal that was in the works that day. I couldn't tell you because he swore me to secrecy, but there was a reason I wasn't worried about what was happening in that office."

And that's when it hit me. "Your father bought *The Bugle*."

He nodded. "He's not interested in keeping it only online. He moved fast, before they could dismantle the printing plant. It's going back to the way it was, with a cash infusion."

The turmoil that had been roiling in my stomach started to settle. "You knew that from the start. That's why you were constantly telling me not to worry."

"I knew, but I couldn't tell you. I made a promise." He held out his hands in supplication. "I'm sorry."

"He was trying to do what's right for everybody at *The Bugle*," Cally said. "He was a moron. The way he went about it was downright stupid, but his heart was in a good place."

"It was stupid," I agreed. Resignation was already washing over me. I knew what this would mean for everybody concerned, especially me. "So, so stupid."

"I'm a moron," Grady agreed as he took a step toward me. "That's always been my greatest weakness. But I want to get better. I want to be better. I want to be what you need. That's all I've ever wanted."

I ran my tongue over my teeth, debating. The crusty wall that had surrounded my heart a week ago when I was fired had completely collapsed. I knew what he was trying to do. Did he go about it in the right way? No, but nobody was perfect.

"The best time of my life was going on adventures with you," he said. "Even when you puked on me, it was the highlight of my day."

Oh, well, that was too much. "Let's not go overboard," I said. "You were not happy that day."

"But I was. I had so much fun with you. I loved every moment of it. I loved the cooking…and the barhopping…and the cruise. I loved the tours…and the float…and I really loved the parades. Do you know what I loved most?"

I shook my head.

"Cutting video together with you at your kitchen table. Laughing over gumbo. Just walking with you after dark. Shay, all I wanted was to be with you. I made a horrible mistake."

I opened my mouth to speak.

"Several horrible mistakes," he corrected. "I want to be better. I want to get all those things back, only this time we can do them for us and not for others." He took a determined step in my direction. "I want us to be together because the best thing I've ever done in my life is love you. I can't go back to how it was before. I can't not have you in my life."

I pressed the heel of my hand to my forehead. Emotions I'd been determined to cast aside roared back with a vengeance. I'd told myself I didn't love him, that it was stupid to open myself up to him. I might've been right about opening myself up, but I got slapped for my efforts. The love, though, was something else.

"I liked you too," I finally squeaked.

"What?" Grady looked as if he was straining to hear.

"I liked you the first day I met you, but I didn't want you to know. I was trying to play it cool. The more you teased me, the cooler I got. I think that might've been the wrong decision, because it's obvious now that if we'd just told each other how we felt from the beginning we could've saved a lot of people tons of heartache."

"Especially us." Grady took the final step. Now he was directly in front of me. The fingers on the hand not holding the microphone were soft as they cascaded down my cheek. "I really do love you. Please give me another chance."

The lump in my throat was too big to speak around, but when I met his gaze, I nodded.

"Is that a yes?" The hope in his eyes was almost enough to bring me to my knees.

I struggled to find my voice. "It's a yes, but from now on you have to run all your stupid ideas past me. It's the law."

He blew out a relieved sigh and dropped the microphone, both of his hands swooping in to cup my chin. "It's the law," he agreed. "I've never wanted to be a law-abiding citizen more." With that, he kissed me.

Explosions went off behind my eyes. Dimly, I knew that the crowd was still watching. I heard thunderous applause. There were even people sniffling back tears. I was fairly certain Cally was one of them.

When I finally pulled back, my lips on fire, I pinned him with a serious look. "We need to work on your flirting. You're bad at it."

He grinned. "You're not much better."

I wrapped my fingers around his wrists. He was still holding my face. "So, we'll do it together?"

"Forever and always."

"Good." I sucked in a breath. "I love you too."

His grin turned sloppy. "That's all I've ever wanted to hear from you."

Epilogue

ONE YEAR LATER

"Lift with your legs, baby."

Grady gave me a dirty look when he saw the way Cally and I were trying to carry the coffee table into our new house.

It was a creole cottage, only two-thousand-square feet, but it boasted a lovely courtyard and guest quarters in the rear. We figured if my parents ever came to visit—something they threatened in a handful of phone calls but never followed through on—that it would be best to host them in a separate building. We also planned to use it as a studio for the videos we kept making. Now they were for us, not the newspaper.

"We are lifting with our legs," I shot back, wiping my sweaty forearm across my forehead. Whoever thought it was a good idea to move in the heat of the day during the summer was an idiot.

By the way, it was me. I was the idiot.

"No, you're lifting with your back." Grady planted his hands on his hips. He seemed amused more than agitated. "That's why you look like you're going to pass out." He lifted his ice-cold bottle of water and pressed it to my forehead.

"Have I mentioned that I love when you get grumpy because of the humidity?"

He clearly wanted me to hurt him. "You're the one who said we had to move today." My voice was shrill. "You're the reason I'm in this state."

"As much as I love getting you hot and bothered, this isn't on me. You said we couldn't keep the rental for an extra week because you didn't want to ask Cally's father for an extension."

"Is that why we're out here in this freaking sweaty armpit?" Cally demanded as she straightened. Her eyes were accusatory.

"Your father has already done enough for us," I complained. "He gave us a month of free rent when we told him we were buying a house. He actually stepped in to smooth things over with the mortgage broker when we were late getting those papers."

"Oh, geez." Resentment lined Cally's pleasing features. "You're unbelievable. It's not as if he placed that call himself. He had one of his underlings do it." She threw her hands in the air. "I can't believe we could've dragged this out and picked a cooler day."

"Yes, I blame Shay." Grady's expression was full of feigned sadness. "Now we're all suffering because of her."

"Keep it up," I warned as I leaned over to grab the end of the coffee table. "Come on, Cally. We can carry this. It's just a table."

The look she shot me promised mayhem later. "If I wasn't so happy that you guys were finally moving forward and buying a place together, I would kill you right now. You might not want to push your luck."

"Duly noted."

. . .

TWO HOURS LATER, THE LAST OF OUR FURNITURE had been dropped in the living room and the people we'd tapped to help move had departed. We'd offered to order pizza for them, but everybody had opted to head out for drinks instead. Grady and I stayed behind to survey our kingdom.

"What are you doing?" Grady asked when he found me spread eagle on the bed. I hadn't made it yet—the sheets were on the floor where I'd dropped them when weariness overcame me—but I needed a break.

"Considering the meaning of life," I replied dryly.

"What have you come up with?"

I slid my eyes to him as he got comfortable next to me. "We have a house." Even saying it sent chills up my spine. "Together. We bought a house together. A year ago, I would've laughed if you told me that was even a possibility."

"A year ago, I was dressed like an idiot declaring my love for you in public. You totally would've moved in with me that day."

"No way. I would've needed at least two weeks."

"If I remember correctly, I spent the night at your place that evening, and we haven't been apart since."

I hated how smug he sounded. I rolled to my side and rested my head on my palm. "Do you regret that day?"

He made an "Oh, come on" face. "What do you think?"

I shrugged. "I don't know. You weren't too happy with me an hour ago when you slipped in the puddle of sweat Grant left on the foyer floor."

Grady smiled at the memory. "Yes, well, we're here now." He turned to face me and leaned in for a kiss. "We're home."

I nodded. "We're home." I brushed his messy hair out of his eyes. "I'm glad we have a home together."

"Me too." He slipped his arm around my waist and

nuzzled the hollow between my shoulder and neck. "If I never have to move again it will be too soon."

"If we ever move again, we're hiring people to do the heavy lifting."

"Good idea." His fingers were light on my waist. "I have to call my father."

As far as transitions went, that one needed work. "I don't know that I'm comfortable that you appear to be thinking about your father when we're wrapped around each other this way. It says a little something about you."

He gave a hearty chuckle. "I just promised I would let him know when Annabelle contacted Edith for a job recommendation. It happened today."

"Oh, really?" I lifted my head in curiosity. Annabelle hadn't made the transition when Grady's father bought *the Bugle*. Somehow, she'd been absent from the list of people called back to work in the office full time. I had no doubt about why, but I never questioned Grady about it. I figured that was his business. "Don't leave me in suspense," I prodded. "Where is she working?"

"Are you sure you want to know?" Grady cocked his head as he regarded me. "She's been out of our lives for a long time now, and it's been blissful."

"It has been blissful," I agreed. "Now that you've made up with Lacey and the Human Resources Department no longer hates you, it's been even more blissful than usual. I'm still curious about where she landed."

"You wouldn't believe me if I told you."

"Try me."

He let loose a dramatic sigh. "She's applying for a position with the vampire store. They want to expand to planned parties. She's trying to be their event coordinator."

My initial reaction was to laugh. Then I thought better of it. "It sort of makes sense," I noted. "The whole schtick of those parties is exclusivity, and there's nothing she loves better than telling people they can't be part of the group."

"That's exactly what I told my father," Grady confirmed as he linked his fingers with mine. "I told him that holding a grudge was unbecoming and that we should just let it go. It's better for us if she finds a new job and puts *The Bugle* in her rearview mirror."

The Bugle was doing better than ever. Er, well, better than I had ever seen it do. I was certain it had been an unstoppable force when people considered it normal to read the newspaper every morning. I was happy with the performance of the paper now, especially because I was working for the bar consortium. I never did go back. That was ultimately for the best, but I remained in contact with *the Bugle* entertainment section multiple times a week.

Grady had kicked up a fuss when I told him I was taking the new job. When I explained I didn't want work to ever get between us again, he reluctantly agreed to stop whining and support my decision. Now, five days a week, we separated in the morning and went to different jobs. By the time we reunited in the evening, we were bursting with stories and ready to focus all of our attention on each other. Oddly enough, despite the change, things were going perfectly on the professional front.

Given the fact that we were in the master bedroom of the new house we'd just purchased together, things were going well on the personal front too.

"So, I was thinking," Grady announced.

"I'll alert the media," I teased.

"I am the media." He kissed the tip of my nose. "I'm serious."

"I'm fine with whatever you want to order for dinner."

He frowned. "I already ordered crawfish boil to be delivered. It will be here in twenty minutes. That's not what I was thinking."

"You ordered crawfish boil?" I pinned him with a serious look. "Not that I won't eat it, but what if I wanted something else? Don't you think you should've asked?"

"I did ask — an hour ago. You said you would eat whatever showed up at the door, including another person."

"Oh, right." I pressed my lips together. I'd forgotten.

"Oh, right." Grady poked my side and caused me to squirm. "Can you focus on me for a second?"

I shifted my eyes to him and immediately lost my head. That smile of his still got to me, each and every time. "Do you want to entertain me until the food comes? I could be up for that."

"I do, but not the way you think." He sat up, pulling me with him. "I have something I need to talk to you about."

He looked so serious that all other thoughts fled my busy brain. "Is something wrong?"

He shot me an exasperated look. "Why do you always jump to that conclusion?"

"Because I'm an alarmist. You know I can't help it."

"True." He cupped my chin and gave me a soft kiss. "Most of the time I find it entertaining. But not today."

"Why not today?"

"Today is the day for serious discussions."

Oh, well, this wouldn't be good. "Just tell me." Something occurred to me. "You haven't changed your mind about buying a house together?"

"No, and look around. We own this place. We signed on the dotted line and everything. It's far too late for that."

That made sense. "So, what's the big deal?"

"Hold out your hand."

I was caught off guard. "What now?"

He chuckled. "Hold out your hand," he repeated.

I did as instructed. He shifted his hand over mine and dropped a small velvet jewelry box in my palm.

My mouth immediately went dry. "What's this?" I sounded like a cartoon mouse on uppers.

"I was going to do it at the fashion show this weekend," he replied. "I thought that because we started at one, and got our second chance at one, it only made sense that we would take the next step at one. Bebe was all for it."

"All for what?" My voice was barely a whisper.

"I love you," he replied. "So, so much. I've loved you since the day I first saw you."

"I've already told you that was lust. It takes at least two weeks to fall in love with someone."

"And I respectfully disagree." He brushed my disheveled hair from my face. "I was going to make a big deal out of it, get down on one knee in Jackson Square, force the crowd to be on my side, and propose in front of everybody. Then there was going to be a big party on Bourbon Street. I was even going to arrange for a parade. But I decided against it."

I clutched the jewelry box tightly, the charms from the stamped metal bracelet I'd bought myself when getting my job tinkling. "Why?" I asked. It seemed the question to ask.

"Because some things should be private, and this is one. I'm more than happy to be the center of attention when it comes to little things—and there's nothing I love more than embarrassing you in public—but this is between us. I want it to be just you and me."

I waited for him to continue. "Aren't you going to say something else?" I asked.

He snorted at my impatience. Then he sobered and his eyes went soft. "You're the love of my life. I knew from the second I saw you that you were it for me. I went about things in the worst way possible, and you still gave me a chance. Then, when I screwed things up again, you gave me a second chance. I don't ever want to screw anything up again."

"Everybody makes mistakes," I pointed out. "It's how you react to those mistakes that matters."

"I know. I figure if you're married to me, you'll be more likely to forgive my mistakes."

"Oh, well, at least you have a good reason," I said on a laugh.

He took the box from me and opened it. Inside was a simple emerald cut diamond, probably two carats, in a white gold setting. It was beautiful, understated, and more than I ever could've hoped for. "I was going to do a big thing in the backyard tonight once everybody was gone. I was going to do candles and cake. But every muscle in my body hurts, so you're stuck with the naked truth."

"Are you going to get naked?" I was hopeful despite my fatigue.

"In a few minutes." He leaned close and rested his forehead against mine. "I love you more than anything. Even now, after a year together, you're still my best friend. I don't want that to ever change. I want to spend my life with you."

"If I say you're my best friend Cally will never forgive me," I fretted.

He pretended he didn't hear me. "Shay Archer, will you marry me?" There was hope in his eyes, and maybe a little fear.

A year ago, his fear would've fueled mine, but I knew that he loved me. I understood that he wanted to be with me no matter what. More than that, I felt the same way about him.

"I wouldn't marry anybody else," I replied when I was reasonably assured I wouldn't start crying. "Yes, I'll be your wife."

His expression lit with joy as he leaned in to kiss me. It was a sweet exchange, although there was the promise of something more to come shimmering beneath the sweetness.

Then the doorbell rang.

"That will be the food." Grady slipped the engagement ring on my finger and gave me a friendly pat on the ass. "Can you get that?"

I glared at him. "Why can't you get it?"

"Because I'm in pain and you just got an expensive engagement ring."

"Fine, but you're going to be the first one doling out massages tonight. You've been warned."

He grinned. "Sure, but that means I'm the first one who gets to test the jetted tub in the master bathroom."

I started to roll off the bed. "Maybe we can share the initial soak."

He grinned. "I plan to share everything with you. That includes food, baths, and the largest viewing audience in New Orleans when we start posting regular pieces on the bars in your consortium."

It was the perfect thing to say. "Please tell me you had Hurricanes delivered too."

"I'm not an idiot."

I paused by the door. "No, you're everything."

"Right back at you, baby. You're my everything too."

I glanced at the ring on my finger. "Forever."

"And always."